Whole in the Heart

WHOLE IN THE HEART

K. W. Román

Editing and Formatting by Anessa Books
Cover Art by Adam Román

AUTHOR'S NOTE

This is a work of fiction. While many of the places mentioned do exist, all descriptions of business operations and all characters were made up by the author. Any similarities to real people or situations are entirely coincidental.

Some potential triggers: this story contains loss and grief trauma, some emotional abuse, and a brief mention of suicidal thoughts (in the past). I wish every reader peace and love, and I hope the warmth of the friendships carries you through—in this story and in your life.

xo

-k

for Carla
Thanks for camping out in my heart
and helping keep their memories with us
always

Kaya

"Ow!" SHE EXCLAIMED. TO no one. "Dammit," Kaya
breathed, as she bent down and gently massaged
the toe she had just stubbed in spectacular fashion
on the threshold of the French doors. Luckily,
Kaya's other hand still held her coffee mug and only
a little had splashed onto the deck outside.

She gingerly stepped her socked feet forward,
testing the sore toe, and pulled her sweatshirt
tighter over her pajamas in the bright, cold
morning. She looked out at the dunes and then
shook her head as if to wake herself from a dream.
It *felt* like a dream.

Was it really just *last night* that she was sitting
with her roommate in their apartment in
Washington watching TV? The late-night drive up
I-95 and down through the New Jersey backroads
had really happened? She was here, in Cape May?

Kaya took a big swallow of coffee and took in her
surroundings. Even though it was December, the
sun was shining brightly. She inhaled deeply in the
cold air. Everything smelled sharper at the shore.
The smell at the beach was always an intoxicating
mix of salt, surf, and dune grass. But in the winter,
she observed, it had an edge—a crispness—whereas

in the summer it was borne along on a cloud of warm, humid mist. She leaned her hip against the deck railing, curling her hands around the mug.

As she took another swallow of coffee, her stomach grumbled loudly. While she hadn't been surprised to find a half bag of coffee in the freezer this morning, Kaya knew there wouldn't be much else in the way of food in the cottage refrigerator or pantry. She figured she would drive out to the Acme later for a proper grocery run. But for now, she couldn't stand the thought of getting back in the car.

Going back inside, she set her mug in the sink and went down to her bedroom to pull on jeans, a turtleneck, hoodie, and a puffy vest. She donned her gloves and a knit cap to guard against the breeze, pushed open the door and skipped down the steps along the side of the house. Her feet crunched the seashell gravel as she walked under the house, fiddled with the lock on the storage space, and opened the door. To get to her bicycle, she had to gently set aside her parents' bikes. Her breath hitched and she wiped tears off her cheeks as the winter air chilled against them. With a heavy sigh, she pulled her bike out, pumped up the tires, locked the storage area, and took off.

Cape May Point was tiny, so she could have easily walked, but she was hungry and biking was the way everyone got around down here. She pedaled around the Cape May Point Park roundabout and over to the red-shingled General Store, leaned her bike against the fence, and pushed the door to step into the bright space full of enticing smells and cheeriness. "Silver Bells" was playing through the speakers. Behind the counter was a middle-aged woman with brown hair streaked with thin ribbons of grey and reading glasses perched on her nose. "Good morning!" she said, looking up when Kaya entered.

"Hi!" Kaya responded. "I was hoping for a cup of coffee and a breakfast sandwich?"

"We can do that," the woman said.

"Are you Mrs. Neville? The owner?" Kaya asked.

"One and the same," the woman said, smiling. "But everyone calls me Tess."

"Gotcha. I don't think I've ever seen you working at the counter before."

"Ah," said Tess, "well then, you must be a summer person. Out of season, there's really not enough business for us to keep any help."

"I guess I am mostly a summer person. My family has a cottage over on Harvard and Coral," Kaya said, gesturing towards the window. "But we haven't used it much in the last couple of years...sometimes rented it in season and closed it up in the off."

Tess handed her the coffee and eyed her carefully. "Wait, you're one of Clare's girls, aren't you?"

Kaya involuntarily winced and her eyes welled up again for the second time already this morning. Tess reached out and touched her arm. "I'm sorry, hon. I was so sad to hear of your mom's passing. Your mother was...oh my goodness, such a ray of sunshine. She made friends with *everyone*. She was just so kind...and so young."

Kaya brushed her tears with one hand, holding the coffee in the other. "Thank you...it's okay. I'm sorry. It's just...I know it's been two years, but I still..." Kaya smiled weakly and gestured to her face. Tess squeezed Kaya's arm and Tess's own eyes welled up a little.

They were both quiet for a beat. "But yes," Kaya responded, "I'm her younger daughter, Kaya."

"Well, welcome back to the Point, Kaya." She released Kaya's arm and went back to the kitchen to make the food order.

Kaya sat at a table by the window in the sun. The last few months—well, years really—had been a total shitstorm. As she'd driven to the shore house late last night she'd wondered if she was crazy. She had certainly surprised herself. She thought about sitting in her little apartment living room last night with her roommate Lynne, watching their latest guilty pleasure YA miniseries on Netflix when she just got up, went into her room and started stuffing clothes into her two largest duffel bags. She recalled the look on Lynne's face when she came in Kaya's room to see what was up.

"I think I have to go," Kaya said.

"Where?" asked Lynne.

"Cape May."

"Now?" replied Lynne, confusion all over her face.

"Yeah..." said Kaya, searching Lynne's face for some sign that Kaya either was or wasn't crazy. After a beat she said, "I gotta get out of here. I love you—I'm sorry—but I think I just need to...go."

Lynne looked at her for a minute, then walked up to her and gave her a hug. "Maybe you do. Drive safe. Call me tomorrow."

Kaya released Lynne from the hug with tears on both their cheeks. "Thank you, my friend."

As she'd made her way from D.C., as it approached and then passed midnight, she questioned her decision to just up and leave. In some ways, this was even harder than she imagined, with memories at every turn. Still, as she sat here this morning, hands wrapped around a hot mug of strong coffee, she was glad she was not in DC.

When her parents first bought the cottage, she was 18 and it was heaven for her family. Now Kaya was twenty-five, recently orphaned and newly dumped. Running away wasn't normally her thing, but suddenly an escape seemed called for.

Tess brought out her sandwich, bringing her back to the present. The woman gestured to the opposite chair. "May I?"

"Of course," Kaya answered. She took a bite of the sandwich.

"What brings you back? In December?" Tess queried.

Kaya swallowed. "This is so good, by the way— thank you." Tess nodded and smiled. "Well, I hate to be a downer so early in the morning," Kaya said with a sort of teary chuckle.

"Not at all," Tess replied. "We're all family out here on the Point, especially in the off-season. We have to look out for each other."

"That's very kind," Kaya replied slowly. She took another bite and swallowed. Tess didn't seem to be in a hurry. Her quiet presence made Kaya feel warm. Safe. "Little Drummer Boy" was now playing softly in the background.

Kaya took a deep breath, marshalling the bravery to say the words. "So, I don't know how much you know?" she started.

"Not much," admitted Tess. "We'd heard she had cancer and word got around when she passed. Everyone loved your mom."

"It was almost two years ago—it was ovarian cancer. She fought like crazy for over two years before she died. And then a little over a year ago, my dad got diagnosed with cancer. Stomach. He was older than my mom, so it wasn't as shocking on that front, but it was pretty aggressive and he passed away in October."

Tess' hand flew to her mouth, but she stayed quiet.

Kaya took another bite, a big breath, and pressed on. "I've been living in DC since I graduated college, but after I went back there—after we dealt with everything with my dad at home in Poughkeepsie, it's just...nothing felt right." She figured mentioning that her boyfriend of three years dumped her was a detail she didn't need to further inflict on this very nice proprietor.

"And the holidays...were going to be tough anyway, so my sister, Callie, and I came up with the idea to come here for Christmas...for a change of scenery...and once we decided, it's like, I just couldn't stay in DC anymore. So I packed up and came early."

"Where does Callie live now?" asked Tess, leaning her forearms on the table. "Is she in DC too?"

"No, she's married, and they live in Providence."

"I see. You've been through a lot," observed Tess.

"Yeah," replied Kaya with an exhale. She turned her head to look out the window at the park across the street. The grass was the faded grey-green of early winter and the trees were bare except for the single giant fir tree.

"Well," Tess said, "is there anything you need at present?"

"This breakfast is a start, thank you," Kaya said, turning back to her and smiling. "I don't have any food in the house yet, so this is great."

"Food we got," Tess said with a chuckle. "Were you planning to work? Jobs can be hard to come by in the off-season."

"I don't really know my plan. I mean, I can work remotely for a while at my current job in DC, and I will for the time being, but..." Kaya trailed off and looked out the window again. She briefly wondered why she was telling Tess Neville any of this, but in the moment, it felt nice to have someone to talk to who knew her mom, who seemed like they cared and wasn't afraid to sit with her and the grief.

"I haven't really said this out loud to anyone yet," Kaya continued, looking back at Tess. "I kinda suddenly hate my job. I used to love the work, and my friends at work, and maybe this is all me still reeling from...everything. I don't want to make rash decisions, but I just feel like I need a break."

"I can understand that," Tess replied, sitting back. "Grief really messes with our heads and our hearts. It's a hell of a thing to process. What is it that you do?"

"I'm a writer," Kaya replied. "I work for a public relations agency, but I have a journalism degree and I mostly write press releases, product placements, and pitches." The bell on the door jingled and they both turned to see a tall, white-haired gentleman push the door open with his foot, as he entered carrying a big cardboard box.

"Gerry, when you get that in, come meet Clare Morgan's daughter, Kaya. She's down for the holidays."

"Sure!" Mr. Neville called good naturedly, disappeared into the backroom. He re-emerged momentarily. "Gerry, this is Kaya Morgan. Her family has that little cottage on Harvard and Coral."

"'Point Taken'!" he said, loudly with a big smile. "I love that place. Clever name!" This was a Point thing. Folks in lots of places name their beach houses, but in this part of Cape May, there were more than a few who couldn't resist a pun. "On Point," "Match Point," and "Tipping Point," all graced wooden signs over doorways in these streets.

"She's a journalist and PR writer," Tess continued. "Do we know anyone who needs that?"

Gerry tilted his head and looked up at the ceiling momentarily. "Not off the top of my head for PR. But maybe a publication? You could stop by Exit Zero. Tell Sloane the Nevilles sent you."

"Oh, great idea!" said Tess. "Sloane and Vance have a weekly, plus the books. Maybe they'd have a project for you, for a change of pace."

Kaya sat still, enjoying the warmth from these people she only tangentially knew, but who were treating her like they really cared. Her blood coursed a little warmer.

When her mother died, her heart had shattered. It had broken apart inside her chest into thousands of shards, like when you tap a hard-boiled egg on the counter. The shell was still on the egg but splintered into pieces. For two years, she had felt like this. But this morning, in this sunny little place, with these people, it felt like at least one tiny piece of her broken heart healed.

Kaya

KAYA WAS ON HER way to the Acme when her phone rang through her Honda's Bluetooth. A photo of she and her big sister, heads together and smiling, filled the console screen. Kaya's shoulders relaxed. This face...the only person left she could be 100% herself with. "Well *hello*," she said, answering.

"Hello yourself!" said Callie. "Did you get there okay?"

"Yeah. On my way to the Acme now."

"In town? Or by the ferry?"

Kaya scoffed. "Ferry. You know I hate to pay for parking downtown."

"Fair. Aren't you going to be lonely out there? We won't come for another almost three weeks. My winter break starts sooner, but Juan can't get off much more than the week between Christmas and New Year's."

"No, it's okay," Kaya replied. "I kind of like the quiet. And I'll be interacting with coworkers and clients on video. Plus, I had a nice chat this morning with the Nevilles over at the General Store."

"Wholesome," Callie teased. "But seriously, I mean, maybe Juan and me could take two cars and I come sooner...? I just...you're all...alone."

"I'm fine really," Kaya said. It was a small lie. She *was* an introvert and really didn't mind doing things by herself. But there was a heaviness to the word "alone" for them now, and Callie knew it. It's a strange thing to be orphaned, even if you're twenty-five or twenty-seven like Kaya and Callie were. No matter how many people you have in your life, there was an aloneness-in-the-world that envelops you—like you're alone in a field in the wind, where your parents used to be there to buffer, and now there's nothing.

But Kaya assured her sister, "It's silly to drive separately all the way from Providence. I mean, I can't wait to see you, but it's really not worth bringing two cars."

"Okay, well, call me every day."

"We talk almost every day anyway," Kaya laughed. It was true—especially since their dad had gotten sick. Whether they were coordinating visits, making arrangements, providing status, or even about nothing. They had always been close, but since their mother died, the texts and calls had felt like a way to hold tighter to each other. The family unit was under attack and the connection provided some sense of safety. "Okay, chica, I'm in the parking lot. These groceries aren't gonna buy themselves."

"Okay love you, bye."

"Love you, bye."

Kaya

I T WAS S UNDAY, SO she didn't need to work today. After she unpacked and put away the groceries, Kaya decided to go for a walk. It had warmed up a little and was a beautiful December afternoon. She didn't need the puffy vest layer, so she just grabbed a sweatshirt. She walked out to the beach and turned left towards the lighthouse and WWII bunker. Cape May Point was separated from Cape May proper by a large wildlife refuge and wetland. To access the Point, you drove or biked around the refuge inland via Sunset Avenue. But the other way to go was on the beach on foot. The beach along the refuge was wide enough that you could walk between Cape May and the Point—a little over a mile.

There was just a light breeze, and the sun was behind her as she made the turn. She tipped her face up to the milky winter sunshine. Her sneakers slipped and shifted in the loose sand. She watched the waves rolling up and breaking into foam. The pattern of the waves was calming—how they just kept rolling, over and over. Kaya figured she'd walk as far as town, just to the cove where Beach Ave started and then turn around.

The little crabs scuttled around on the sand and the gulls soared and dove. She tucked her dark, reddish-brown curls behind her ears to get them out of her eyes as the wind tossed around. As she got closer to town, she saw three men throwing a frisbee with an energetic golden retriever. She spotted them easily because otherwise the beach was empty. They looked to be in their late twenties or early thirties. One had dark hair and appeared Asian—but they were far away, so she wasn't sure. Another was shorter and stockier, with bright blond hair. The third was tall with brown, wavy hair and broad shoulders. She wondered briefly if they were Coasties, although the Coast Guard base was closer to Pittsburgh or Poverty beaches, not down here.

When she got closer, the dog spotted her and came bounding towards her. She generally liked dogs but inwardly groaned. Why were goldens so *exuberant*? She reached out with both hands to scratch its ears and hopefully ward off any jumping or licking by holding its face firm. The tall guy was yelling "Sorry! I'm so sorry!" over the breeze, while the blond one shouted, "Come *here,* Molly! *Molly! Come!*"

Kaya laughed and tried to be good natured. "It's okay!" she called. Molly proceeded to give her a good sniffing and then ran back to her people.

Grateful for having escaped without being slobber-bombed, Kaya decided rather than get any closer, maybe this was the spot to turn around and head back to the Point.

Kaya

THE NEXT MORNING, KAYA made herself breakfast and set up her laptop at the kitchen counter. It was kind of wild being able to sit and work, looking out at the ocean. Heaven. *Almost*.

She glanced at her Outlook calendar and saw the first meeting was at nine, and with people she liked, so it was a nice ease-in to the workweek. She logged on five minutes early, and a few seconds later, her supervisor Melanie's face popped up. Kaya *loved* her boss. Melanie was three years ahead in her career. Kaya shared Melanie's love of putting in the work to do a job right, her zeal for logic and order, and helping everyone on the team succeed. Kaya loved when people called her a "mini-Melanie"—a high compliment in Kaya's book. Plus, she and Melanie got annoyed by all the same types of people and shared an obsessive love of the Oxford comma.

"*Girl*," Melanie said cheerily, her chestnut hair brushed off her shoulders and large, gold earrings swinging. "How—seriously—are you holding up?" she asked. Kaya smiled.

"Well, since it's just us for now, I will say, it's still very much a day-by-day thing, you know? And being here, it's a lot of memories. But it's also the ocean. And as my mom always said..." and they both finished the sentence together: "a bad day at the ocean is still a good day." Kaya laughed lightly. "Yeah." Melanie was from Southern California originally and shared a love of the beach.

"How did it go with Barrie? Does she do virtual?" Melanie asked.

When her mom's passing was imminent, and at the urging of her father, Kaya had found a therapist that her healthcare plan would at least partially cover. Barrie was a slight, wiry woman in her early sixties, with short, spiky silver hair, and black framed glasses. She started appointments as early as 6:30 a.m. and played tennis three times a week. Her office in downtown DC had a radiator that was broken so that it was always on. Barrie cracked a window so there was this odd juxtaposition of blasting heat and a cold draft. There was a plant in the corner that always looked like it was in pain, but never actually died.

Barrie was fantastic. She asked direct questions that left Kaya no room to hide. She was kind, but she had a way of driving right to the point...she'd wait patiently for answers, but she was not going to let Kaya off the hook. More often than not, a session would include Kaya sighing and saying "we're going there?" or "please don't make me go there," to which Barrie would respond, "we're going there."

Kaya reflected that Barrie was the biggest factor in her getting some semblance of her life back. Barrie helped her probe all the ways her relationship with her mother continued to help her, the things she needed to let go, and whether the stories she told herself were serving her. Barrie helped her see that her abandonment fears were a thing she experienced, but weren't all she was. And she helped her with tools to try to appease these fears. It helped.

Every time they finished a session, Barrie asked, "Would you like to come back?" The answer was yes, weekly, for several months. Then it was every other week, then monthly, until one day, while feeling pretty good but anxiously eyeing her rent and student loan obligations, she told Barrie maybe they'd pause. "Well, you know where to find me," Barrie had said. Her bony arms came around Kaya in a hug, and Kaya simply said, "Thank you."

Then Kaya's father died. She felt the old familiar panic setting in and thought she'd seek out some more Barrie time to help her through.

"Mel," Kaya said. "You are not going to believe this, and I will preface by saying you absolutely must laugh because otherwise I will cry and I am the authority on this."

"Oh no, what?" Melanie replied.

"So, last week I called her office to get back on her appointment schedule, and you know what they said?"

"No—Oh God, what?"

"She retired. And they asked would I like to schedule with another therapist. She *retired*, Mel."

"What. The. Fuck." Melanie breathed.

"I *know*, right?" Kaya exclaimed. "I think I might have actually even said 'what the fuck'—maybe not—I don't remember, but something along those lines, and they said, 'well we coordinated with all her standing appointments, but you haven't been in in over a year'. I was speechless. I think I might have hung up on them, I was so shocked."

"Shocked, and *triggered* for fuck's sake," replied Melanie. "Like, *hello* people. Have a little sense. You have a patient who was in therapy for abandonment issues, and you just drop, 'oh sorry your therapist abandoned you'? What is *wrong* with people?"

"You gotta laugh. I insist you laugh," Kaya pleaded.

"For you, I will laugh," said Melanie, giggling a little as she said it. "But I also stand by 'what the fuck'."

"Valid," Kaya said.

Kaya

KAYA LOGGED OFF EARLY, finished with her work for the day. She didn't have any errands to run, and she found herself restless. She considered going for a run, but decided to hop on her bicycle instead. On a wave of nostalgia, she biked back to Cape May proper. She wound through town, by the shops, restaurants, and Victorian houses so familiar to her from coming here every year while growing up. She eventually found herself at Beach Avenue and turned left, up the shore until the hotels ended and the big, old houses lorded over the oceanfront. It was quiet up here.

The two big old hotels—Congress Hall and the Chalfonte—and several of the smaller ones stayed pretty busy through Christmas. Some of the beachfront hotels closer to town also had people around them. But the beach hotels at this end were practically empty, and very few of the houses up at this end were year-rounders. Some families might come use them over the holidays, but not yet in early December. She saw no one for blocks.

Just past Baltimore Avenue, she stopped, turned her gaze away from the ocean and looked between two stately homes on Beach Ave, at the tall, tan dwelling behind and between them. Then she got back on her bike and went up Baltimore and turned right on New Jersey Avenue, stopping in front of the tan property. 1506 New Jersey Ave.

Her family had started going to Cape May every summer when she and Callie were young. Their father, Greg Morgan, was from New Jersey and had been in the Coast Guard, so he always had a soft spot for the town. Also, he didn't have much patience for "boardwalk towns," as he called them, where the boardwalk was the main drag and there wasn't much else except t-shirt shacks and bars. He liked that Cape May was a real, permanent town—propped up in part by the US Coast Guard Training Center, but it had a year-round feel. There were churches, and a few museums, a couple libraries, that sort of thing. Plus, it is the very southern tip of New Jersey, so no one just "passed through" Cape May. You went there on purpose.

They always rented, and always the same place—a condo at the four-unit 1506 New Jersey Ave, one block up from the beach. It was comprised of two mirror buildings that shared a driveway space between them. Each building had two units—one in front, and one in the back. Her family always had the unit on the right in the back, towards the ocean. Clare Morgan was very organized so she never neglected to call her property agent, Joey, on the first day reservations were available and book it. (She also had a box of Jonathan apples shipped to him a week before because they are most local to Poughkeepsie and Joey loved them.)

1506 fit the Morgans and Aunt Peggy perfectly. Kaya and Callie loved their mom's sister, Peggy, and the fact that she always joined them at the beach. At 1506, the top floor was an open concept kitchen, dining, and living room with lots of light and sliding glass doors to a deck on the back. Being situated the block behind, but between two big Beach Avenue mansions provided a straight shot view from the 1506 back deck to the dunes and the ocean. It was amazing.

Kaya was a junior in high school when Aunt Peggy passed away. They didn't go to Cape May that summer. It was too painful. For the first time it was Joey who called Clare first, and she said, "Not this year, Joey." They never went back to 1506.

As Kaya stood and gazed at it, the memories washed over her like the waves she could hear from beyond the dunes. Every brick in the driveway was familiar. The path they wore down the side lawn to the outdoor shower. The tears came again, unbidden, but familiar now. It hurt, deep in her chest, thinking how happy they had been here—as a family—and she wept for the girls who didn't know that family wouldn't survive into their adulthood.

She looked around at the quiet, empty street. It was like all that happiness had just vanished. She got back on her bicycle and pedaled away.

Kaya

THE NEXT MORNING, KAYA didn't have any meetings until the afternoon, and she had still not been given a full workload since she came back from bereavement leave, so she biked over to Beach Plum Farm. Beach Plum was close to the Point, tucked away on Stevens Street, off Sunset. It used to be just a farm to supply some of the food for the big, historic Congress Hall hotel, but the owners invested in making it a proper destination, adding a store, market café, landscaping, and eventually cottages people could rent. Their hospitality empire was expanding, Kaya reflected.

When Kaya entered the market, there were a couple employees stocking fridge cases. She approached the counter. The guy at the counter was tall and, she noted, totally cute. He had thick, brown, wavy hair that was a little long, but well-kempt, sitting in waves behind his ears and a bit down his neck. He had light blue eyes that were almost grey. He was wearing a black button-down shirt with the Beach Plum logo, with the sleeves rolled up to the elbow and broad shoulders. He was looking at her, smiling widely as she approached. Kaya found herself staring.

"Hi!" he said. He sounded so...she wasn't sure. She got the sense that he was happy to see her, but that made no sense. She also knew she needed to stop staring but there was something familiar about him. "I'm glad you're here. Can I get you something?" he asked, still smiling openly. Wow, he had adorable dimples.

"Uh, yes," she stammered. "Sorry," she said, shaking her head and laughing at herself to ease the embarrassment. "Coffee, please. Large? With room?"

"Okay, anything else?"

"Yes, um, a bagel please, toasted, with, um, cream cheese?" Why was she losing the ability to talk properly? But he was *so* good looking, and she was trying to place him, and then it hit her—one of the golden retriever guys from the beach. Okay, definitely not a Coastie, then, if he was working here. "I think I saw you?" she started. "The other day? On the beach—was that your dog?"

He blinked at her as his face stilled in thought. "Oh, wow, was that you? You were too far away for me to recognize you. But yes! Now, I totally see it was you! No, definitely not my dog," he said, laughing. "Molly is my friend Casey's dog." He rang up her order.

"Ah," she said tapping her phone to the payment device. "Well, I'm Kaya."

His eyes lit up and he smiled that broad, dimpled smile again. It melted her. "Well hello,

Kaya," he replied. "It's nice to finally be introduced. I'm Lucas."

Huh? Finally? She took another beat, head cocked to the side, until a worker jostled her shoulder with a box of supplies and said, "Oh! Sorry." She ducked her head, smiled, said, "Nice to meet you, Lucas," and walked to the pick-up counter to wait. *Finally?*

He kept glancing over at her and grinning, even as he helped another customer. She kind of wanted to hang around and talk to him more, but she didn't really have any excuse to, so after another worker handed her the bagel, she reluctantly went back to the cottage.

Lucas

IT'S HER! LUCAS WANTED to talk to her longer, but there were more customers. He watched helplessly as she shot him another shy glance and walked out. *Damn.* It had been a long time since he'd thought about her—Kaya—and her family. He knew her name, of course. He used to hear her and her sister, Callie, playing, laughing, and talking every time they were outside. He'd hear them out on their porch. They stayed for two weeks every summer, from the summer he was nine or so, through the at least that one summer he came home from college. They always rented the unit directly across the driveway from his family's home.

He hadn't recognized her the other day on the beach—she'd been too far away, and he certainly wasn't expecting to see her—to ever see her again, honestly. He couldn't believe she was here—back in Cape May! And in December. He was so curious why, as he set the two shot glasses under the espresso spouts and turned on the machine. When she'd walked in this morning and he saw her face, he knew it was her. She'd grown up, of course, but he'd recognized her. That same curly hair. A little taller. Lucas swirled the pitcher of milk on the frother before setting it down, dumping the shots into a paper coffee mug and covering them with the steamed milk. "Here you go," he said with a smile as he handed the coffee to the next customer.

There were no more customers immediately in line. "Hey, Carol," he called out to the associate who was stocking cases. "Can you watch the counter for a sec?"

Carol looked back at him. "Sure, no problem."

Before the sentence fully left Carol's mouth, Lucas had darted around the counter and out the door. He looked around the parking lot and down the lane that led back to Stevens Street. Empty.

With a disappointed sigh, he walked back inside and to the counter. Kaya had seemed reserved. Maybe that was fair. Lucas had spent a lot more time furtively watching Kaya, her sister, and their family back then than they likely spent noticing him, he reflected. Which sounded creepy, he admitted to himself as the thought crossed his mind. But it was true. When he'd observed them from his window or the shadows of his top deck, he had been fascinated and a little envious of the raucous happiness and freedom they seemed to enjoy. Lucas' brows knit together unwittingly as he reflected on his own childhood, which was...the opposite of that.

"What's the frown about?" Carol's voice jolted him out of his thoughts.

He smoothed out his expression and gave her a smile. "Nothing. Just that girl who was in here earlier—I know her from when we were kids. I was hoping to find out where she's staying so we can catch up, but she was gone."

"Ah," replied Carol. "Well, it's a small town. If she's staying around, I'm sure you'll see her again."

"Hope so." He really *really* hoped so.

Kaya

IT GOT DARK EARLY and a cold wind had whipped up, so instead of going for a run or walk after her work was finished, she facetimed Callie.

"Helllooooo," sung Callie.

"I have news," replied Kaya.

"I like news. Spill."

"Well, I went over to Beach Plum Farm this morning, and maybe this isn't that interesting, but one of the guys who works there is a total smoke show."

"Oh, *really*. This definitely sounds like it's interesting for *you*," Callie teased.

Kaya smiled and momentarily ducked her head. She responded, "I feel like maybe it's wrong to even be thinking about something like that, so soon after...with what's been going on." This grief thing, it was tricky. After her mom died, she was too broken to function most of the time. She would go out with her boyfriend Charlie and her friends, but it's like she had to make herself do it. It was hard to find joy in daily life. Over time, and with therapy, it got a little better.

Losing her dad was a huge blow, and it had only been two months at this point, so she almost felt guilty if she wasn't sad all the time. But, having lived through losing her mom, it wasn't so destabilizing this time. She felt more alone in the world, but not so debilitated. Maybe it was numbness. Was it wrong? She didn't know.

"Hey," Callie said, pausing until Kaya looked up again. "Neither of them would want us to shut ourselves away. They wanted us to be happy. They would want you to find someone."

"Well, it's *way* too early for talking about finding 'the one' or anything. I'm pretty sure I'm broken in that department. Just ask Charlie," Kaya huffed.

"That's crap. Charlie is an immature child. He was fun in the good times, but he was *never* going to be able to be there for you. We're in trauma here. I'm glad he's out of your life. You'll find someone. Maybe it's Beach Plum barista."

"*Mom* didn't think I'd find someone."

"Why would you say that?" blurted Callie.

"Callie, when they were buying their burial site, she asked if they should get a three-plot. *Three*, Cal. She assumed I wouldn't have anyone to eventually be *buried* with. She preserved your wedding dress after you got married. *Preserved* it. Even though she knew I want to wear it. That means she didn't think I'd be wearing it until like a million years from now, if ever!"

"Well, the facts that she asked about the plot and preserved the dress are true," Callie allowed. "But that didn't mean she didn't have faith."

"Yeah, well," Kaya replied, "we can table my marrying anyone for now. I just happened to notice that this guy was super cute and we introduced ourselves, because I asked him if he was one of the guys I saw on the beach the other day. His name is Lucas."

"Excellent name. Ok, I gotta go pick up Juan from the train. Get a snap of him and send to me."

"What? *No.* I cannot do that and maintain any sort of chill."

"Fine. But when we get down there, Beach Plum Barista is getting a full big sister drive-by."

Kaya

KAYA FELL INTO A routine over the days until Christmas. Since the daylight was so scarce, if it wasn't too cold or wet, she ran, walked, or biked in the morning. She did her work for Alston Group. She started cooking more. Kaya and Lynne could both cook the basics. But here, alone, with all her time to herself, Kaya started to see dinner as an opportunity. She started looking at YouTube videos and reading cooking blogs. Saving links to recipes she tried and liked. She burned her first attempt at a roux and had to throw it all out. (Her second attempt was better.) She made her own tomato sauce for the first time in her life. Kaya made notes of what she could make when Callie and Juan came. It was the family cottage, but Kaya felt like she was the host and she wanted Christmas to be perfect.

She got the cottage ready for them. She fished out linens and washed them to shake out any dust or damp. She made the beds and stocked the bathrooms. It had been a while since Point Taken was really lived in. After Aunt Peggy died, the Morgans didn't return to Cape May, and no one really talked about whether they ever would again. It was sad to go, but, Kaya thought, sadder not to.

But she and Callie were busy with school; it wasn't at the top of their minds. She and her sister were both surprised when, at Christmas Kaya's freshman year at university, their parents announced they were buying a place of their own in Cape May. Kaya couldn't quite believe it. Their *own* place. They could stay longer than a week! They could go any time!

It was in Cape May Point, where they'd never spent much time beyond an annual bike ride to the lighthouse at one end, and a visit to Sunset Beach at the other, but never really in the neighborhood. The cottage was modest—more modest than 1506 in town. It was right on Harvard Ave, across the street from the dunes, steps from the Coral Ave beach access. Kaya loved it from the second she saw it. It had a storage room and space for the car at ground level under the house, along with an outdoor shower. Up a flight of stairs on the side of the house led to the main door. There were three bedrooms on the first floor.

Upstairs was an open space common room like 1506. But the Point house was older, with weathered grey shingles instead of crisp siding at the newer 1506, the appliances were a little older, too. But the space was flooded with light and perfect for them. There was an open deck on the top floor, front of the house that faced the ocean. From this height, you could see the waves over the dunes.

It wasn't as fancy as 1506, but it was theirs, and they all fell in love with it, and with the Point. There had been plans to use this house long into Clare's and Greg's retirements—but, well, life had other plans.

There were more year-rounders and active owners on the Point, but the Morgans had never been out here at Christmastime. Christmas in Poughkeepsie was a festive season full of traditions, family, and friends. As Kaya settled in on the Point, and the days ticked by until Callie's arrival, she decided she should decorate Point Taken for Christmas.

The lampposts on the Washington Mall were decked out with green garlands and red bows, and the General Store had lights strung across the edge of its roof. It seemed to Kaya a shame if she didn't do a little something to make it festive for Callie and Juan...and herself.

One afternoon, she went downtown. She found a parking spot and headed towards Swains. It was a hardware store in name, but she knew they'd have a lot of what she needed. They had Christmas trees propped up on stands out front. There was no way she could pull off a full-sized tree, since she was on her own and didn't have any ornaments or anything. But maybe a small one? She went inside first and loaded up a small basket with some festive hand towels, a couple of candles, an evergreen wreath, some Christmas lights, and a random copper reindeer that struck her as pretty. Her heart was aching thinking about how much her mom loved Christmas, but it also made Kaya feel a little better to get into the spirit. "Jingle Bell Rock" was blaring over the sound system.

Yes, she decided, she would get a small tree. She picked up a stand and took everything outside to pick out her tree and pay for her finds. She found one advertised as "tabletop"—a little under four feet tall, and she drank in the pine smell. "You'll do," she said to herself with a smile. "I believe you'll do."

"Excuse me, but did you just talk to a tree?" Kaya whirled around at the sound of the deep voice. Her eyes widened when she found Lucas standing behind her, in a navy fleece quarter-zip and jeans, hands in his pockets, smiling. *Still cute.* Her heart fluttered a little. And she became instantly self-conscious. He was standing there looking like a catalog model, and she was in running leggings and her old University of Rochester sweatshirt under her puffer vest. Her hair was in a frizzy ponytail. There hadn't been much thought put into this outfit. Certainly not *I might see Lucas* thought.

"Maybe?" Kaya laughed. "I mean, how do I know if it's sufficiently deserving to be in my house?"

"Well, that's true," he replied. "Maybe I haven't been talking *enough* to trees in my life." They stood smiling at each other, which should have been awkward, but Kaya just felt...warm. After a beat, he asked, "Hey, do you need help getting all this to your car?"

"Actually," Kaya said, "that would be awesome. I guess I really didn't think that part through. Do you mind taking the tree? I think I can get the rest and I'm just over there."

Kaya paid and Lucas grabbed some twine and the tree. They loaded up Kaya's car, and Lucas helpfully secured the little tree to her roof. "Hey," he said as he finished, "do you want me to go back with you to help unload?" Kaya blinked. Come home with her? I mean, she knew he just meant to help, but, like, *what?*

"Sorry," Lucas laughed, shoving his hands into his pockets. "Is that weird?"

Kaya laughed too. "I wouldn't want to inconvenience you—you were headed into Swain's for some purpose, presumably."

"Oh, yeah, but it's not urgent. I need some filters for the furnace but not, like, immediately. I just thought you might need some help. I don't know where you're staying but nothing is far away here."

"That's true—I'm on the Point. And if you're sure..."

"I'm sure," he said quickly. She gave him her cross streets. He nodded and jogged backwards as he said, "I'll know I've found it when I see your car with the tree."

On the way home, she called Callie. Before Callie could even say "hello," Kaya shouted, *"He's coming home with me!"*

"What is even happening here?" Callie said. "Who is going where? Is this about Beach Plum Barista?"

"Yes," Kaya breathed. "I ran into him at Swains and he helped me load up some stuff into my car

and then he volunteered to come back to the house to help me unload it! He's coming to the cottage!"

"Wait. How do we know this is safe? We don't know him at all!"

"Oh, he gives off zero creepy vibe," Kaya said. "He's giving, like, a boy scout or Wegmans employee—super-helpful. Like, it made his day to be of help? It's hard to explain but I don't think I'm in any danger."

"But it's so quiet out there——no one to even shout out to."

Kaya sighed heavily as she turned off Sunset Ave onto Seagrove Ave. "There *are* neighbors, for the record. But seriously, I promise you, it's awkward and a little weird, but it is not dangerous."

"Okay, well...call me after."

"Promise. Love you, bye."

Lucas

LUCAS WAS GRINNING EAR to ear as he got in his car and pulled out of Swain's lot, turning right to head out to Sunset. This evening had been entirely unremarkable until it wasn't. Running errands, maybe the gym later, nothing special. But when he'd gotten out of his car and saw her—at least he thought it was her—his heartrate picked up. It looked like her hair, but it was back in a ponytail.

As he got closer, he thought—or really hoped—it had to be her. Then he heard her voice, talking to herself, and he knew he'd been right. He had been hoping for a little information on what she was up to, but *this* situation exceeded his expectations. He was beyond thrilled that she'd accepted his offer to go to her house and help. *Way to go, Lucas!*

Lucas navigated his Subaru Outback through Cape May Point. He pulled up slowly to the intersection she'd given him and parked on the side of the road opposite the dunes. He jogged up to her, looked at the roof of her Honda and said, "Well hello again, tree." Kaya laughed. "Cute place," he said looking up.

"Thanks," she said. "My parents bought it, like, seven years ago."

"Ah, so you're out here now," he said.

"Yeah?" she said, sounding a little confused, he thought. He was about to elaborate but she just went on, "But we've never come out for Christmas. I thought I'd decorate a little."

"Makes sense. Where do you want it to go?" he asked as he pulled a Swiss Army knife out of his pocket and started cutting the twine. "And if you want, let's put it in the stand first—we can get it standing straight out here where it won't drop as many needles on your floors, and then bring it in already in the stand."

"Smart," she replied. He gave her a quick sideways glance and smiled.

"Here, hold it upright where you want it, and I'll tighten the screws," he offered. Lucas crouched down and stabilized the little tree in its base. "Okay, we're good," he said, smiling again at her as he stood up. Her curls were piled on top of her head, and she was wearing a sweatshirt with a vest over it. She was looking at him with an expression he couldn't quite place—like she didn't know quite what to make of all of this. It was cute as hell.

"Um, okay, this way," she said, heading towards the stairs along the side of the house. Kaya led the way up the stairs with the other supplies and unlocked the door. Lucas followed her inside and up to the top floor of the house with the tree. He tried not to check her out, but it was hard when her butt in those yoga pants was at his eye level as they climbed the stairs. He could feel a flush creep into his face.

They emerged into a sort of great room on the top floor.

"Um, I guess just put it there for now," Kaya said. "I wasn't really thinking I was getting a tree, so I haven't really cleared space yet. But this little guy is small enough I should be able to move him." She gestured towards the corner of the room, beside some French doors. Lucas carried the tree across the room.

"So," she said, when he turned around. Lucas gestured to the sink to question if he could wash his hands. She nodded as she said, "Yes, totally. So...barista and off-duty boy scout? Do you also help old ladies cross the street and rescue cats from trees?"

He washed his hands and dried them, glancing back over his shoulder at her and chuckled. Then he turned around to face her, leaning back against her farmhouse sink. "Barista is part of the job. I'm actually a full-time employee of Cape Resorts."

"The ownership company for Beach Plum and Congress Hall?" Kaya asked.

"Yep, among other properties. I have a degree in hospitality from Cornell and I interned with Cape Resorts during college. They hired me after."

"They have a reputation for being sort of..." Kaya faltered and he saw a blush blossom over her cheeks.

"Douchey?" he offered, feeling the edges of his mouth quirk up.

"Yeah, something like that."

"They can be," he said, and looked at her, raising his eyebrows. "Safe space here?"

"Totally off the record," Kaya confirmed.

"The two sons—Tripp and Justin—are pretty entitled and vying for control. One of them will eventually probably get it. There are no other siblings and Mr. MacFarlane wants the business to stay in the family. But Mrs. MacFarlane really likes me, and she likes that I'm not afraid to do the work, that I love the place. Diane thinks I'm a good 'balancing force'—her words," he said, making air quotes.

"I told her I wanted some skin in the game—so when she and Mr. MacFarlane are gone, I will have some say with Tripp and Justin for company decisions. So, the parents have agreed to let me buy in. I've been saving and I'm pretty close to the good-faith deposit. The MacFarlanes will help me finance the rest of the buy-in."

"Wow," said Kaya. "So less 'barista' and more hospitality industry almost-mogul." Her eyes were large and deep brown. He noticed flecks of light, almost sparkles when she teased him. He smiled and looked down. Her voice brought his gaze back up. "Hey, do you want anything? Like tea, or water, or soda? Or wine maybe?"

He searched her eyes. He shouldn't abuse her hospitality. But then again, he really wanted an excuse to stay, to find out why she was back and what her life was like now. "That would be really nice, actually. Sure."

He watched her take off her vest and put it over the back of a counter stool. Grabbing a bottle of red wine from the pantry, she crossed to a drawer and got out a corkscrew. It just felt so *comfortable* being around her. He couldn't believe he was finally getting to hang out with her, after all these years.

Lucas shoved off the sink, took off his fleece, and set it over the same stool as Kaya's coat. He got a whiff of pine scent and...lavender maybe...when he passed her to walk around the living room. Lucas paused at a credenza behind the couch with family pictures on it and picked up one of her family. He immediately recognized her parents, Kaya, and her sister, Callie. "Ah, your family." There was another male in the picture he didn't recognize, with a warm smile, deeply tanned or brown skin, close-cut hair. "Who's this?" he asked, pointing to the guy.

Kaya glanced over from the island. Her eyes narrowed for just a second before she looked back down at the corkscrew. "My sister's husband, Juan. He's awesome."

"Ah," he replied. "That's great." He watched her pull out two stemless wine glasses, pour some wine into both glasses and hand one to him as he put down the picture. "Cheers," he said. "To talking to trees."

"And helpful baristas," she returned.

"What about you?" he asked, hoping his tone was as casual as he was trying to make it. He took a sip of wine for cover but kept his eyes on her. "Husband, boyfriend?" Lucas was annoyed to find his pulse quicken.

She sighed as they sat down at opposite ends of the couch.

"This, my new friend, is a sob story for which you did not sign up."

"Eh, try me," he countered, shifting his glance downward.

"Okay, well, we'll sum it up thusly," she said and paused to sip her wine. He was briefly distracted by her lips. "I was dating a guy for the last almost-three years. But my mother died two years ago and my father a couple months ago. Charlie decided I wasn't fun anymore and dumped me."

Lucas looked up and felt like all the blood drained from his face. *What?* "Your parents...are *gone*?"

Kaya

KAYA NOTICED THAT HE got a little choked up on the last word—which, considering he didn't know her parents, seemed suddenly, incredibly sweet. She flushed a little—*I'm sure from the wine*, and definitely not because this very nice, handsome man seemed truly invested in her life's tragedy.

"Yes, cancer. We got through COVID unscathed, but cancer apparently comes for the Morgan family. It's been a really awful go for a while." She let that sit, knowing that this was the part where most people got extremely uncomfortable and changed the subject, or offered some platitude like "at least they're together now," or "now they're at peace." *Bullshit, people.* I mean, yeah, she hoped her parents were having a cocktail on some mystical deck together in heaven, but the pain down here was real, folks.

To her surprise, though, Lucas stayed right there. "I know every loss is unique so I will not say I know how you feel," he said. *Wow. This guy...gets it?* "I will only say that that is incredibly devastating. I can't imagine what you and your sister have been through. And I hope, if you let me be your friend, that you'll never feel you have to hide or downplay your pain. That...I don't mind when you have bad days, and you'll let me celebrate with you on the good ones."

Kaya just blinked her now-teary eyes at this speech. She took a sip of wine and tried to process the overwhelming empathy coming off this man.

"Now, this Charlie person," he said, taking a swallow of wine. "I have a whole other set of feelings about."

"Honestly," Kaya said, swiping her eyes from the inside outward with her thumbs, "I wouldn't waste any energy even thinking about it. We were work friends; we hit it off." She paused, but something about Lucas' declaration has emboldened her. It felt good to open up to someone—like that day at the General Store with Tess.

"He's funny and generous, an outgoing guy who was always the social organizer, which was great because I'm an introvert. We had a lot of fun for a while. I thought it might be serious. Then...my mom got a lot worse—when the chemo stopped working. I went through phases where I didn't feel like eating. He would take me to dinner and try to make me laugh, and I was grateful for that." She fell quiet, lost in thought. Shaking her head to clear it, Kaya looked up. Lucas was watching her with soft eyes. He didn't seem bothered by the silence, which felt...nice.

"After she died, I was really reeling—kind of a shadow of myself, you know?" Kaya continued. "He didn't know how to support me, and I didn't have the emotional energy to know what I wanted or how to ask. It was starting to get better, but then my dad died, and about a month later, Charlie broke up with me saying that 'we've changed'." She also did the air quotes and then picked up her wine glass. "He meant me, I'd changed, and honestly, I can't deny that. Anyway, he said he was sorry, it'd been like this for a while for him, but that he didn't want to break up while my dad was sick."

"But he did it after your dad *died*?" Lucas choked out, aghast.

"That's what I said to him," Kaya answered with a sad laugh. She paused. "I've had a lot of time alone to think, and compared to losing my parents, this thing with Charlie was a lot easier to get over. Perspective, I guess. I have kind of realized I'm not upset about losing Charlie. He wasn't going to be any type of good long term in my life. I just think it was the loss itself—someone else leaving me." She never talked this much—especially to strangers. But something about his quiet strength and kind eyes, and how he was not running in discomfort from this pain...it was all drawing her out.

"But most of our work friends treated me weird because of...all of it...everyone tip-toed around me. I was really tired, and my sister and I decided to do Christmas here for change of pace, so I just kind of chucked it all and came out early."

"Ah," said Lucas, sipping from his wine and putting the glass back on the coffee table. "Are you working somewhere here?"

"I write copy and campaigns for a PR agency in DC. I'm working remotely. We'll see." They sat quietly. It was strangely not awkward. Kaya had always been comfortable with silence, but she also appreciated anyone who could be in it as well. She glanced over at him. A wave of his hair had fallen over his forehead and he was looking down contemplatively at his hands. Kaya followed his gaze. They were very nice hands. Long fingers curved around the glass. She flushed again.

He looked at her and stood up, so she did too. She watched as he crossed the room and picked up his fleece. "This has been really nice—thank you for the wine."

"Thank *you* for the help with the tree and everything." As he pulled his fleece over his head, his t-shirt caught a bit and she saw a little glimpse of horizontal muscle definition on his abs. *Whoa. Kaya! Keep it together*. He took a step towards her and put one hand very lightly on her forearm. He smelled like the Christmas tree and something minty. His gaze bored into hers.

"Thank you for telling me about your losses. I'm really sorry you're going through that. It sucks," he said. Her eyes darted back and forth between his while they held the gaze.

"Thank you," she said softly, finally. He nodded slightly and headed down the stairs. She followed him down to the first floor and showed him out. He walked down into the crisp, dark night, the sound of waves crashing, and the feeling it might snow.

The air was cold, but she still felt warm where he'd touched her arm.

Lucas

HER PARENTS ARE GONE. Lucas' thoughts were all over the place as he got in his car and headed back towards Sunset. He didn't know them, of course, not really. But he'd spent so much time watching them. There were renters all summer at that unit. But Kaya's family held a special fascination for him. More than any others, their joy was palpable.

And so young, or at least he assumed. Her parents had seemed about the same ages as his. This seemingly perfect family unit was...destroyed. It didn't seem fair.

Lucas turned onto Lafayette Street. On a whim, he grabbed his phone and hit his mother's number.

Her voice came over the car's speakers. "Lucas? Is everything alright?"

"Hi, Mom. Yes, everything is fine."

"Are you driving? What's wrong?"

Lucas absent-mindedly rubbed the bridge of his nose with one hand. "Nothing is wrong. I have a small-world story for you."

"Oh," she replied, her voice softening. "It's lovely to hear from you. What's the story?"

"So, I ran into a woman called Kaya. I don't know if you remember her. Her family used to rent unit three at 1506."

"Oh, Lucas, so many families rented that place when we lived there."

"Dad didn't like this family."

"You're going to have to narrow it down a bit more, I'm afraid."

Lucas chuckled hollowly. "Two girls," he started slowly. "Brown hair. Maybe a little younger than me. They stayed for at least two weeks every year. The mom was always smiling," he felt his voice catch and took a breath. "I think you liked her—the mom. The mom's sister came with them too. Sidewalk chalk. Silver Volvo station wagon. Dance parties on the back deck."

"Oh..." his mother replied. "I *do* remember them. Her name was Clare. She was very friendly. You ran into one of the daughters?"

"Yes." He navigated around the traffic circle at Washington Street and headed over the bridge. There was little traffic coming into Cape May at this hour on a weekday in December. He made the left easily onto his street.

"The younger one, Kaya. I saw her at Beach Plum and then again at Swains. I guess her family bought a place on the Point."

"Oh, really?" His mother's voice perked up. "They own down there now?"

Lucas turned his car into the driveway space under his building and turned off the engine. "Well, Kaya is staying at the family's house. But her parents...they passed away."

"They...really? Goodness. Covid?"

"Cancer."

"How sad," his mother replied. Lucas dragged a hand down his face. "Well," his mother continued briskly, "I'm sure your father is wondering where I've gone. I should go. Everything well with you? Job good?"

Lucas exhaled and placed his forehead briefly on the steering wheel. "Yeah, Mom. Everything's good. Say hi to Dad."

"I will. Goodnight, sweetheart."

"Goodnight, Mom."

Kaya

KAYA JOLTED AWAKE. IT was pitch dark outside. No moon. She jumped out of bed and pulled aside the curtain. It was snowing lightly. Her heart was racing wildly. *A dream*, she told herself. *It had just been a dream.*

She was outside on the deck of 1506, pressing her nose against the glass looking into the living room. People were milling about, laughing and talking. Many faces she didn't recognize—a dream blur. But some of them came into focus—Charlie, Barrie, Aunt Peggy, Dad...Mom.

She went to the bathroom, downed a glass of water and tried to go back to sleep, but she couldn't. The clock said 4:20. She just stared at the ceiling until it was time to get up.

Kaya

KAYA GOT UP, RESTLESS. She needed cold air; to get out of the house. She checked her schedule—no video calls this morning, so she packed up her laptop and biked to the General Store. Pushing open the door, she looked around. There was a family taking up two tables. More people were starting to come to the Point the closer they got to the holidays. But the other tables were open. Kaya ordered her coffee and settled in by the window, opening her laptop and connecting to the wifi. The family eventually left.

"Tess," called Kaya thoughtfully.

"Yes, hon?" responded Tess, the grey streaks on top of her head visible as she stocked jelly jars in the corner. The store was warm and bright, and festively decorated with many of the shelves and counters accented with red bows and gold bells.

"Do you know a guy called Lucas who works over at Beach Plum? Do you know his last name?" Tess stopped what she was doing, paused a second and then turned around.

"Of course, Lucas Andre. He's not just Beach Plum. I hear he's gone deep into the Congress Hall club over there."

"Yeah, we've run into each other a few times and I know he works with them." She was hesitant to say more, given her promise to Lucas that it was "off the record."

"Well," Tess said, "he's a really steady kid." She laughed almost to herself. "Kid. I mean, he must be thirty?..." She trailed off, probably doing the math, Kaya thought, compared to Tess' own kids' ages and where they all fell in school. Kaya stayed quiet. She wanted to know more about Lucas but wasn't sure what to ask. *What's with how nice he is, is he dating anyone* and *isn't he super hot* didn't seem exactly...*appropriate.*

Luckily, Tess picked up her own thread. "The Andre family was here a long, long time. Dr. Andre is sort of locally famous—some sort of trauma therapist. He's a civilian, but before he retired was kind of a big deal over at the Coast Guard and several other bases and educational facilities up the shore and over on the Delmarva. Lots of stories on how much he helped people—Coasties, other military, students, you know. But around here, the Andres mostly kept to themselves.

"Especially once Lucas started college, he didn't come home a lot. So it's kind of been nice to see him out and about, getting involved in the community operations."

"That seems like him," said Kaya. "He's certainly very helpful. That's why I was asking," she added quickly. "I ran into him last week at Swains and he helped me with my Christmas tree."

"That tracks for sure," replied Tess.

Kaya turned back to her laptop, but the words on the copy she was writing weren't nearly as energizing to her brain as Lucas. Lucas Andre.

Kaya

Kaya woke with a start and sat up. Today! Callie and Juan were coming! The days had been crawling lately with her anticipation. She decorated the little tree with the lights she bought, and she passed the time cutting plain white paper in dozens of little, intricate snowflakes that she nestled in the little tree's boughs. She was quite pleased with the effect. She set out the candles, the reindeer, the towels, and hung the wreath above the fireplace. But now she was downright impatient. She texted them both, since she was not sure who would be driving at any given time.

Followed by a Christmas tree emoji. Juan responded.

4ish? making good
time

Kaya checked the time—only 1:15. She decided to go for a run to burn off the impatient energy. It was a nice day out so she wound up going to Sunset

Beach, then back up to the West End Garage before looping back to the Point.

After she cooled down and showered, she still had time, so she forced herself to read to take her mind off the wait. It worked and she was engrossed in the latest Annabel Monaghan novel when she heard a car crunch on the shell gravel. They were here!

Suddenly there was all hugging, and energy, and laughing. Juan and Callie had gotten married young—a month after they graduated from Brown. Everyone *loved* Juan. He always asked everyone about themselves and how they were doing, even when he had his own shit going on. He was tall with light brown skin, sandy brown hair, and a big laugh that took up his whole face. His eyes crinkled and he often threw his head back when he laughed. And he *adored* Callie, which was what won Kaya over when she first met him.

They all unloaded the car, Juan leading with a box of spirits and cocktail paraphernalia. Juan always did some sort of themed cocktail for holidays and parties. Kaya was a pretty simple girl—she usually just drank wine. Even when she went out with her Alston Group friends and everyone ordered grown-up-sounding things like martinis and gin-and-tonics, Kaya never really got into spirits. She didn't really know what to order or what she would like, so she kept it simple. But she had yet to dislike anything Juan made.

When they'd brought in the bags, they gathered back on the top floor. Juan started poking around to see what snacks Kaya had on hand. Callie walked over to Kaya and looped arms with her. Kaya looked at her. "You look fantastic. I love your hair shorter," she said. Callie's hair was cut to just above her shoulders.

The sisters looked alike enough for people to believe they were related, but Kaya had always thought of herself as a starker, messier version of Callie. Though neither of them were considered short, Callie was an inch taller; her brown hair was a lighter shade than Kaya's and her brown eyes were as well. Kaya's eyes were a very dark brown, while Callie's were a dreamy caramel. Callie's hair was also a perfect beachy wave without much effort. Kaya always admired that. Hers was curlier, which she liked on good days, but didn't enjoy that it didn't need much help to skew frizzy.

"Yeah, well," Callie sighed, "I let it go for too long towards the end there with Dad, and afterward...there wasn't much time for self-care." They gazed at each other in perfect understanding. "But I've since gotten it done—as soon as winter break started." Callie was an elementary school music teacher, which was almost cliché, given that Callie often exuded sunshine and tended to greet people with a singing lilt in her voice.

Juan called from the kitchen area. "Who needs a cocktail?" The sisters turned around and raised their hands. Then Callie slowly turned, taking in the room. Tears came into her eyes.

"It's weird, being back here..."

"Yeah, I know," said Kaya. She squeezed her sister's arm a little tighter. "I know, the memories are..."

"It's just..." Callie started. "Like, we were so happy here, so I'm happy, and then I get hit with the...emptiness." Callie pulled a cuff of her sweater over her hand and wiped at her eyes. "I'm sorry..." she trailed off, shaking her head.

"Don't be. I feel it every day," Kaya replied with a small smile as she picked up a box of tissues from the end table and handed it to her sister.

Callie sniffled and shook her head again. "The tree is adorable. It's so festive—thank you for doing all this!"

"You're welcome. I know we all said we needed a change of pace, but it's still Christmas, you know?"

The evening wiled away. Kaya made a chili and cornbread, and they ate, laughed, cried, and reminisced. "I have something for you," Callie said. "Juan, can you get the thing?" Juan disappeared downstairs and came back up shortly. Kaya looked at her sister with her head cocked to the side.

"Mysterious."

"It is," Callie said softly. She took the small, rectangular box from Juan and gave it to Kaya.

"What is it?"

"Open it," answered Callie. "When we were cleaning things out in Poughkeepsie, I found two of these boxes, identical, in his closet. I looked inside and I can only assume that these were going to be Christmas gifts...for both of us," she said, choking lightly on the last words. Kaya carefully opened the box. It was two beautifully detailed ships in bottles nestled in protective cushioning—tiny tall ship models in glass orbs, corked, with red satin ribbon tied around the necks.

"Ornaments," breathed Kaya. "He loved ships," she said, looking up at Callie with glistening eyes. All three of them were crying now. "Thank you. Thank you for bringing me this."

"Of course," she said, as they dried their eyes and hung Kaya's set of ornaments on the little tree.

"Hey," Callie said suddenly. "When do we get to meet Beach Plum Barista? I mean, I know you said he is a junior executive or something, but to me he'll always be the BPB."

"I haven't seen him since the tree night. I don't really know his work schedule, but we can go over there any time you want. You just have to promise me you'll be cool."

Callie squealed a little and clasped her hands together. "Let's go tomorrow! Okay, no. Tomorrow is Christmas. Let's go the day after!!"

"None of this is giving 'cool'," Kaya sighed, gesturing at Callie.

Kaya

EVEN AFTER A NIGHT of maybe one too many cocktails, the Morgan girls were never late sleepers. So Kaya wasn't surprised when she came upstairs rubbing the sleep out of her eyes to see Callie already sitting at the counter with a cup of coffee, gazing out at the ocean.

"Morning," said Kaya.

"Heyyyyyy," Callie sang softly. She got up hugged Kaya. "Did you sleep okay?"

"Yes, actually," Kaya replied.

"Actually?" Callie asked as she sat back down and watched Kaya pour herself some coffee and join her on the adjacent stool.

"I have bouts of insomnia, crazy dreams, that type of thing. Not every night, but sometimes. It's okay because I can usually nap during the day if I have to. Turns out I'm a much more efficient worker when there's no one stopping by my cube, or wanting to go for coffee…"

"I know what you mean," Callie offered. "I'm not having dreams, really, that I recall, but sometimes I just can't turn my brain off. You know."

"I know."

They sat in silence—a comfortable, shared silence, bonded by blood. And loss. And grief. Still looking out at the water, Callie said, "I know we have some time to talk about this, but do you need anything from Poughkeepsie? I think I have everything that was personal stored in our basement in Providence, but if there's something you're attached to...just before we engage the real estate and estate sale people..." her voice trailed off.

"Thank you," said Kaya slowly, thinking. "I don't think so. I cleaned out a lot when I first moved to Washington. You and I already sorted Mom's stuff. I'm sure you've pulled the right things. I had grabbed a couple of his sketches after the funeral. I think I'm good?" she looked at her sister and smiled sadly. "I'm just sorry you're dealing with all that. If there's anything I can do to help, let me know."

Callie gazed out at the dunes and then back to Kaya, also smiling. She covered Kaya's hand with hers. "No, of course not. I've got Juan to help, we live closer than you, and honestly, we're going to have the estate management people do everything. I don't know how you feel, but I've said my goodbyes to that house. It's not the same without them."

"Exactly," said Kaya.

"Plus," Callie went on, "you know we have neighbors and friends there who would willingly help with any last-minute stuff the estate folks need. I am hopeful it just comes down to me telling you when we have offers to buy it so we can decide together which to accept."

"Okay," said Kaya, and they both turned as Juan came up the stairs, blinking sleep out of his eyes.

"Merry Christmas!" he called, spirited but sleepy. Kaya and Callie looked back at each other and burst out laughing.

"Merry Christmas!" they said to each other. Callie laughed, "I totally forgot."

Kaya responded, "Me too. I mean obviously I knew it was Christmas, but the excitement of having you arrive, and this being a whole crazy new routine down here, it just slipped my mind this morning!"

"Well, it's Christmas now!" Juan declared and they all exchanged hugs.

After they make a huge breakfast with eggs, bacon, pastries Callie grabbed from Madisons on the way in the day before and lots of coffee, they exchanged presents. They had agreed to keep it all low key this year. Kaya gave Callie a new, pretty messenger bag for work, while Callie gave Kaya a cheery, blue, Lodge clay pot. "I know you're getting into cooking more..." she offered hesitantly.

Kaya hugged her, saying, "I love it. It's true! It's just me, I'm not in anyone's way and I have lots of time. I'm really enjoying teaching myself things, new recipes. I don't have a big heavy pot yet and I know I'm going to use it."

A different Christmas for sure, but looking at her little family, Kaya smiled.

"Tomorrow." said Callie, looking mischievous.

"Tomorrow?" asked Kaya.

"Tomorrow, we go searching for BPB."

Lucas

THE DOORBELL RANG. LUCAS glanced towards the door of his condo. It was Christmas morning. He wasn't expecting anyone. He had just come back from a run because the gym was closed for the holiday. He set down his glass of water and went to answer the door. Molly, the big golden retriever hopped up from where she was snoozing and pricked up her ears.

"Hey," he said. His friend, Tim Lee, was standing on the threshold. Lucas stepped aside and held the door open. "Come in. What are you doing here?"

Tim entered and eased off his loafers. The dog came bounding up to the visitor. Tim laughed, reached down and scratched the dog's ears. "What is *she* doing here?"

Lucas chuckled as he walked back to the island and swallowed some more water. "Casey's with his folks. He flew this time." Lucas shrugged. "Couldn't take the dog."

"But aren't you going to your parents' today?" Tim asked, straightening up.

"Yeah. You want something? Water?"

"Nah, I'm good. So what are *you* going to do with Molly?"

"Take her?"

Tim looked at his friend. His eyebrows shot up. "Take her," he repeated incredulously. "Your parents will flip. Do they know?"

Lucas sighed and ran a hand through his sweaty hair. "No. Once again, Casey's logistics were somewhat last-minute. I couldn't say no to him."

"You can. You could. You just never do."

"Right."

"Look, man, I'll take her," Tim offered. "It's just for the day, right?"

Lucas' eyes snapped to his friend's. "I can't ask you to do that."

"You didn't ask. I'm offering. Merry Christmas."

"Tim..." Lucas started.

"Bro," Tim interrupted, his voice soft, "it's Christmas. It's usually a shit show surviving time with your dad under normal circumstances. Throw in a holiday and a dog he will not want in his perfect house—and a big dog at that—I don't want that for you. My mom and grandma won't care. Plus my mom has a fenced-in yard. Molly will be so much happier."

Lucas' shoulders dropped. "Are you sure?"

"I'm *sure.*" Tim turned to where Molly was sitting and looking up at him with her big, brown eyes. "See? She wants to come with me." As if on cue, Molly gave a short bark.

Lucas laughed. "Okay. I really appreciate the help. I can take her back tonight. Honestly, I *was* kind of dreading showing up with her." He didn't really have a plan. No way his dad would let her in the house. Lucas was sort of assuming he'd have to leave Molly in his parents' garage. But he wasn't entirely sure they'd even allow that. It might have been the car, which felt cruel.

He grabbed her leash from a hook by the door and put it in a tote bag that already had her bowl and food in it. "Give her a heaping cup of this around six tonight and put a bowl of water where she can get it. Otherwise, she doesn't need much," Lucas shared. "I *really* appreciate this."

"No problem. And hey, it looks like you need a shower before you get on the road, so I won't keep you."

"Yeah, why did you come over? I mean it's nice to see you and Merry Christmas, but..." Lucas trailed off.

Tim laughed. "I knew Casey left town. I figured Molly was probably here and if she was, I figured that would put you in a jam."

Lucas looked at his friend. "Thank you, man. That's really nice of you."

"You're welcome. You're always doing everything for everyone else. I was free. This is easy."

"Sorry I'm sweaty, dude, but I'm totally gonna hug you right now," Lucas said with a chuckle. They gripped hands and hugged each other with their free arms. "Merry Christmas. I'll see you later tonight," he added as he pulled back.

"You got it," Tim replied.

Lucas

LUCAS PULLED INTO THE driveway of his parents' home on the Main Line outside Philadelphia. He followed the drive around to the side of the house. He noticed another car was already there. Probably some friends of his parents. He didn't recognize the car, but that said, he wouldn't really know what cars his parents' various friends were driving. Getting out of the car, he shook out his suit pants and smoothed the front of the sweater he had on over a button-down shirt. He ran a hand through his hair and crossed to the side door.

He entered through the mudroom and followed the sound of voices to the main living room at the front of the house. "Hello," he called.

"Lucas!" his mother exclaimed, jumping to her feet. "Merry Christmas, sweetheart." She embraced him and he caught her signature scent of Shalimar perfume.

"Merry Christmas," he replied. He pulled back and handed her the bottle of red wine he was carrying.

"Oh thank you," she gushed. "One of your favorites?"

"Yeah, a relatively new relationship, but they're making interesting wines and we're going to buy more of them. They operate out of Cape May County but get some of their grapes from other vineyards."

"Lovely," she replied. Lucas turned to the rest of the room as his mother disappeared with the wine.

"Merry Christmas," he said. His father walked towards him with his hand outstretched. Lucas took the hand and shook it firmly. "Sir," Lucas said. His father just nodded at him. Lucas pursed his lips slightly and turned to the other couple who were on their feet as well. "Hi, Mr. Sullivan, Mrs. Sullivan. Please, sit," he said. "Mind if I make myself a drink, Dad?" he asked as the three sat back down.

"Go ahead," his father replied before turning back to his company. "As I was saying, Jack, they're revamping the whole program. I'd just be a consultant."

"Doesn't sound like a 'just' to me," Mr. Sullivan replied.

Lucas didn't know what program they were discussing and frankly he didn't care. Some new opportunity for his dad to be *important*. He busied himself across the room at the bar cart. One strong drink should do it. Take a little of the edge off this gathering and still be able to drive home later after dinner. He made himself a gin martini (*double*).

He turned back towards the company, but stayed standing at the side of the room. His gaze swept over his parents well-appointed living room. He took in the large Christmas tree in the corner. Faux, but a high quality faux that looked real. Perfectly color-coordinated and matched ornaments. Small, white lights. Lucas knew his mother had it set up and decorated by a professional designer. He sighed to himself. It was beautiful, *but...*

Lucas had yearned as a kid for a real, irregular tree that filled the room with pine smell and was decorated with his art projects, pictures, souvenirs from trips, colored lights...the kinds of trees some of his friends had. Personality. But that was never going to happen in the Andre house.

His mother re-entered the room. "Lucas, join us," she called. He crossed the room and took a seat on the sofa beside her. "How is work?" she asked, patting his thigh.

He took a sip of his drink. "Very good, actually," he answered. "I'm headed back to Congress Hall, the mother ship." It was good—closer to the MacFarlanes, he would be part of more meetings, have more interaction, and eventually get to back of house and operations. It crossed his mind that the one downside of leaving Beach Plum Farm was that Kaya wouldn't know where to find him. Assuming she'd be looking, that is. *I really hope she's looking.* His mouth tugged into a smile as he thought about her.

"What is it that you're doing now?" he heard Mrs. Sullivan ask him.

"I'm still at the hotel," he replied, taking another sip of his drink. The gin burned in a satisfying way as he swallowed.

"How interesting," she said politely.

"I like hospitality," he said. "I like being of service."

His father scoffed lightly. "You make coffee."

"I'm sure it's very good coffee..." Mrs. Sullivan started but Lucas quickly interjected, looking at his father, "...among the many other things I do."

"Your father's just teasing, sweetheart," said his mother, patting his thigh again. Lucas gave her a quick glance over the top of his glass as took another sip of his cocktail. He set the glass down on the coffee table and took a deep breath, determined to keep his tone mild. He looked back at his father. "In another year I'll be bought in. So yes," he said turning his gaze back to his mother and smiling at her, "work is going well."

"Or," said his father, taking a large drink of a dark amber liquid—probably bourbon, "the MacFarlanes are bluffing."

"How's that?" Lucas replied, feeling his chest tightening.

"Taking advantage of you. I don't see Robert really handing over the reins. That's his business. His family."

Lucas looked back at his father. Lucas would not capitulate, but neither would he argue. His inner voice might be screaming but he kept his tone measured. "I have no reason to believe they are dealing with me in anything other than good faith."

His father leveled his stare at Lucas. "You should hope so. Don't make a fool of us."

Lucas exhaled and looked at his mother. They held each other's eyes. Hers had a sadness that probably only Lucas could see, for a fleeting moment, before she smiled and said, "Lucas, I ran into Margaret Scott at the hospital gala—they were giving your father an award this year..."

Of course they were.

"...and Margaret's daughter Kennedy was on the planning committee. She is so impressive. I don't know where she finds the time—she's a lawyer at a big firm. But it was such a wonderful event. She really is something. Do you know her? I could connect you two."

Lucas felt his mouth twitch up at the ends.

"Oh yes," Mrs. Sullivan gushed. Lucas turned his gaze to her. "I know them, too. Kennedy Scott is very smart and *so* lovely. Just a stunning girl. You should meet her, Lucas."

"Thank you, both," he said looking back at his mother and smiling. "I appreciate you looking out for me. I'm all set right now."

"Well if you change your mind..." his mother trailed off before looking back at her company. "Who needs another drink?"

Kaya

KAYA AND CALLIE SAT in the front of Kaya's Honda with Juan in the back seat. They drove the short distance to Beach Plum Farm, because it was too cold to bike. They argued about the least embarrassing way to do this drive-by. Well, Kaya wanted to avoid embarrassment. Callie seemed wildly undeterred.

"We just go in and you introduce me," Callie said.

"What? No. I can't be all 'we've bumped into each other a couple times and I spilled my guts to you in my living room, and now I think it's the right time for you to meet my family'!"

"I don't see the problem. You said there's a connection—that you feel a connection with him," Callie protested.

"I do!" Kaya responded with a huge sigh as she turned into the Beach Plum entrance. "But I don't know what he felt! And I don't even know if he's here! And it's still too soon!"

"Okay," said Callie. "Well, I'll just go in alone and check him out."

"Fine," said Kaya, pulling into a parking spot.

"But wait, how will I know which one is him? I guess I can ask."

"*What*? No. You can't ask. Why would you be asking for him?"

"Okay, Juan can go in and ask."

Juan looked startled. "What?" he asked while simultaneously Kaya barked, "why would *Juan* be asking for him?"

Kaya put the car in park and turned to face her sister. "Okay, enough. You guys wait here. I will go in and get a coffee. If he's working, I'll come back out, and you guys can go in without me to get a look at him. Deal?"

"We look a lot alike, Kay," said Callie, eyes dancing.

"Well, this is my best offer."

"Okay, fine."

Kaya pushed through the door into the festive warmth of the barn-like market building. Her spirit fell briefly when she looked behind the counter and it was a young woman. She approached a mid-30s woman who looked like she might be more in charge, with pretty braids, folding merchandise shirts and tea towels on the displays.

"Excuse me," Kaya ventured.

The woman looked up, smiling. "Yes?"

"I was wondering, is Lucas Andre working today?" Kaya felt like this woman had got to be seeing right into her soul and Kaya flushed like a schoolgirl with a crush.

But the woman's eyes danced as she shook her head. "No, sorry. Lucas has moved on."

"Moved on?" Kaya breathed.

The woman laughed, "I just mean that they sent him over to Congress Hall. He's done with our rotation."

"Ah," Kaya said. "Well, thank you for the information."

"Good luck," the woman said over her shoulder, grinning, as she turned back to the merch.

Kaya returned to the car and shared this news, at which Callie said, "Off to Congress Hall for us!" Juan rolled his eyes. Then he opened his car door. "No," he said.

Callie and Kaya both whirled around and stared at him, mouths agape. "I mean, *yes*," he said quickly, laughing. "Of course we'll go, but I need breakfast. I'm *hungry*," he said as he swung one leg out of the car. The sisters looked back at each other and snort-laughed.

"Okay," said Kaya, "but I can't go back in there. Grab me an egg sandwich?" she asked, hopefully.

"Make it two!" called Callie cheerfully.

After a quick sustenance in the parking lot of Beach Plum, they drove into town.

"Okay, what's the new plan?" asked Callie.

"I guess..." Kaya started, thinking, "...that we can all go in, since it's the hotel. Like we could realistically be going to Congress Hall to look at the

Christmas decorations. He wouldn't yet know that I know he's working here..."

"That's right," Callie picked up the thread. "If we do run into him, he can't assume you've brought your family to meet him, because he doesn't know that you know that he is here, so you can't have come here to find him."

"This is getting dizzying," Juan said mildly.

She found a parking spot in the lot behind the Washington Mall. They crossed the street towards the hotel. Congress Hall was seriously done up for Christmas. Garlands and lights wound around the giant columns, there was an enormous wreath and oversized ornaments hanging over the main entrance. Inside the entryway were giant pots of poinsettias.

Kaya eyes swept around the lobby. "We have no idea where he'd be," she said as her gaze came back to her sister.

"Ask!" said Callie, cheerfully and started towards the desk. Kaya grabbed her arm.

"No!" she hissed in a whisper. "We can't just ask. We don't really have any business with him!"

"Relax," Callie said. "This place is huge and busy. There are so many people. For all these people know..." she gestured towards the concierge stand. "...maybe you do actually have business with him. Let me just make a small inquiry," said Callie, shaking free of Kaya before Kaya could stop her.

Callie strode up to the desk. "Hi," she started. "Is Lucas Andre working front of house anywhere today?" Kaya's cheeks burned with embarrassment. She actually *doesn't* have any business with him. If they asked, she was sure that *I need him so my sister can check him out* was beyond the reasonable request of staff, even in the hospitality business.

"Lucas?" the guy behind the desk repeated, looking blank. Kaya watched nervously from a distance, while Juan wandered around checking out the art in the lobby. A very efficient-looking young woman with a perfectly styled blond ponytail, in a crisp blouse and suit jacket stood next to the guy Callie had asked, typing away on her computer. Without looking up, she offered to him, "Lucas Andre. New exec train." She looked up at Callie. "Try the coffee shop." And immediately went back to her screen.

Kaya exhaled. She didn't realize she'd been holding her breath. Callie returned to her, with a triumphant smile. They both headed over to Juan.

"Okay, what now?" Kaya asked. She gestured with her head towards the colonnade of shops that included the Congress Hall coffee café. Answering her own question, she said, "Same plan? I go in first to confirm if he's there, and then..."

"No," said Callie. "We've covered this. He doesn't know that you know he's here. We're all just here for coffee!" she said with a huge smile, and sailed down to the café.

Lucas

LUCAS TAPPED THE CUSTOMER'S order into the console and spun it around so they could choose their options for tip and payment. He glanced up quickly towards the door, sensing new customers. He glanced down but then did a double-take back up and felt a broad smile rip across his face. *Kaya.* The other customer walked away, and Lucas watched the next guests approach. Callie, like Kaya, looked much as he remembered, just a bit older. Lucas couldn't recall exactly what the brother-in-law looked like from the brief glance at the photo at Kaya's house when he was helping with the tree, but he assumed this was him.

"Hi," said Kaya. The prettiest blush crept across her face.

"You found me," Lucas said. He could feel his grin, but couldn't stop it.

"I did...I mean, I uh, I had no idea you were working here...we, uh...we came for coffee," she stammered. Lucas felt his smile drop. "But I'm happy to find you here," she hastily added. His mouth curved back into a smile. She looked so cute. Her hair was down, with a purple knit cap on. She was wearing a black turtleneck sweater, jeans, and a navy wool coat hanging open, her hands thrust in her pockets.

"It's really nice to see you," said Lucas. He held her gaze for a beat and then glanced over her shoulder at her family.

Kaya stammered, "Oh...sorry..." and stepped to the side. "Um, guys, this is Lucas...Andre." *Hmm had he told her his last name?* "Lucas, this is my sister and brother-in-law, Callie and Juan Ramos."

"Really great to meet you, Juan," said Lucas, extending his hand across the counter, which Juan shook. "And wonderful to be introduced to you, Callie."

"Um," said Callie, "back atcha?"

"What can I get for you all?" he asked. They ordered their coffees, and Callie stepped up to pay. Lucas looked back at Kaya and found her gaze on him. "Merry Christmas," he said.

"Merry Christmas, Lucas," she replied. He held her gaze, her big brown eyes locked on his before she turned away. The next customers were waiting expectantly. Regretfully, he turned back towards the counter. He saw them leaving out of the corner of his eye. He looked over to catch her. He gave her a nod and a little wave. She waved back. A grin ripped across his face. He couldn't help it.

Kaya

AS THEY WALKED OUT, Callie said, "What's up with the nice-to-be-introduced-to-you business? Is that some more formal way to say nice-to-meet-you?"

"Honestly, I don't know," Kaya responded. "He said something similar when I met him too." She shrugged.

"Okay, well, you were not lying—he's seriously cute," she said, at which Juan good-naturedly rolled his eyes and groaned, "I'm *right here*!"

Callie turned to Juan and put a hand on his forearm. "You're adorable, babe," she placated before turning back to Kaya. "And he lit up when you walked in, so, congratulations." Kaya looked down and smiled.

They crossed the street to the top of the Washington Mall—the three-block stretch of boutique shops and restaurants in the center of Cape May. Kaya and Juan should have known what was coming next...Callie clapped her hands together and declared, "Okay, let's shop!" They looked at each other and laughed.

Kaya

THE LAST NIGHT BEFORE Callie and Juan left to go home, after the dishes were washed and put away, they all sat around the fireplace with a bottle of wine. There was a lull in conversation when Kaya said, "Guys..." They both looked up at her.

"It has been really good for me, being here, the last month. And, I'm wondering if I can...stay for a while. Like, give up my apartment in DC and live here for the time being." Callie and Juan looked briefly at each other in surprise and then back at Kaya.

"I know," she continued, "that you'll probably want the rental income if we rent it in the season..."

Callie cut her off. "No, that is actually the last thing on my mind. I'm just worried that you're doing something rash. It would be a...big step."

"Yes," said Kaya. "But not a permanent one. I'm not saying I'll never go back to DC. I just...I feel like I don't want to leave here yet. I think it could be good for me. And if I'm staying for a while, it seems like a waste to keep paying rent back in DC."

Juan cleared his throat. "I think you should do whatever you think is best for you, and I agree with Cal that we don't care about the rental income. But

I would just worry that you're down here alone. If there's trouble, or really rough weather, if things break..." he trailed off.

"Then, I'll facetime you and you can show me how to tighten towel bars with an allen wrench, or whatever. And for bigger things, I guess I'll have to adult and call someone. Or consult YouTube," she smiled at him. "I'm not worried about being alone, though. I have people already who will help me like the Nevilles, and I'm planning to get a job—or at least try."

"Wait, you're quitting your job too?" Callie asked, her brow furrowing slightly.

"I've been thinking about this for a while," Kaya said slowly. "I could probably keep working remotely, but it's ultimately not best for the Alston Group. They're being really nice letting me do it for now, and all the bereavement leave before, but I don't see how it's sustainable. I can do the work, but I can't do as well on developing the staff or myself...or client management and sales from here. Plus, I want to take a break. We have a little money from the trust, and we'll have the sale of the house in Poughkeepsie. I don't plan to live just on that, but it's not like we're desperate. I can pay off my student loans and I live pretty simply here. I want to look for a job writing down here—probably part time is all I can get, but then I can get a rando job in season to pad my accounts for the next year."

Callie and Juan were quiet and looked at each other. Kaya watched them peer at each other as they seemed to have a wordless conversation. "Okay." Callie said, her expression smoothing out as she turned back to Kaya.

"Okay?" Kaya asked, her brows shooting up.

"Okay. If there's anything I've learned over the past two years is that you just never know how life is going to go. If you feel good here—and it sounds like you do—then you do you. Just let us know what you need." Kaya's eyes welled up. She leapt to her feet and pulled her sister up off the couch to wrap her arms around her. Kaya felt Callie's arms tighten around her torso. When Kaya pulled back, she saw Callie's eyes were also misty. Juan had stood up. Kaya turned to hug him too, her tears melting against his t shirt.

"I love you guys."

"We love you, too," Callie replied.

"And I guess it doesn't hurt," Callie said, "that hot BPB is here too."

"It doesn't hurt," Kaya said, smiling into her brother-in-law's shoulder.

Kaya

AFTER CALLIE AND JUAN pulled out of the drive, the cottage felt too quiet. It would take some time to get used to being alone again. Kaya called her old boss, Melanie. She answered on the third ring.

"Kay! Happy new year! Are you back?"

"Happy new year," Kaya responded. "No, I'm still in Cape May. How are things?"

"Things..." Mel paused for a minute. "Well, I would be happy to regale you with holiday stories of my crazy mother and crazier sister, but that should really pair with wine or something stronger. How's by you?"

"Oh, it was really nice having Callie and Juan here. It was quiet, and...different, but ultimately really nice."

"That does sound nice. When are you coming home?"

"Hmm, well, I have some news, and you're not going to like it, I'm afraid," Kaya said tentatively.

"Well," said Mel, "then let's have it out."

"I think I'm going to resign..."

Before Kaya even finished, Mel cut her off. "No. Unacceptable." She didn't sound angry, exactly, but like she was going to marshal an argument to change Kaya's mind. "I have told you this for almost four years. We are a team. No one props me up like you do." She was chuckling while she said it, though, almost like she knew it wouldn't work.

Kaya laughed and then sighed. Mel's voice softened. "What's going on?"

"It's no one thing," Kaya started. She knew she was safe. Melanie wouldn't like working without her, but she would totally understand.

"Well, I know it's not that tool, Charlie." Melanie snorted.

"That is actually true. That sucked in sort of a I-can't-believe-you're-doing-this-now way, but in the grand scheme of things, I've been over it. I think...uggghhh I don't know how to say this."

"Just say it," said Mel.

"I think on some level, after my mom died, I've been going through the motions and work was a great distraction."

"Well, nothing in the quality of your work has screamed 'distracted'," Mel said loyally.

"I appreciate you saying that. I do. It's actually been so wonderful, working with you and the team, and having things to do. But then since my dad passed away, I've been restless. Like...I don't know. Life is short. And where I used to take solace in the work, now it feels increasingly meaningless. And I hate feeling that way. You and the team and our clients deserve better, you know?" Kaya rushed on, almost afraid to pause because she didn't want to disappoint Melanie. "And I think I'm going to stay here. Remote work forever has even less meaning for me and is even less fair to you...and I'm just trying to increase my...purpose, or my happy or something...so...that's where I'm at. Am I crazy?" she finished with a deep sigh.

"Well," Melanie said quietly, looking directly into the camera. "You know I love you and I will always want what's best for you. So I won't try to talk you out of it."

"Thank you," Kaya said quietly.

"But 'crazy' is still in play." They both laughed. "And you know you can always come back if you want," Melanie added.

"I really, really appreciate that." They were both quiet for a beat. "I'll let you know when I'm coming back. I'll have to put stuff from my apartment in storage and get a few things from the office..."

"Good. There will be wine with your name on it."

"Perfect."

The text from Melanie came later that day.

> Told Margaret. She understands but is sad. And seriously this is a direct quote from her: 'pls say it isn't bc of that idiot in events bc I can fire him' lol I told her def not bc of Charlie

Kaya smiled to herself.

Ha def not. Thx for telling her. I'm sorry to let her down. I'll send her a note as well

Don't worry, she understands. She also said u are welcome back any time.

Lucas

"LUCAS, DO YOU HAVE thoughts?" Robert MacFarlane's voice jolted him. Lucas had been totally lost, thinking about Kaya. Wishing she'd come in again. He knew where she lived, of course, but he didn't have her contact information. He couldn't just show up at her house unannounced, but it was driving him crazy that she hadn't come around.

He hadn't seen her since the day after Christmas. And that was almost two weeks ago now. He wasn't sure why he was so fixated on her. She was cute, yes, but it was more knowing that she was here somewhere, in pain...reeling from the loss of her family. He was worried about her. He wanted to mourn with her somehow. That family meant something to him, too, in some small way. Living vicariously through the laughter, the freedom, the joy.

But now his boss was speaking to him, and he had no idea what he'd missed. "I'm sorry, sir, what was the question?"

"The cottages at Beach Plum. It was your idea originally. Do you have thoughts on expansion?"

He *did*, actually. This project had been his baby.
They were sitting on ample land out on Stevens
Road. The original idea had been to expand the
farm, but Lucas had run the financial models to
show they could partner with other farms to get
more varied and local produce more cheaply than
they could scale their farm. His idea had been to
build guest cottages and expand the restaurant to
create a unique hospitality experience on the
acreage.

"Yes," he replied. "The first four cottages did
very well in terms of profitability last year, and I
think we can make it an even more enticing
destination. We should put in a pool for the
exclusive use of cottage guests and do more with
the café. I'm thinking if we put up a permanent tent
structure, we can host themed dinners or tasting
experiences."

"Just for guests?" Mr. MacFarlane asked.

"Not necessarily," mused Lucas. "We could give
guests first crack, but we could open them to the
public as well."

"That doesn't make sense." Lucas turned to his
right to find Tripp MacFarlane leaning forward,
arms on the boardroom table, staring him down. "If
people are staying in a whole house, why would
they want to come to the café to eat? They can just
cook for themselves at the cottages."

"Do *you*?" Lucas fired back. He watched with
some satisfaction as Tripp reared back in his chair.
"Tell me," Lucas pressed on, casually, "when you

stayed at that villa in Italy last fall, did you cook your meals?"

"Of course not. There was a chef."

Lucas leaned back in his chair, looked down and allowed the edges of his mouth to quirk up. It was too easy.

Tripp's brother, Justin, said, "Right, not everyone wants to cook when they're on vacation. Because they take the whole cottage doesn't necessarily mean they want to cook there."

Lucas turned to Justin and smiled. "Exactly. The data show that people like places like the cottages, or AirBNBs because they have the privacy, and the *option* to cook for themselves. To fix breakfast or keep snacks. But a lot of people won't want to grocery shop for all the ingredients for dinners, only to have a lot of it go to waste. Or they just don't want the work."

Tripp scoffed, but didn't reply. Lucas, dressed in his Congress Hall café yellow polo shirt and khakis, observed Tripp—dark blonde hair slicked back away from his face. He wore an expensive suit and silk tie. Lucas wasn't entirely sure what Tripp and Justin did all day but he didn't care. Lucas knew *he* was useful and that was all that mattered right now.

"Write up the projections," Diane MacFarlane said. She sat at the end of the table, flanked by Justin and her assistant, a petite raven-haired woman named Tracy. "Put together the concept and we'll discuss at next week's meeting."

"I look forward to the discussion," Robert MacFarlane said from the other end of the table. "If this goes well, we should think about doing something similar at the Shelter Island property. That's all for today." His chair scraped back on the wooden floor as he stood. Tripp shoved his chair back aggressively and strode out of the room. Robert stood, started for the door, but paused beside Lucas. Robert put a hand on Lucas' shoulder. "Good work, son."

Kaya

THE TRIP BACK TO DC to organize her things into "take back to the cottage," "put in storage," and "throw/give away" turned out to be easier than she had been fearing. Several of her friends and some assorted friends' partners were surprisingly helpful and efficient in the heavy lifting.

Her week back in Washington concluded with a big, free-wheeling "happy hour" at Mi Vida at the Wharf, which in truth was a four-hour affair because friends and co-workers who wanted to say goodbye all had different obligations and times they could meet. Even Charlie came by, and Kaya found herself rather dispassionate about that turn of events. He kissed her on the cheek and told her good luck, and looked a little relieved when she said she wished him well, too, and thanked him for coming.

At one point, Melanie approached Kaya, clinked her margarita glass against Kaya's, leaned towards her and whispered, "You're doing really well."

Kaya drew back and faced her, her head cocked to one side. "What do you mean?"

Melanie laughed lightly. "With this," she said gesturing around. "You *hate* farewell happy hours.

You hate elongated goodbyes. Hell, you hate goodbyes altogether." Kaya looked slightly down, over the top of her margarita into the middle distance.

"I do," she admitted, looking back at Melanie. "You're right. But it's more specific than that. I get triggered by people leaving *me* or the team. As it turns out," she paused, took a sip of her drink, and smiled wryly, "I really don't have any issues with being the leave-er."

"Ah!" responded Melanie. "Well that explains it!"

Kaya drank lots of water along the way, and everyone seemed to over-pay whenever they left, so she wound up being not too tipsy and owing nothing when the bill finally came due. She issued everyone invites to Point Taken. There was hugging, some crying, and lots of laughing and promises to stay in touch.

For the most part, the emotional ease of the trip only validated for Kaya that this was the right thing for her right now. The hard part was with her old roommate Lynne. She tried to tell herself that it was okay—Lynne was getting serious with Evan and was around the apartment a lot less already for the six months or so before Kaya left for Poughkeepsie and then the Point. But they were close—they would always be close.

Kaya remembered when her phone rang in their apartment in the wee hours that May morning, both of them jolting awake knowing there was only one reason the phone would ring that early—the same reason Kaya had stopped putting her phone on "do not disturb" at night. Kaya answered her father's call, heard him say the words, told him she'd get a flight that morning, and hung up. Lynne had crept into Kaya's room, crawled into her bed, and hugged her tight while she sobbed.

Lynne drove her to her office to grab some things she'd need over the hiatus, helped her pack, and drove her to the airport. And a week later, Lynne stood by her side, or off to the side, but always near, through the endless hours of Clare's viewing, funeral, and wake.

A friend like that was not nothing.

Lynne was, of course, totally supportive of Kaya's move for Kaya's sake. She didn't so much care about finding a new roommate—she said she might be moving in with Evan anyway. But she confirmed she was going to miss Kaya like crazy. Kaya reminded Lynne the upside was she had a free place to stay at the beach any time she wanted. (Lynne *loved* the beach.) "I mean," Kaya said, "I know how you treasure our day trips to Ocean City with Imagine Dragons blaring, but maybe a multi-day, free stay at a nice cottage right on the beach at the Jersey Shore can suffice?" They laughed through their tears.

Kaya

KAYA RETURNED TO CAPE May mid-way through January. The closer she got to the shore, she could feel her heart lifting. It always had when she was a kid, because it meant a summer vacation in her happy place. Now she felt something else. She *lived* here now...she was coming...home.

She was tingling with anticipation and lightness, as she counted down the last few exits on the Garden State...three...two...one...and, then she was there. Exit zero. Driving over the canal and on to the cape, she lowered her window just a little to smell the salt air. As she wound into and through town and out the other end towards the Point, she wondered where Lucas lived. She wondered what he might be doing now.

She wondered if she might need some coffee sometime...soon.

Kaya popped into the General Store the day after she returned from Washington.

"Hi, Tess!" she called.

"Welcome back, hon!" she responded.

"Thank you. Hey, I was thinking about following up on Gerry's idea today—about Exit Zero Publishing? Is it okay if I use your names?"

"Of course!" said Tess. "We wouldn't have offered otherwise. Sloane and Vance are good friends. Tell them we said hello."

"Okay, will do. Also, I know it's only January, but I'm going to look for a job for in-season too. You don't happen to know your plans yet for the summer?"

"Well, I think I do. Both my kids are coming back, and one is bringing a friend. They all want hours, and I usually keep a spot open for the O'Brien kid over on Lake Lily. So we are planning to be full up at this point. But I will definitely keep my ears open, and if you are approaching any other place, come ask first if I know anyone there. I'll help as much as I can."

Kaya flushed at the generosity. "Thank you, Tess, that's really kind."

"Think nothing of it," Tess said, flourishing her hand in the manner of a Shakespearean character. They both laughed.

There was kindness and goodness in the world, all around, thought Kaya. Another little shard of her heart healed itself.

Kaya

SHE PUSHED OPEN THE door of the Exit Zero Filling Station and looked around. It was early, so lunch service wouldn't have started, and it was off-season, but she was still surprised to find the shop so quiet. No one appeared to be here. "Hello?" she called.

"I'll be right down," someone called from upstairs. Presently, down the stairs came an older woman with greying, light red hair and warm green eyes. She smiled at Kaya. "How can I help you?" she asked. She was wearing khaki pleated pants, a sweater with pastel flowers on it, and Keds sneakers. It reminded Kaya of the kinds of things her mother would wear. Her heart twisted a little.

"I'm looking for Sloane Spencer?" ventured Kaya.

"Oh, Sloane is probably in back and didn't hear the door. I'm Maureen," she said, holding out her hand. Kaya shook it and couldn't help smiling back at the woman.

"I'm Kaya."

"It is lovely to meet you. Is there something I can help you with in the meantime? You look like you are a bit on a mission and it's fabulous," mused Maureen with a smile.

Kaya flushed a little and looked down briefly and then back up. She had picked out a pair of black dress pants she used to wear to work in DC, with a pink blouse and black cardigan. "I am, thank you," she started. "Do you work with Sloane? I was hoping to speak to her or someone here about potentially joining the team."

"I do work with Sloane!" said Maureen brightly. "I've worked here since the beginning. But I don't make hiring decisions."

"Do you write?" asked Kaya eagerly.

Maureen laughed—a bright, trilling laugh. "A little," she said. "But I mostly lead the research. I have been in Cape May County my entire life, so I suppose Sloane figured if there's anything to know that I can't find out, well, maybe then we just don't need to know it!" She laughed again, and Kaya couldn't help but laugh too. "I also help with editing," Maureen added.

"That's so cool," Kaya responded. Kaya was transfixed. It seemed like it would be impossible to be so taken with someone she just met, but the older woman's mix of self-confidence, transparency, and warmth were intoxicating. It was like a balm over Kaya's heart. She'd already wanted this job, but now she *really* wanted this job. She wanted Maureen for a co-worker.

With another smile, Maureen reached out and patted Kaya's shoulder. "Well, my dear, we're a small operation, but let me go and see if I can find Sloane and see if you can get yourself that job!"

Kaya watched as Maureen disappeared into the back of the store. She mused over how utterly delightful Maureen seemed until she heard voices returning. She saw Maureen come back, trailing a light-skinned Black woman, with smooth hair tied back in a low ponytail. She was probably in her early 40s. She was wearing slim jeans and a chunky sweater. "Sloane, this young woman wanted to speak with you," said Maureen. "I will leave you to it," she added. As she turned to head back up the stairs, Maureen smiled at Kaya and gave her a quick wink. Kaya smiled.

"Hi, I'm Sloane Spencer," said Sloane, holding out her hand. Kaya's gaze snapped back to Sloane. She felt suddenly nervous. There weren't a lot of writing gigs in town and she wanted this one. She took a breath and tried to put herself in the mindset like she's talking to a potential client. "I'm Kaya Morgan," she said, taking the handshake with what she hoped was professional firmness but not squeezy.

Sloane tilted her head. "An unusual name—how do you spell it?"

"Yeah, I get that a lot," Kaya said. "It's K-A-Y-A, and most people want to pronounce it 'Kye-ah' like 'kayak', but it's 'Kay-uh' like 'okay' and with an 'a' on the end. I think my mom wanted to give us unusual first names to make up for 'Morgan' being so boring," she finished, laughing.

Sloane chuckled. "Well, I'm a Spencer, so I feel you," she said. "So K-A-Y-A Kaya, what is it I can do for you?"

"Thanks, yeah," Kaya said. "The Nevilles gave me your name. I'm a writer. For personal reasons, I've recently moved to my family's house here on the Point and I intend to live here year-round. Until recently, I've been a writer at the Alston Group, a PR agency in Washington, DC. I majored in journalism at University of Rochester, and I would love to know if you are hiring writers—staff or freelance—in any capacity." She thought she delivered that pretty well. Didn't feel like she rushed it. Sloane gave her a quick once-over.

"I see. Do you have a resume?"

"I do!" Kaya said brightly. She pulled one out of her bag. Tess was nice enough to let her use the printer in the office of the General Store. Sloane reviewing her resume right in front of her was a little nerve-wracking, but she tried to keep her sangfroid. She focused on the pretty bangle bracelets on Sloane's slender wrist and tried to stay calm.

"Well K-A-Y-A Kaya," Sloane said smiling at her, "this *might* be your lucky day."

"Really?" Kaya asked, trying to keep the squeal out of her voice.

"Might," said Sloane with a laugh. "I actually do need someone. You probably know about *Cool Cape May*, the coffee table book we publish annually with all the business listings?"

"Yes," said Kaya eagerly. "It was always in the house we rented before we bought our cottage."

"Well, I have a couple other book projects going on, and the guy I hired to do the Exit Zero weekly magazine is on the new side and won't have bandwidth to do both. No one works full-time. I have been trying to sort out how I'm going to get *Cool Cape May* done before the publishing deadline this year, so figuring that out was going to become a priority rather soon. So, I'd say your timing is impeccable. And if you're used to writing product placements, describing all our great businesses should be a snap."

Kaya had unconsciously clasped her hands in front of her in a decidedly "GOODY!" posture. Sloane laughed at her and continued, "*But.* The reason I say 'might' is that I won't make any decision until I've seen some writing samples. And I'm a small operation, but it would be great if I could have a reference from your agency to speak to your trade writing."

"Of course!" Kaya said eagerly. "I have a portfolio I can email to you as soon as I get home, and I can provide multiple references!"

Sloane laughed. "One is fine. I don't want to call the entire DC PR world. But one other thing, and I hope you don't mind, but I just want to know what I'm getting into." She paused and peered at Kaya. "Do you mind telling me the personal reasons why you've moved out here?" Kaya blinked. She willed herself not to turn into waterworks today. She took a deep breath.

"I don't mind." Kaya tried to keep her voice matter of fact and professional. "My family has a cottage and I love it here—which is the 'why here' part of the answer. But the 'why' and 'why now' is that we lost my mother two years ago and my father last fall. My PR work, against this backdrop, was feeling less meaningful to me and I like feeling a purpose to my work. I also felt that processing my grief was going to require a change of scenery. And in the short time I've been back, I have felt that this is a great place for me."

Sloane was quiet. "Thank you for sharing that with me," she said finally. "I am very sorry for your losses."

"Thank you," Kaya replied simply.

"Please pardon one last intrusion," Sloane said.

"Of course," Kaya replied.

"This is an important project for me—sales of this book to the hotels and home rentals are an important pillar in our annual revenue. I appreciate that you're in a fragile place and that doesn't bother me. I'm glad you're seeking work you're more passionate about. It's just...can you give me any comfort that you won't have a painful day at some point, change your mind on the next breeze, and flee back to DC or Tahiti or whatever? I want someone to see this through."

Kaya laughed—practically a snort that surprised herself. "Well," she said in reply, "I broke my lease, pre-paid a year on a storage unit, have broken up with my DC boyfriend, and very possibly have an enormous crush on a year-rounder barista here."

Sloane flat-out grinned. "Okay, Kay," she put out her hand to shake again. "Send me those samples and references and I'll be back in touch."

"You got it, boss," Kaya replied, smiling.

Kaya

AFTER SLOANE CALLED TO make the official offer, Kaya squealed to herself. She literally hopped up and down with her hands clasped. She was so excited. It was times like this that made living alone not as attractive. She immediately grabbed her phone and tried Callie. No answer. She tried Lynne—straight to voicemail. Oh! She knew who she should call.

"Hey!" said Melanie after the third ring. "What's up?"

"Hey!" said Kaya. "First off, thank you so much for being a reference for me!"

"My pleasure," said Mel cheerily. "Did you get the job?"

"I did!" Kaya blurted.

"Oh, yay! That's awesome!" said Mel.

"I really appreciate all your help and support," said Kaya. "I know it wasn't exactly cool of me to leave your team and then ask you to put in a good word for my next gig."

"Oh, *please*. You moved to Cape May. It's not like you stayed in DC and went to Morris or something," said Mel, referencing a (vastly inferior, of course) rival firm. "This may come as a surprise to you but I actually *like* you. We are *friends*. I want you to be *happy*." Mel had always been so ridiculously pragmatic. And loyal. And generous of spirit.

"Well, thank you for answering. It is fun to tell you."

"Of course! So have you seen the dude you were telling me about?"

Kaya laughed and sighed. "No, but really it's only been a couple days that I've been back."

"True, I guess," said Mel.

"And honestly," Kaya confessed, "I'm not really sure of the next move. Like, if he still works at the coffee shop, I can go in and see him, but it's not like he can hang out if he's working. And am I just being annoying at that point?"

"Can't you go in, and if it's not busy, just ask him out?"

"Oh, wow," Kaya shot back. "I don't know that I could do that..."

Melanie laughed. "Yeah, maybe being that direct is not your style. I confuse us sometimes," she said laughing.

"I guess I'll just...keep my eyes open around town. But I really want to start strong with this job, anyway."

"Sure, sure, Kay. Go get 'em."

Kaya

LOCALS TALKED ABOUT THE "Cape May bubble"—
how when storms swept across the area, clouds
often seemed to part when they passed over Cape
May. Not that it never rained—it did—but it didn't
hit as often as the surrounding areas. And because
it was surrounded by more temperate water, snow
was even more of a rarity—especially snow that
stuck. But one morning Kaya blinked awake and
sensed an immediate difference in the light coming
through the window. It was brighter. *Whiter*. Snow!

Snow might be a rarity in Cape May, and DC, but
it was not in Poughkeepsie. So there was still
something magical about it that transported Kaya
back to her childhood. She jumped out of bed,
pulled on sweats, a hoodie and her puffer vest. A
knit hat, boots, and mittens completed the outfit. It
was just a couple of inches, but the snow wasn't as
wet as she would have thought—it was light and
cold. She pushed it aside by sweeping left and right
with her feet as she descended the outside stairs
and clomped her way down the driveway, across the
street and up the stairs at the Coral beach access
point.

She crossed the dunes and marveled. It was as if the dunes and the beach were spray-painted white. It was surreal. She'd gotten used to the beach in the cold weather, but there was still something so connected in her brain with the beach and summer that it was taking her time to make sense of it.

Other hearty souls had already been out, she could see by the boot and paw prints crossing in front of her. She stepped forward towards the ocean. It was beyond beautiful. The waves broke, crashed and pulled back like they always did. But now the surf, snow, and sand crashed and combined into a beigey-white frothy mix. She gazed at it, losing all track of time. Another painful shard in her heart repaired itself into just a quiet ache.

Lucas

THE MANAGEMENT SUITE OF Congress Hall was quiet when Lucas entered. Sometimes the assistant, Tracy, was at a desk in the reception room, but she wasn't here at the moment. Diane MacFarlane had asked to meet with Lucas, but he wasn't sure if he should knock on her office door, or wait. Lucas glanced at his watch. He was right on time. He chose to knock.

"Come in."

Lucas eased open the dark oak door and let himself in to Mrs. MacFarlane's inner office. Sunlight poured through her giant windows. The MacFarlane's suite was right at the "elbow" of the L-shaped building, on the second floor. "Lucas, please sit," she said, smiling and gesturing to a chair. Her thick, grey hair was always perfectly straight and blunt cut, hanging just to her chin. She was wearing a deep purple turtleneck sweater.

Lucas eased himself into a leather chair opposite her desk. "You wanted to see me?"

"Yes, I wanted to talk about how everything is going. Check in."

"Oh," Lucas replied thoughtfully. What exactly did she want to know? Was he in trouble? He waited for her to continue.

"How are things at the café? Any observations for improvements or feedback for us? You had such good ideas out at Beach Plum." Lucas cocked his head slightly as the realization rolled through him that she wanted his opinion. *Valued* his opinion. It still surprised him.

"Things are good," he started. "I think baked goods have been slightly over-ordered for this part of the year. There was more waste than I'd like, so I thought it was worth the risk of running out to scale back. It has been good, and we have not run out yet—at least not of everything. Guests who wanted something have had choices."

"Good. And how are the staff?"

"Good for the most part. There are a couple of the newer kids who I have to watch and remind not to be on their phones where customers could see them."

"Oh, these young people and their phones!" exclaimed Diane. "Thank you for being on top of that."

Lucas smiled to himself. He thought of himself as "young," too, but Mrs. MacFarlane addressing him as more of a peer felt good. "I hope it's okay, but I actually do let them scroll their phones if it's slow. I just usually ask them to do it in the storeroom. I don't want them on their phones if a guest could walk by or come in."

Diane nodded. "That makes sense, I suppose. I defer to you." Lucas felt the edges of his mouth pulling up. Diane leaned forward, resting her arms on her desk. "We haven't discussed your timeline for ownership lately. I wanted to check in on that. I assume your intentions have not changed?"

"Not at all," Lucas confirmed. "I'm still very committed."

"Good," she replied smoothly, her hair swinging slightly as she nodded. "This will be an important year. After you finish retail here, you'll do front of house, then operations, and finish up in general management. I estimate that next year at this time, you'll be our partner."

Lucas couldn't stop a full grin from ripping across his face. "I really appreciate the chance you and Robert are taking with me, Diane—the opportunity you're giving me. I probably don't thank you enough."

Diane stood up, so Lucas followed suit. "I really don't see it as taking a chance. That makes it sound like you're a risk. You're anything but, Mr. Andre. You have the technical knowledge, work ethic, hospitality gene, and attitude for this work. If anything, you might be *too* helpful sometimes. I'm not sure *all* the cups needed stacking at eight in the evening." Lucas chuckled and looked down. "But there is no risk in investing in you. We need you."

He looked back up at his boss. His heart was awash with so much gratitude. "Thank you," he said simply. She nodded.

Closing her office door behind him, Lucas saw Tripp striding into the reception room, fixing Lucas with a hard stare. "What's your business with my mother?"

Lucas paused and dropped his hands into the pockets of his khakis. "We were discussing the concepts for the new resort in Hilton Head."

Tripp's eyebrows shot up. "What? We're building a resort in Hilton Head?"

"No." Lucas couldn't stop the edges of his mouth quirking up.

"You dick. My mother has a soft spot for you, Andre. But don't think that means you're part of this family."

Lucas blinked, remembering the disastrous conversation with his father at Christmas. He took a breath. Then, he laughed, air rushing through his nose as his mouth curved back up. Tripp scowled.

"This is my *job*, Tripp," Lucas said quietly, stepping forward, closing the gap between them. Lucas was nearly a head taller than Tripp and took the opportunity to loom over Tripp a little. "A job I care a lot about." Lucas held Tripp's gaze. "And now, I need to get back to work." Lucas patted Tripp's upper arm, stepped around him, and left.

Kaya

EXIT ZERO TURNED OUT to be all the good things Kaya was hoping. Towards the end of her first week, she climbed the stairs to the office space above the Filling Station store and restaurant. The workspace was large, open, and sunny. Sloane had an office with a door, as did her finance guy and husband, Vance. Vance was quiet and thoughtful, and incredibly nice to everyone. Sloane and Vance didn't seem to be around today, but when she turned towards the worktables, Kaya was thrilled to see Maureen.

"Maureen!" she exclaimed, setting her bag down across the table from the older woman. The space had a couple work stations with multiple oversized monitors reserved for working on graphics, off to the side a large table dominated the middle where they had meetings and anyone could work. "You've not been here the other days I was here...?"

Maureen smiled. "I know and I couldn't wait to see you," she answered. "I was so happy when Sloane said she'd hired you. I just liked the look of you," she laughed, conspiratorially. "I also work at the library, and am often out talking to people for my work here, so I'm not always around," she explained.

"Well, I can't wait to learn from you," Kaya admitted. "I was trained as a journalist, but I've never really worked as one. I know the business listings won't be hard for me, but I am looking forward to any book or magazine work."

"And I can't wait to work with *you*," Maureen replied. "I'll be happy to share any sources or tips with you, but I love having you young people around for the energy. And so this old dog can learn some new tricks too! Especially how fast you all seem to be able to find people through social media. I'm getting the hang of it, but there's a lot to learn," she said. "How are you getting settled?"

Kaya sighed. "Here, really well. Everyone is super nice and helpful. And Cape May generally, pretty well. I have some projects at my cottage I need to get done, but it's good and I like the quiet."

"You live on your own?" inquired Maureen.

"Yes," Kaya answered. "You?"

"I have my husband and my dog, but otherwise the nest is empty. We have three children, but they're grown and left the county. I'm proud of them, of course, but it still feels a little too quiet sometimes," she said wistfully. "I bet your parents are proud of you," she said with a smile. But then her face fell when she saw Kaya quickly look down. "Oh no," said Maureen, her voice a little softer. "I've troubled you."

Kaya looked back up. "No, it's okay," she started. "Sloane knows and it's not a secret. It's just that my mother died a couple years ago and my father this past fall...both from cancer. I'm here because I needed a bit of a change and Cape May is my happy place," she finished with a weak smile. Maureen didn't say anything. She just gazed warmly at Kaya.

"It's funny," Kaya continued, "when my mom first died, the grief was so intense that I felt like surely people must notice...as I walked down the sidewalk...or, or on the subway. Like it must *show*. I know that sounds silly."

"It doesn't," Maureen replied.

"Anyway," Kaya said, trying for lightness, "I guess it still catches me off guard."

"I thought there seemed something...a little lost about you when you came in that day, but I couldn't quite put my finger on it, and of course our conversation was so short," Maureen mused. "But we have found you and you are on our team now, and I couldn't be more pleased."

Kaya's eyes filled slightly, not with sadness this time, but with gratitude. She brushed away the tears as they heard someone coming up the stairs.

"Morning!" announced Callum, emerging at the top of the stairs. Callum was the new guy working on the weekly. Sloane brought him on in the off-season deliberately so that he'd be hitting his stride by the time spring came and readership and circulation started to tick up. He was a few years younger than Kaya, funny and outgoing, and relentlessly optimistic. He was working on a bachelor's degree online, but otherwise was dedicated to Exit Zero.

There were two other freelancers whose ranks Kaya joined, in addition to her running lead on *Cool Cape May*. The other freelancers, Lucy and Adam, contributed to all the publications. They were year-rounders who grew up here and got sent Sloane's way by the English teacher at the high school—Lucy a few years ago, and Adam more recently. Adam worked sometimes in person, and often remote, and had a full-time job in-season at Uncle Bill's Pancake House—which all made him enough money to feed his sport rock climbing habit at a gym in Philadelphia. "His writing is really good, though," sighed an exasperated Sloane. Lucy was a nurse at the assisted living facility downtown, but the part-time writing, Lucy had shared, "keeps her sane."

Mateo was the graphics guy. He was a firefighter and EMT locally and dropped in to do graphics work at Exit Zero because he was good at it and loved the creative work "as stress release," although there weren't too many dangerous fires in Cape May County—most of his job entailed shutting down illegal bonfires, answering medical calls, and people thinking they smelled gas. (Most of the time, false alarms.)

A week later, Kaya, Callum, and Maureen were working quietly, when Callum broke the silence. "It's pretty amazing how fast you got up to speed, Kay," he said, leaning his chair back on the back two legs and running a hand through his unruly corkscrew curls. "I've been here almost two months longer than you, and I still feel like I'm not getting it."

"That's sweet," she replied, "but my stuff is pretty straight-forward and all the things I've done before make this work familiar." Kaya was supposed to contact every business in the database from last year via a mass email, confirming they wanted to participate and asking them to submit any changes for this year's edition. Then, she started working the list of anyone who didn't respond to the email. As she collected responses and confirmed payment, she created the write-ups to entice the tourists to patronize the businesses.

"Okay," Callum replied, "I guess I get that, but you're also so good on the writing and you just got here!"

"Kaya is an excellent writer, that's true," replied Maureen, looking up. Kaya flushed and looked down.

"I love writing," Kaya confessed. She looked back at Callum. "And don't feel bad—I've had a lot of practice. I studied journalism in college, and I wrote a ton for my old job. You wouldn't believe the ridiculous stuff that went down."

Callum dropped the front two legs of the chair down and leaned his forearms on the table. "Like what?"

Kaya laughed and tilted her head in thought. "Oh! There was this one campaign for Under Armour…"

"The athletic clothes?"

"Yeah, they're based in Baltimore and they hired us. They had been dragging their feet on approving the copy—the taglines, press release, print and digital ads—all of it. So our manager told us to just write it up. She figured missing deadline would be worse. There were seven reporters ready to give us earned press the next day. So we turned everything in at, like six and went out for drinks. We're at the bar and at, like, maybe eight, all our phones started pinging. Under Armour finally looked at it and wanted it all changed."

Callum's eyebrows shot up. "No way. *All* of it?"

Kaya laughed. "They didn't hate everything, but they chose a different tagline. One of the other ones we'd suggested a couple weeks before. And since the tagline is central to the campaign, everything had to be if not totally re-written, certainly heavily tweaked."

"No *way*."

"Yeah, so we all went back to the office, started dividing and conquering. We'd stop and show each other what we were doing to make sure we stayed in synch. Finished around one-thirty in the morning. I've never been so happy to have honed the skill to write on deadline. And honestly, maybe being a little tipsy helped. Kept us loose," Kaya finished with a chuckle.

Callum threw his head back and laughed. "That is crazy."

"There was tons of stuff like that. By comparison, this is certainly...calmer. But I like it," Kaya said looking back at Maureen.

Maureen smiled. "I could use your help on the book on the history of the railroad in southern Jersey." Kaya felt her face fall. "What is it?" asked Maureen.

Kaya waited a beat and then replied, "Nothing...just that my dad loved railroads and would have gotten such a kick out of this project." They were all quiet for a moment—whether from sympathy or the awkwardness of not knowing what to say, Kaya wasn't sure. She turned and smiled at both of them, but then said to Maureen, "It feels like I'll never get over the instinct to want to call them and tell them things."

"You can still tell them things, dear," replied Maureen, her eyes soft. "Just not on the phone."

"I suppose that's true," answered Kaya. She sighed. She wasn't sure if this was ever going to get easier, but for today at least, she felt a little less alone.

Kaya

ON A BRIGHT DAY in early February, Kaya was out at the big, Ace hardware in North Cape May. She had a list of things she wanted to fix, repair, or shore up at the cottage now that she decided she was living there for the foreseeable future. Extend the pulls on the ceiling fans. Touch up paint on the door jams. Repair a screen. Clean the grout on the backsplash... She was feeling oddly energetic. She woke up feeling close to her parents. She almost felt as if they were with her in her little missions. Cheering her on.

She used to love going to the hardware store with her dad in Poughkeepsie. It was small and the same family had owned it for decades. It was packed with stuff. Narrow aisles with merchandise all the way to the ceiling. It had a smell of sawdust and a mild but not unpleasant chemical. She loved following her dad around while he looked for whatever he needed for a given project. Sometimes he knew right where to head, but more often he asked someone for the location. She loved how he explained to her what each specific thing was used for and why it was different than the other things.

Phillips vs. flathead, different types of nails and anchoring screws.

She felt prepared today. She'd called Juan the day before. She usually talked to Juan only when on speaker with her sister, but yesterday she called him directly.

"Kaya? Is everything alright?" he had asked, surprised, as he picked up.

"A hundred percent. I just need some advice," she replied cheerfully.

"Oh! Okay. What's up?"

"Well, I've got a bunch of things I want to fix or do, and you're super-handy, so do you have a minute?" she asked.

"Sure!" he answered with enthusiasm. *Juan is such a good dude.* He patiently worked through her list with her, giving her useful advice. It was his idea for her to come to this hardware store. He wasn't completely sure she could find everything she needed at Swains in town, so he encouraged her to come to the larger, newer store.

She wandered the aisles, jamming out to Li'l Nas X's *THATS WHAT I WANT* playing over the store's sound system. She was singing along, "I *want*...someone to looovvvve me. I *want*..." when she rounded a corner to find...Lucas. *Lucas*! It took her breath away a little. He was here. And not just in her mind, this time. In the flesh.

Lucas

SHE WAS *SINGING*. HE smiled—he couldn't help himself. He watched her hand fly to her hair and over her ponytail. She was wearing jeans and a sweatshirt, adorably casual. Lucas was suddenly glad he'd shaved this morning.

"Hi!" she said.

His heart was thrumming happily but he tried to keep his cool. "Well, hello yourself," he replied.

"We have to stop meeting like this," she said.

"Do we?" he said, still smiling. "I rather enjoy it."

She blushed. "Not working today?" Kaya asked.

"Not until later," Lucas replied, then nodded at the shopping basket she's carrying. "Whatcha working on?"

Kaya glanced down, then back up at him. "I have a bunch of little things I want to knock out at the house."

"Anything you need help with?" Lucas asked, searching her eyes.

She looked briefly startled. She blinked, then quickly recovered. "Oh...no, thank you. That's really nice of you, but this is all pretty straightforward. Just time and a little elbow grease for most of my list." He probably shouldn't be so intent on getting invited over again, but he would have loved to help her with whatever she was doing. "What are you up to?" she said, gesturing to him.

Lucas opened his hand to reveal a bathroom sink drain kit. "A small plumbing project. And I also just need some wall hooks to hang some pictures."

"That's on my list too!" Kaya said.

"Lead the way," he said, smiling. They walked down the aisle towards the back of the store. Lucas tried unsuccessfully not to notice how cute her ass looked in those jeans. When they got to the right area, they selected what they needed.

"Anything else on your list?" Lucas asked casually. He didn't want to let her go just yet.

"Just one more thing—ceiling fan pull chain extensions."

"Let's go," he said cheerfully, heading towards the ceiling fans. "Did you have a nice holiday with your sister?" he asked.

"What? Oh! Yes, thank you," she replied. "I'm sorry we didn't get a chance to chat more at Congress Hall. I mean, I know you were working. But she was happy to meet you...I'd... mentioned you to her," said Kaya. Lucas glanced sideways at her. Her eyes were forward. *She'd talked to her sister about him before they came in.* He did a mental fist pump.

"I'm glad you mentioned me. And I'm glad I was there to be found when you came in," he said with a quick wink. *Too much?*

He watched Kaya shift her tote bag on her shoulder. "Did you have a nice holiday? Do you have family here?" she asked.

He tilted his head as he looked at her. She would have no reason to know that his parents had moved away, but her wording was funny, like she didn't know he had *ever* had family here. "Well no, they're not here anymore. I did see my parents, briefly, up in Philadelphia, but mostly I was working. I don't mind. I love the work, and my friends were around," he finished. She picked out what she needed from a display. "Are you sure you don't need any help with anything?" he asked again.

She smiled at him. *God, she had a pretty smile.* "I'm sure. But it's very nice of you to offer. I'm actually looking forward to my little projects," she said with a laugh.

His mind was flying...he tried to think of some excuse, some reason to extend this chance meeting. But they were in a strip mall in North Cape May. There was no coffee shop or anything he could suggest popping into. There was maybe a Subway sandwich shop but that hardly seemed like the move. She was just gazing at him, with those gorgeous brown eyes. He realized he was out of ideas. And now out of time.

They headed towards the checkout and made their purchases. Standing at the door, she turned to face him. "It was really nice seeing you."

"Made my day, Kaya," he said, smiling at her for a beat. He watched her smile back, and turn to go.

Kaya

A COUPLE DAYS LATER, she was cycling to work, reliving the hardware store encounter. He just looked so...*good*, with those shoulders, and his hair laying beautifully away from his face in a soft swoop. He had been clean shaven and smelled good—she'd clocked his aftershave—it made her think of spring rain and something minty. She was second-guessing turning down his offer to help her with her projects. She really had wanted a reason to get together. *But*, she didn't want him to just do things at her house. That wasn't a dynamic she was interested in having with him.

She smiled to herself as she recalled their parting. *Made his day.*

As she pedaled up Sunset, her thoughts turned to her birthday...and how birthdays—hers, her parents, her sister's—anniversaries of any kind after you lose people close to you are often sad hallmarks in time. Remembering celebrations of the past and missing the traditions and the presence of those you used to celebrate with. This week was going to be hard, she reflected with a heavy exhale, her breath visible in the cold. She had a choice—pass the day in quiet, or...not. Kaya thought she would choose the latter.

Tentatively, she brought it up at Exit Zero. "So, um, guys," she said to the center of the room. Callum, Maureen, and Lucy paused their typing and looked up. "My birthday is this week." Their faces lit up, so, encouraged, Kaya went on. "I was wondering, um, if you guys might want to do drinks at the Mad Batter on Thursday?" She quickly added, "Like, no gifts or anything, but just go out with me to celebrate?"

"Fuck, yes!" cried Callum, grinning. "Oh, sorry Maureen," he added sheepishly, glancing at the older woman who, for her part, was suppressing a grin. "I'll get Adam too," said Callum. "He's always down." Kaya breathed out a little in relief. Callum leapt into planning. "I'll text Mateo too. If he's not working, he'll come and maybe bring his boyfriend. Like, six-ish good for everyone? You're in, right Lucy?" he asked, looking at her as he picked up his phone.

Lucy nodded. "Thursday? Yeah, that time works."

Kaya fell into thought at who she *also* wanted to invite and how she might make that happen. She sat at her computer, thoughtfully eyeing the email address of her *Cool Cape May* contact at Cape Resorts. Nancy DeVine. n.devine@caperesorts.com

So, if that was the format, wouldn't it make sense for the address to be l.andre at same? Heart racing—and I mean *why*, it was just an email?—she typed the address in. What subject should she put? Hoping it hit the right blend of casual but also "hi I'm emailing you for the first time out of the blue," she typed "Hello and birthday" and hoped it hit the mark. In the body she typed:

Hi Lucas! (was the exclamation point too much?)

Took a chance that this might be your email. I am working now with Exit Zero publications and I have a contact at Cape Resorts whose email uses this format...let me know if I've found you? (She figured she might as well be honest because this was so random.)

If you're reading this, I just wanted to reach out because my birthday is this Thursday and some of my new friends from work and I are going to the Mad Batter for drinks. Not a "party" per se—like, no gifts or anything—just meeting for drinks after work, around 6. If you're not busy, I would love to see you. Feel free to bring friends—it's totally casual. If you have any questions or anything last minute, my mobile is below in my signature block.

Hope you're well.

-K

After she hit send, she second-guessed all of it. "Hope you're well?" Was that crazy formal? And she felt like she had to mention friends, because, *God*, he might be dating someone. The dude was hot and kind, so it was entirely likely he was...but she really hoped he wasn't. But also, she didn't want him to feel like he was showing up to a bunch of people he didn't know. The year-round community was small—he probably knew, or at least knew of people she worked with, but she wasn't going to ask anyone if they knew him—way too embarrassing. Was "I would love to see you" too much? And was it too forward to point out her mobile number?

While she was stewing over what she wrote, a new message hit her box. *Whoa. That was fast.*

Lucas

IT WAS SLOW IN the coffee shop. Lucas was wiping down the frother and steaming equipment when he looked up to see Tripp walking towards him. He groaned inwardly.

"Andre," Tripp drawled. "I'll take an espresso." *Ugh, this buy-in couldn't come fast enough.*

Lucas tapped his fingers lightly on the counter and cocked his head. "Hey, Tripp. I don't know if you want to trust me to make it just the way you like it. You're welcome to come back here," Lucas said, gesturing to the area behind the counter.

Tripp just stared at him. *You have no idea how to use this equipment.*

"Um, no," Tripp stammered. "I'm fine with you making it. It's just an espresso."

Lucas was not the type to pawn his work off on someone else, but there were two other associates on this shift and the shop was otherwise quiet. He turned to one of his shiftmates, a young guy named Edgar who was leaning against the counter surreptitiously scrolling through his phone.

"Hey Edgar," he said with a smile. Edgar looked up and quickly pocketed his phone.

"Yeah, boss?"

"Would you mind making Tripp an espresso? I need to stop by the office for a moment."

He probably should have said "Mr. MacFarlane," but today Lucas found himself with too few fucks to give. Lucas caught Tripp's scowl as Lucas edged his way around the counter and out into the hall. Without looking back, he walked into the main lobby and up the stairs. He jogged up a second set of stairs and then a third, and made his way down the hall to his little office, tucked under the eaves at the far end of the original building.

Lucas might move in to the second-floor management suite at some point, but for now he was perfectly content with his space on the top floor. Former servant's quarters, and relatively low ceilings, but he loved it. It was quiet, and his window looked out at the ocean, and it was all his.

He moved the mouse to wake up his computer screen and navigated to his email. *What?* "Kaya Morgan" in bold, unread font at the top of his inbox. His pulse surged and he felt his face tug into a smile. His eyes scanned her note, his smile broadening with every line.

She had a job here in Cape May! At Exit Zero! This was a new development. And her birthday was this week. He leaned back in his chair as he re-read her note. Lucas thrilled with an excuse to see her again, but he also considered that it was her first birthday here. Without her friends and family. Her first one without her father. It had to be hard. No way he was not going to help make this a fun one.

Hell yes, Kaya, I'm coming to your birthday party.

He leaned forward and his hands flew to the keyboard to type his reply.

Kaya!

You found me! How cool to see your name pop up and that's awesome you're working at Exit Zero. Between that and your home repairs, I hope that means you're sticking around for a while. 😊

I am honored you are including me in your birthday celebration and I will 100% be there. I'll text you NLT Wednesday on time. I'll know my work schedule by then so I can give you an ETA and let you know if I'm bringing anyone so you can plan numbers. But either way, I am totally in.

Can't wait.

-Lucas

He leaned back again, finding it impossible to wipe the smile from his face. He knew, in his heart, that deep down, Kaya knew joy. He'd seen it every summer. She was carrying around some heavy shit right now, but she deserved to get back in touch with her light. He wanted a chance to bring some of that light back to her. He picked up a pen and absent-mindedly twirled it, when he saw a new email pop on his screen.

Hi again,

Glad I had the right email and that you can come! See you soon.

-K

He smiled. Lucas picked up his phone to send her a text but stopped himself. *Too soon, dude. Don't scare her off.* He texted Tim and Casey instead.

> Drinks Thursday? It's a bday thing for a girl I met

Casey wrote back immediately.

> Can't. Out of town

And then again:

> Actually can u watch molly?

And again:

> You met a girl?

Lucas rolled his eyes as he replied.

> Yes on molly. just let me know when you're bringing her over and for how long

A reply rolled in from Tim.

> I think I'm good for Thurs. Barring any emergency calls.

> And what he said - u met a girl?

Lucas laughed, thumbs-upped Tim's yes to Thursday and set his phone down. He made himself wait until the next morning to send Kaya a text. He sat, watching the time on his phone, his knee bobbing. When the phone flipped from seven fifty-nine to eight, he let the message fly.

Kaya

KAYA WOKE UP THINKING about Lucas and his "can't wait" email. She rolled over and picked up her phone off the nightstand. She navigated to her email to see if he had replied to her last note. Nothing yet. A few responses for *Cool Cape May*, but nothing from Lucas. She hopped out of bed and pulled a sweatshirt over her head in the cold.

She peed and tried not to stress out too much about the "if I'm bringing anyone." It could totally mean just friends. Because otherwise, the rest of the message was him being excited to see her, right? She brushed her teeth, grabbed her phone and headed upstairs to make coffee. As she was pouring water into the coffee maker, she heard her phone buzz on the counter. After turning on the machine, she picked up her phone. A new text.

> Hi it's L. put my # in your phone right now! 😊 I'll see you thurs prob by 6:30 and I'm prob bringing my friend Tim aka one of the guys from the beach with the dog

> C U then can't wait
> happy early bd

She couldn't stop smiling. He was bringing *Tim*. Again, with the "can't wait"! They were now texting friends!

> Hi! So cool that u can come and roger on Tim—the more the merrier

She hit send on that and felt like she needed to say something else to match his "can't wait" because honestly *she* couldn't wait either! She sent a quick

> Looking forward to seeing u

before she could overthink it. She saw the three dots and held her breath.

> Me too

She exhaled and smiled.

Kaya

SHE TRIED HARD TO concentrate on the conversations, as she snuck glances towards the door. "Who else are you expecting?" asked Lucy, as they waited for their drinks at the bar on her birthday at the Mad Batter. The restaurant was in an old Victorian house in the middle of town that was now a small hotel called the Lewis Carroll Inn. The entire first floor was the restaurant, with a large section in the middle dedicated to the bar. The color scheme was chaotic—loud hues and brightly contrasting trim. The group had snagged a large table in the corner.

"What?" Kaya asked, snapping her gaze back to Lucy, guilt registering.

"You keep looking towards the door," shrugged Lucy. "Just wondering who else you invited."

"Oh, do you know Lucas Andre?" asked Kaya in what she hoped was a nonchalant tone.

Lucy thought for a minute. "Oh! Yes, I know Luke. He went to high school with my brother. Always seemed like a nice guy, but I don't know him well. I think I saw him out for a run once, but I don't see him much around." They turned towards the bar. "How do you know Luke?" Lucy asked.

"I met him when he was working at Beach Plum, and we've run into each other a couple times. It was sort of a last-minute decision. I just don't know that many people here, so I told him about it. He said he might come with a friend of his." The bartender handed them their drinks and Lucy turned and walked back to the group. The whole Exit Zero crew was here—even Maureen came out.

Kaya paused to take a sip of her wine. Then, as if his mention conjured him, Lucas appeared at her right elbow. He nudged her gently, shoulder to shoulder, and said, "Hey, birthday girl."

"You came!" said Kaya, beaming. She hoped she wasn't smiling so hard that it was goofy. She was so very aware of how good he looked. He wore jeans and a black sweater with a high v-neck; sleeves pushed up to just below the elbow. His hair was all combed back and there was just a hint of stubble across his jaw.

"I told you I would," he said. The bartender came over and after Lucas confirmed that Kaya already had a fresh drink, he ordered a beer. "How have you been?" he asked turning his face towards her, but, Kaya noticed, not breaking the light contact they had between their arms. She tried not to notice the heat. It was like a crackle of electricity. She had come from work and, although Exit Zero was super-casual, it was her birthday so she'd dressed up a little. She wore a grey, knit turtleneck dress over black tights. Her sleeves were long, but she was aware of the pressure of her arm against his bare forearm.

"Good. I like Exit Zero. It's fun writing product pieces that are places and experiences I know and love for a change. I mean, I liked my clients at the agency, but I get a lot more excited writing up, say, Morey's Piers or the Salt Marsh Safari, than the latest offerings of some government contractor or credit card company."

"That does sound like fun," Lucas said. "So...you quit your DC job entirely?"

"I did," said Kaya as she took a sip of wine and looked at him. Their faces were really close...and she loved it. He smelled good. She tried not to close her eyes and breathe him in. They said nothing but held eye contact. His eyes bored into hers and the corners of his mouth twitched up into a smile.

It seemed like he didn't want to ask, but she hoped he wanted to know, so she ventured forth. "I don't really know how long I'm staying but I don't have any plans to leave. I talked to Callie over Christmas. I'm going to live here for the time being. I'm hoping to do more writing—my boss, Sloane, connected me with the editor at the *Cape May County Herald* and he said he'll send me freelance feature assignments too. It doesn't pay a ton but I'll hopefully pick up a seasonal job with lots of hours to save up for next off-season. I just feel...better here." He peered at her quietly and took a sip of his beer, never breaking eye contact.

"I'm glad," he said finally. "I'm glad you're staying for now and I'm glad you're doing...better. You deserve it." It seemed like a funny thing to say

from someone who barely knew her, but Kaya's
heart swelled a little.

Lucas

LUCAS FELT SOMEONE GRASP his shoulder. He looked back. "Tim!" he said and turned around. "Kaya, this is my friend Tim Lee. Tim, this is Kaya Morgan, aka birthday girl."

"Nice to meet you and happy birthday!" said Tim. He had a huge smile.

"Likewise and thank you," said Kaya. "I'm glad you're here. I don't know a lot of people here yet...it's really nice for you to come out tonight," she said.

"No worries at all. I was totally up for it!" he replied.

"What do you do?" Kaya asked.

"Coast Guard," Tim replied cheerfully.

"Oh! Are you an instructor? My dad was in bootcamp here back in the day," she said.

He laughed. "God, no. I'm attached to the boats out of the station here. Mostly SAR—search and rescue. I would be terrible at teaching or commanding recruits. I'm way too much of a pushover. I barely survived it myself!"

"He's being humble," said Lucas, smiling at his friend.

An elegant Black woman and younger white guy approached the bar on Kaya's left. Kaya turned away from Lucas and Tim to greet what must be some of her coworkers. Lucas turned to Tim. "Thanks for coming," he said.

"No problem. You know I'm always down if I'm not on call." Tim collected a pint glass from the bartender and slid a couple dollars across the bar. Lucas leaned with his back against the bar, facing Tim. Kaya was beside him, her forearms resting on the bar as she chatted with her colleagues while they ordered another round. Although they were facing opposite directions, Lucas shifted slightly so his right hip was in contact with Kaya's right hip. He found himself hyper-aware of the feel of the bone of her hip through the thin sweater fabric of her dress and tights, even through the denim of his jeans.

He watched her co-workers get their drinks and rejoin what he assumed were her work friends. Kaya didn't follow them. It was like Kaya and he were stuck like magnets and it felt really good. Kaya broke contact and Lucas felt suddenly cold. But when she turned around so her back was now also to the bar, Lucas felt her softly placed her left hip back against his again. Lucas smiled as he crossed his arms over his chest with the beer bottle in one hand and settled firmly against her.

"It was really nice of both of you to come out," Kaya said, smiling up at him and then at Tim. Her hair was down around her shoulders and he could see she had put on makeup. He'd never seen her this dressed up. He thought she was beautiful without makeup and hair in a ponytail, but she also looked really nice like this.

"Our pleasure," Lucas replied.

"I should introduce you to my co-workers," Kaya said slowly. She didn't sound convinced and frankly, Lucas was perfectly happy having her mostly to himself. Tim glanced back over his shoulder to where her colleagues were standing around two high-top tables. Lucas' gaze followed Tim's.

"Lucy, the one with the long brown hair back in a braid—she said she went to high school with you," Kaya offered.

"With us?" asked Tim. "Huh."

"Well, she said her brother was in class with you," Kaya said, again tilting her head up to Lucas. He was briefly distracted by her big brown eyes. "Her last name is Torres."

"Oh, Marty Torres," said Tim. "That's right. He did have a sister. I'm gonna go say hi."

"I should probably go, too," Kaya said, but didn't move and held Lucas' gaze.

"Lead the way," he replied, also not moving. He thought he heard her sigh as she finally pushed off the bar. She smiled at him and led him back to her group.

Lucas was mostly quiet as he observed her with her colleagues. The Black woman was apparently the boss—Sloane. Lucas was briefly concerned at how good-looking two of the guys were—the one called Mateo—warm brown skin, close cropped hair, looked ripped—and the one called Michael—dark skin, meticulously shaped hair, intentional light beard across his jaw...but then Lucas realized the two men were a couple. The two other guys from her work seemed younger and were goofing around with each other—not appearing to flirt at all with Kaya. So, there didn't seem to be competition here, he told himself.

After a half hour or so, the boss and an older white woman introduced as Maureen said their goodbyes. "You young people have fun," Maureen had said with a smile as she left.

Tim was chatting everyone up. It seemed like everyone but Kaya had gone to Lower Cape May Regional High School. Apparently, the brother of one of the younger guys was Scott Jones, who Lucas remembered as a year behind him and Tim in high school and was also now in the Coast Guard.

He watched Kaya closely. Sometimes she'd catch Lucas' eye and smile, which sent a jolt through him. Kaya seemed a little sad at times, which he could understand, but it was clear that her co-workers—however new they might be—already really liked and respected her. He was glad to see it.

Around ten, the party started to break up. Lucas stayed close to her as they descended the stairs to the sidewalk. He waited patiently as everyone said their goodbyes and happy birthdays to Kaya. Then, it was just the two of them.

She turned around to face him. "Thank you, again, for coming," she said, beaming up at him.

"It was my pleasure. I'm glad you did this—birthdays deserve to be celebrated. I hope you had fun, but also, I can't imagine this was an entirely easy day."

Kaya blinked at him, her eyes a little glassy and her lips slightly parted as she exhaled. "It wasn't..." she whispered. "Thank you for saying that."

Lucas was itching to touch her. "Are you okay to get home? Where are you parked?" he asked, looking around the street.

"Yes, I'm okay," she said quietly. "And I'm just over in the lot behind the mall."

She was just peering at him. His heart was scrambling for purchase. He couldn't keep her here—had to let her go, but it just felt...incomplete. He sighed inwardly. *Fuck it.* He reached out, put his arms around her waist, and pulled her into a hug before he could second-guess himself.

His heart did a backflip when he felt her arms come around his neck, returning the hug. "Happy birthday," he said against her hair.

"Thank you," she said as they came apart. "I'm really glad you came."

"Me too."

Kaya

WELL, THIS *BIRTHDAY SHAPED up quite nicely.* Her work friends, Lucas, and Tim either already knew each other, knew *of* each other, or had a sufficiently low number of degrees separation that the group had easy camaraderie. She'd had fun, she reflected as she washed her face and changed into her pajamas.

On some level, birthdays would always suck. No one else got as excited about your birthday as your mother. Her mom used to always say she celebrated too. "It's the day I brought you into the world," she'd say in her sing-song voice. Birthdays now were bittersweet. *And Lucas gets that.*

But sadness can coexist with happiness in the moment. She headed to bed feeling grateful most of all. For all the wonderful birthdays she had as a kid, and the new friends who had made this year's a nice celebration.

Kaya laid on her back thinking of how good Lucas smelled. The zings she felt with all the physical contact. The feel of his jeans through her dress when they were hip to hip. The hug. When he put his arms around her, being flush against the solidness of him, she felt buzzy all over. The light scrape of his stubble against her cheek when he pulled away.

As she plugged in her phone and set her alarm, she saw she had more unread texts. Her heart skipped a beat when she saw Lucas' name in her notifications. She forced herself to take a deep breath and read the other texts first.

From Callie:

> okay one last happy birthday that you'll see when you go to bed. So glad you had a good day! Call me tomorrow to tell me all about Mad Batter and Luuuuuuuuuucas

followed by the heart eye emoji.

Kaya grinned to herself and hearted the message.

From Lynne:

> HBD!!! Sorry so late! Been thinking about you all day but just never got a moment. Hope you had a great day! Miss you

Kaya smiled again and hearted that message as well. Now, time to read the one from Lucas.

> ty for inviting me—rly fun
> and great to see you

She noticed it came in just five minutes ago. She paused a second and responded.

> ty for coming! I'm glad
> you did

> also Tim is so nice—nice
> of him to come to some
> rando's bday thing ha

Three dots appeared!

> well he knows you're not
> a rando to me

She felt warm all over.

> very kind of u

well I will let you go—it's late—but I just wanted to say thx and goodnight and you looked great tonight

Ahhhhh!

u didn't look so bad yourself and thx to you too!

night

night

Kaya

THE WEATHER WAS HIGHLY variable in February. It had been a few days since her birthday, and, except for the texts, Kaya hadn't heard from Lucas. She finished the things she wanted to get written and edited for the day, but found herself restless. Maybe she'd go for a run.

She checked her phone...air temperature: 34. Not too bad. She put on warm leggings, a t-shirt and a quarter zip, plus a knit cap and gloves. She laced up her sneakers and headed out around the Point.

Kaya didn't usually run with music. Even though she was alone a lot of the time, running gave her brain a different sort of quiet. The motion, the deep breathing—something about it loosened up parts of her mind. She didn't hurt as much when she was running. Her mind wandered to more creative places. Sure enough, as she headed around the Point, she thought about a new research angle for the railroad project that she hadn't thought of before.

When she turned left onto Sunset Ave towards the beach, though, she immediately felt the wind coming harder at her. Thick grey clouds blotted out the sun. It felt colder than she had anticipated. She pulled back down the sleeves she'd pushed up and zipped her top all the way up. When she got to where the road dead-ended at Sunset Beach, she stopped, looking at the water, hands behind her head to try to open up her chest. She found herself wheezing a little. She needed to catch her breath.

Out of the corner of her eye, she saw another runner pull up and stop as well. The parking lot at the end of the road here was a common place for runners and cyclists to stop and take a breather before turning around. She glanced at the woman, and they caught each other's eyes and smiled in greeting.

The woman was taller than Kaya, with light ash-brown hair and a short ponytail sticking out the back of a baseball cap. She had shorts on over leggings and a sweatshirt. She looked about Kaya's age. She also appeared to be catching her breath.

The woman gestured to the ocean. "Always so pretty isn't it?" she huffed, hands on hips.

"It is," agreed Kaya. "But, if I'm being honest," she continued with a chuckle and another gasp for air, hands still on the back of her head, "I'm gonna take in the view extra today because I totally underestimated how cold it would be out here—I don't always breathe well when I exercise in the cold."

The woman nodded. "I get that. Although I have the opposite issue. I hate when it gets too hot and muggy. The cold I don't mind. But also, I always welcome a break," she said with a grin. Kaya smiled and looked back at the water. The woman asked, "Are you okay though? Do you have an inhaler or something you use?"

Kaya looked at her again. "That's really nice of you—I'm fine. I just need to catch my breath. I have an inhaler at home. I'll probably go home from here instead of doing my normal miles, so I don't push it."

"How many miles do you usually do?" the woman asked.

"Depends. I guess my 'normal' would be about four. But sometimes more, sometimes less."

"Same," said the woman. "I come out here a lot— I feel like I've maybe seen you or passed you on Sunset," she said, gesturing her head to the road behind them. "I'm Alexis, by the way."

"Kaya," said Kaya in reply. "And we probably have seen each other. But I'm just usually zoned out in my thoughts, so I'm terrible at noticing things around me," she added, laughing. Her breathing started to deepen and calm again. She lowered her hands. "I hope I'm not holding you up or making you get a chill."

"I'm okay," said Alexis, "but I don't want to hold you up, either."

"I think I might head back walking for a bit," said Kaya.

"I can walk with you," said Alexis and they fell into step back up Sunset.

"I think I came out too fast today, too," said Kaya. "That probably also made me short of breath."

"How fast do you usually go?" Alexis asked.

"Oh, I'm slow," laughed Kaya. "ten-half, maybe eleven-minute mile?"

"That's about what I do too. I don't mean to be weird, but if you ever want a running buddy, that'd be cool. I run to kill time and exercise, but it's a lot more fun for me when I'm not on my own."

Alexis exuded a laid-back, chill demeanor. Kaya pictured having a friend like this to run with, and her face lit up. "That actually does sound fun. Do you live close by?"

"Not at all," said Alexis, laughing. "I live about forty minutes up the shore. Thirty if traffic is good. But I'm down here for work—I'm a tech at that vet hospital on Sandman Boulevard. I like to work double shifts for the money, but they mandate that you have to take at least one and a half hours off between shifts. So, to kill time, sometimes I run."

"Well, that sounds like a fun job, and I'd totally go running with you some time."

Alexis grinned. "I would love that, because some days I plan to, but I wind up just getting a chai and wasting time on my phone. If I have plans to go *with* someone, it makes me do it."

They got to where Cape Ave intersected on the right, leading back into the Point. Kaya waved her hand in that direction. "I live out this way and I think I'm gonna head back and cut it short today. But let's get each other's info," she said pulling out her phone. Alexis did the same.

"So, at some point, text me your work schedule and we'll find a day," Kaya said.

"Sounds good," Alexis replied. "Hey, nice meeting you."

"You too!" Kaya said, and realized she meant it. Alexis resumed jogging up Sunset. As Kaya walked home, she marveled a little at how easy it felt to just...make a friend.

Lucas

"I LIKED KAYA." TIM called. Tim, Casey, and Lucas were throwing a frisbee around on Poverty Beach. Molly was bounding around trying to intercept it.

Lucas laughed. "I like Kaya, too." He caught the disc and rifled it over to Casey.

"Do you have a picture?" Casey called as he hopped to the side to catch it.

"No, jackass, I do not," Lucas replied. "I mean, I've seen her Instagram profile pic..."

Casey looked back at Lucas. "Yeah, I *bet* you have."

"You asshole," called Lucas, also laughing. Casey threw the frisbee to Tim, who caught it and sent it to Lucas in one motion. It flew high on a gust of wind. Lucas jumped and used all his height to snag it out of the air.

"Is she hot?" asked Casey.

"She's cute," Lucas said before taking a couple steps and sending the disc back to Tim.

"She's hot," Tim called. "But in, like, a normal way."

Lucas laughed. "Right. I mean, she's just so...real. Most girls are so fake, or at least really closed off, which I get when you're getting to know someone. But she just *owns* her feelings in a way that is so...I dunno. Refreshing, I guess. Makes it really easy to be around her."

"Have you talked to her since?" Tim asked as he sent the disc back to Lucas.

"No," Lucas replied.

"Sorry I couldn't meet her when you all went out. Why haven't you talked to her?" Casey asked, jumping to grab the disc from Lucas and sending it over to Tim.

"I don't know, honestly," Lucas admitted. "I want to. I feel this connection with her. But she's really going through a hard time, and I don't know if I should leave her alone or what."

"Dude," called Tim, sending the disc towards Lucas. "She invited you to her birthday party. I doubt she wants you to leave her alone."

"Yeah, I know," Lucas replied. Tim's throw went short and Molly pounced. Lucas jogged up to the dog to wrestle the frisbee from her teeth. "Gross," he muttered, brushing the disc against the sand to try to wipe off some of the slobber.

He arced it back to Casey. "But that was a group outing. Do I go right from there to a date? Seems too much too soon. I don't want to make her uncomfortable."

"Wanna double date?" Casey asked. "Wendy and I could do something with you."

"That's still a date," Lucas replied. He *did* want to ask her out. All the joy centers of his brain lit up when he thought about her, closely followed by pain thinking about all she had lost. In a way, he was grieving the loss of that family too. He couldn't imagine what she and her sister must be going through. He didn't want to add to her stress, even as he craved wanting to be near her.

"I'll figure something out," he said.

Kaya

KAYA AND ALEXIS MADE plans to meet a few days later. They arranged to meet up at the Exit Zero parking lot, since it was between their locations and Kaya knew it would be easy for Alexis to find a parking spot, at least while it was still off-season. The day they picked was a good ten degrees warmer than the day they had met, and there was just a light breeze with full sun. Kaya arrived by bike and locked it up. She spotted Alexis getting out of her car.

"Hi!" Kaya called, pulling on her gloves as they walked towards each other. "I know we said about four miles? Is that still good?"

"Sure, works for me," Alexis replied.

"I mapped out a couple routes, do you have a preference?" she asked, holding out her phone to show the options to Alexis.

Alexis laughed. "No, no preference. And I'm not nearly that prepared!"

Kaya laughed too. "Okay, then we'll do this loop out to Sunset again. Ready?"

"Ready." They started jogging. At first, they just chatted about the weather, their histories with running as exercise, the houses they ran by. There were periods of silence too—an easy silence.

"I'm an introvert," said Kaya. "I don't mind going hours without talking to people. It's peaceful...but," Kaya continued, "this is really nice. Having someone to run with...to talk with."

Alexis glanced sideways, grinning. "Yeah, like I said the other day, I like having a commitment I have to keep. But I also just think it's more fun with a buddy. I have a roommate and she's fine, but she mostly keeps to herself...we don't really do stuff together."

"Ah, got it," said Kaya as they turned onto Sunset towards the beach.

"Do you have roommates?" Alexis asked.

"No. I did when I lived in DC—my best friend, Lynne. But I moved down here at the beginning of December. My parents bought this place almost ten years ago. None of us ever lived here year-round, but I am really liking it."

"Do your parents come down and visit?" Alexis asked.

Kaya was quiet as they jogged along. She found that she didn't tear up. She didn't feel as raw today, while in motion. But she was hesitant to be the one to bring the light conversation down. Still, no point in holding back the truth. "No, and I'm sorry—this is gonna be really sad, so I'm sorry to drop this on you when we've just met!" she started.

But Alexis quickly replied, "No, please don't apologize. You don't have to tell me anything you don't want to. I'm sorry I asked!"

"It's okay—there is literally no way you could have known," Kaya said smiling and glancing sideways briefly. "My mom died almost three years ago and my dad died this past fall. I quit my job and moved here because I just seriously needed a change of pace." They were quiet except for their breathing. She had warmed up by now, so Kaya tugged off the gloves and zipped them in her pockets as she jogged along.

"That sucks that that happened," said Alexis finally. "But thank you for telling me, and I think it's really cool that you did that—like, deciding to make a big change. I think it's awesome." Kaya grinned at Alexis.

"What?" asked Alexis with a sideways glance.

"It's just cool, how you reacted," Kaya said flicking her own glance sideways. "Like, it's just my life, it's part of me, and I hate when people feel like they have to tiptoe around me, you know? A lot of my old coworkers did that. But you're just like '*that sucks*' and you're so nice about it, and I think it's awesome," Kaya finished with a goofy smile.

Alexis laughed. "I don't have a lot of tolerance for BS, but it also means I kinda say whatever I'm thinking, so, buckle up, running buddy."

Kaya laughed. "So, yeah, I don't have any roommates," she said. They ran a few more minutes in silence before Kaya asked, "You don't by any chance know a guy here called Lucas Andre?"

Alexis thought for a minute. "No," she answered. "But I don't really know anyone down here except some clients and my co-workers, and most of *them* don't live here either—it's expensive down here! I come down for work and then go back to Middle Township. All my friends live up there. Why?"

Kaya felt herself blushing, even though her face was already red from exercise. "I think I have a really dumb crush."

"Oh, *really*," teased Alexis, laughing. "I can already tell you are going to be a fantastic running buddy for the gossip alone." Kaya burst into a genuine chortle. Alexis smiled. "I don't think crushes are dumb. Do tell."

"Yeah, well," Kaya started, "I've run into him around a few times, he's crazy handsome, and super kind, and thoughtful, and always wanting to do nice things for me."

"But?" asked Alexis as they looped back towards Exit Zero.

"No 'but', I just invited him out with a group of people for drinks for my birthday…"

"It was your birthday?" Alexis interrupted. "Happy birthday! I love birthdays! How old are you?"

"Thanks," answered Kaya, laughing. "I turned twenty-six."

"You sweet, sweet summer child!" laughed Alexis back.

"You can't be that much older than me!" Kaya exclaimed.

"I am twenty-eight. Very old. Very sage. Quite your elder." They were both giggling now between breaths. "Okay, so, the guy. Your birthday," Alexis said. "Let's get back on track."

"So it was a group for drinks. I invited him. He came and I thought it was fun, and he texted me that night to say thanks. But now it's been, like, a week and I haven't heard anything from him. Just trying to figure out my next move, if any."

"Well," said Alexis, thoughtfully, "I'm not into guys, but if it were me, and I really liked a cute girl in this type of situation, I'd probably reach out again. Like, I wouldn't worry about 'trading' invites or whatever."

"You wouldn't?" asked Kaya.

"Definitely not," assured Alexis. "I mean, I think you should try at least one more time? I wouldn't assume he's ghosting you yet," she added. They came back to where they met, and came to a stop in the parking lot. "But like I said, I tend to take everything at face value."

Kaya looked up at the sky, with her hands on her hips, letting her breath start to slow down. She wiped at the sweat on her face with her forearm, and looked back at Alexis. "Thanks," she said, smiling, "for the encouragement. I'm not sure how brave I am yet, but I will definitely think about it."

"You're welcome," said Alexis, grinning. "This was fun."

"This *was* fun. Let's do it again."

Lucas

THE MACFARLANES, LUCAS, AND the assistant, Tracy were sitting around the conference table in their suite at Congress Hall. The topic was final logistics for the "friends and family" pre-season event they threw every year to give the seasonal staff a sort of dry run of summer and event season. It also doubled as advertising for their properties.

As the meeting adjourned, Tripp and Justin fell into conversation with their father. Lucas followed Diane out of the room. "Diane, do you have a moment?"

She turned around to face him. "Of course."

"I was wondering if I could invite someone from Exit Zero publishing to the event?"

Mrs. MacFarlane's eyes went up and to the side as she considered his words. "I believe Sloane and Vance Spencer are already on the list." She turned to Tracy who had also left the conference room and headed to her desk in the reception room. "Tracy, do you have an RSVP status for the Spencers?"

Tracy tapped her iPad and looked up. "They're a 'no' this year."

"Who did you have in mind?" Mrs. MacFarlane asked, looking back at Lucas.

"The staff writer who handles *Cool Cape May*. Her name is Kaya Morgan."

"I see. I think that would be fine. If you know her, feel free to extend the invite. If you don't, Tracy can do it."

"Thank you," he said, trying to keep a grin off his face. Lucas left the suite and jogged up to his office. He opened a new email and typed it out.

Hey Kaya,

Been a minute since your birthday, hope you're good. No pressure, but I wanted to invite you to the pre-season event at Congress Hall. It's a friends and family gala. The attire is cocktail I'm told...

Kaya

KAYA STOOD IN FRONT of the full-length mirror in her room. She had found an oxblood-colored cocktail dress at a consignment store downtown. It had wide straps and an Empire waist. She felt...pretty. Her curls were relatively smooth tonight, but to be safe, she pulled the top away in a clasp for a half-up, half-down 'do.' She exhaled. Time to go.

She had been so excited to get Lucas' email, but she wasn't sure what to expect tonight. As she stepped into the ballroom of Congress Hall, it occurred to her that "friends and family" of the Cape Resorts property company was the entire year-round population of what felt like all of Cape May County.

She took a flute of champagne from the tray of a passing server and took a sip as she took in the huge room and throngs of people. She felt a light tap on her elbow and turned to see Lucas standing right beside her. He wore a dark navy suit with a slim fit trouser, tailored *excellently*. He had a grey shirt and a blue-grey-purple striped tie. He looked *good*.

"Hello!" she said, maybe a little too brightly? "Um, wow. You clean up well." She was annoyed to feel her cheeks flushing.

He grinned. His eyes briefly flitted down and up. "You look amazing," he said, leaning towards her slightly. His hand was still on her elbow. All the heat in her body seemed to zoom towards the point of contact. She gazed at him, like she was stunned. His blue eyes were mesmerizing.

"Thank you," she said softly.

For a moment, it was as if everyone else disappeared. But the moment broke when another man their age, with slicked-back blonde hair, in a dark suit with a loud teal paisley pocket square strode up to them. "Andre," he said curtly, addressing Lucas but his eyes took in Kaya. Something in the deadness of his eyes made her want to shiver as he made no attempt to hide his eyes dragging down and back up her body. He continued to look only at her while speaking to Lucas. "This a new vendor? Party planner? Mass-booking customer? Or did you not understand the assignment?" Kaya looked at Lucas. A look of annoyance crossed his face before he readjusted it to neutral. He tightened slightly his grip on her elbow, protectively.

"Kaya, this is Tripp MacFarlane, my colleague. Tripp, this is Kaya Morgan. She writes the business entries for *Cool Cape May*. Including *our* entry," he said with emphasis.

"Pleasure," Tripp said, continuing to look at Kaya. He took a step closer to her, turning his shoulder in between her and Lucas, forcing Lucas to let go of her arm. It felt cold in the absence of his touch. "Do let me know if there's anything I can do you for you that my *colleague* can't handle." He flashed a wolfish smile with one side of his mouth and strode away.

"Sorry about that," said Lucas weakly. He looked openly irritated.

Kaya took another sip of champagne and smiled at him over her glass. "Like you said."

"I said...?" he asked, confused.

"When we first discussed them. Douchey."

"Ah, yes," he said, chuckling. "Definitely. Now you have independent confirmation." They smiled goofy smiles at each other until they were separated by more people approaching Lucas commanding his time and attention. He apologized, but she waved him off gesturing with her champagne flute. He was working, after all. She leaned back against the wall and enjoyed watching him walk away.

Lucas

LUCAS GLANCED BACK APOLOGETICALLY at Kaya. She smiled at him. Was this a terrible idea? He *had* wanted to see her. But now there were all these people who wanted to talk to him, and it was his job to do so. He was listening to Pat from Magarity's Lawn Services tell him to please put a good word in with the MacFarlane's about switching to his company. *No, we're not ditching Jones Landscaping*, he thought to himself.

Lucas felt someone slip their arm through his. He turned and looked down. A petite blonde woman with blood red nails laying possessively on his forearm. She had a flute of champagne in the other hand. She was wearing a black cocktail dress that plunged in front. He swallowed and looked back over his shoulder to where Kaya had been. She wasn't there anymore.

"Lucas," the woman purred.

"Good evening, Mrs. Whitmore," he said with a slight emphasis on the "*Mrs*."

"It's Rebecca, Lucas," she said with a small pout. "And soon to be Rebecca Vito again."

"I'm...sorry?" Lucas stammered. She leaned conspiratorially into him. He inwardly flinched but outwardly stayed neutral.

"Divorce is in the works, but I consider myself already back the market. Let's go out. It'll be fun. You would never go out with me in high school," she whispered against his ear.

Lucas forced a chuckle and put some distance between them. "And ruin an old friendship?" he said, withdrawing his arm and placing his palm on his chest. "Enjoy the party. Excuse me," he said with a smile as he turned away.

He spotted Kaya at the bar, chatting with the server, Helen. That seemed like her—bond with the help as opposed to hobnobbing. He watched her tilt her head up and laugh at something Helen must have said. He threaded his way through the crowd. Lucas wanted to be in on that joke, whatever it was. To hear her laugh—to try to *make* her laugh. He couldn't quite identify the root of this compulsion but seeing her lighter like this was doing things to him he didn't fully understand.

Before he could reach her, though, Mr. MacFarlane called his name.

"Sir?" Lucas replied, turning to his boss.

"Son, I need you to explain the expansion plan for the Beach Plum cottages to Hernán from the Chamber of Commerce. You know the details better than any of us."

"Of course," Lucas replied. "Where is he?" Mr. MacFarlane pointed across the room. The opposite direction from Kaya. Lucas nodded. Before he turned though, he looked back at Kaya. She was looking at him and smiling. She raised her glass. He smiled, shrugged and returned the gesture.

Kaya

KAYA FOUND HERSELF LOOKING forward to the runs with Alexis. There was something almost magical about it—something about being in constant motion, side by side, made the conversation feel like it was fleeting—not in a way that it disappeared, but rather that it wasn't tied down to any particular place. It was like their runs were a protective bubble where they could float through the rest of the world.

Alexis' easy-going manner helped, too, and Kaya found that she could open up. It was nice to have someone *here* she could talk to regularly. Callie and her DC friends were great, but had their lives in other places. And she liked her new work friends, but she didn't really confide in them. Maureen came closest, as a type of mother-figure, with her advice and warmth. Kaya genuinely liked spending time with all of them, but, still. And it didn't hurt that Alexis seemed to delight in stories of drama.

Even in this short amount of time, the friendship with Alexis happened so naturally. Kaya found that she loved it.

"Hey," Kaya said, walking up to Alexis. They met today by the Coast Guard station. "I'm sorry but I might be slow—is it okay if we see how it goes?"

"Of course," said Alexis. "This is now officially a running club rule. Anyone can ask to slow down without judgment. And we should probably also ban the use of 'I'm sorry' unless we actually need to apologize for something," she said, laughing. This had become an inside joke—that the two of them comprised a running "club," and they came up with rules while they were jogging, like: it's always allowable to stop and take a picture of something pretty. No running in temperatures under twenty-eight degrees. You're always allowed to call off a run if you drink too much the night before. No members shall be added to the club without express permission of the founding members (though neither of them really anticipated *expansion*). It was a very easy friendship.

"But what's up?" asked Alexis. "Are you not feeling well?"

"I'm fine, just tired," responded Kaya as they started jogging. "I couldn't sleep last night."

"Thinking about *Lucas*?" teased Alexis.

"Ha," responded Kaya. She *had* been, truthfully. While last night was really just regular-grade insomnia, she'd be lying if she said she didn't spend many of those awake hours thinking about him.

"Insomnia and I are old friends," Kaya offered.

"Anything major on your mind?" Alexis asked with a sideways glance as they jogged along the harbor.

"Everything major?" Kaya said and laughed through her nose. "Do you ever just have a sense of panic, like everything is wrong?"

Alexis was quiet for a moment before answering. "I don't know that I've felt exactly that. I've worried about things. I mean, everyone has. What do you think is wrong?"

"I guess, I just feel a little unsteady, unmoored since I lost my parents. Not all the time, but things pile up. Like, was I right to move here? Quit my job? I don't know. Maybe I'm alone too much with my thoughts." Kaya listened to the sounds of their sneakers hitting the hard sand and gravel along the side of the road. "Maybe everything seems worse at three in the morning."

"That is *definitely* true," Alexis replied. "And I'm sorry you're not sleeping. But selfishly, I'm happy you moved here." She glanced at Kaya with a smile. "But seriously, any Lucas news?"

"He texted me," Kaya said.

"Whoa!" responded Alexis. "When? I thought you said you didn't hear anything after the fancy party the other week?"

"Yeah, but then I did a couple days later."

"What did he say?"

"Not much. I mean basically that he was glad I could come and he was super-apologetic that he couldn't spend more time with me at the event. I just said it was fine, thanked him again for inviting me, and said I totally didn't expect him to have time to hang with me."

"That's it?" Alexis huffed out as she jogged.

"Well…" said Kaya.

"*Now* we're getting somewhere," teased Alexis.

"He did say he thought I had looked amazing."

"'Amazing' is good!" squealed Alexis. "What did you reply?"

"I just reiterated what I told him at the event—that he cleans up really well, and I put a winking emoji." They jogged on and Kaya added, almost wistfully, "He really did look good that night."

Alexis hmphed. "You need to be braver. Reach out to him."

"Thank you," said Kaya, glancing sideways at Alexis.

"For what?"

"For continuing to think of me as someone who is braver than I actually am."

"Well, you're welcome. Because you are. You just have to figure it out."

Kaya

KAYA TRIED TO GO to bed early to try to make up some sleep, but her mind was turning over what Alexis said. Brave. Maybe she could be. She picked up her phone and navigated to the thread with Lucas.

Hey

she wrote. Nothing happened. She glanced at the time—it wasn't late, only 9:30. Maybe he was working, and she tried to will herself not to panic. She put down her phone and looked up at the ceiling. This is silly, she tried to tell herself. He was so freaking cute, and empathetic and kind, and she really wanted to get to know him better. She felt so *drawn* to him, somehow, whenever she was near him.

He always seemed happy to see her when they bumped into each other. And she knew she wasn't imagining all the physical contact at her birthday. She went over the memory of when they first saw each other at the Congress Hall event. She was pretty sure she had read his expression right when his eyes took her in...he did tell her she looked "amazing," right?

But then, why hadn't he asked her out? Kaya was not old-fashioned. It was not that she was waiting for *him* to ask *her* out, necessarily. So, what was her hesitation? Maybe she just felt like she was too broken to be interesting enough for him...then her phone vibrated.

> Hey! What's up

> Nothing—sorry, did I get you from something?

Kaya immediately panicked. Did that sound like she was asking him if he was *with* someone? *Shit shit shit.*

> Not at all. Just got back from the gym—what are you up to?

Well, hell. Her heart kept racing when she couldn't stop an image of a toned Lucas in a sweat-soaked t-shirt from popping into her head. *Lord.*

Not much—was going to try to go to sleep early since I didn't sleep well last night, but I'm not tired

Yeah that's frustrating when it happens to me—like when I want to get a good sleep because I have an early start, but I can't fall asleep. Sucks

sorry

it's okay but thanks

just thought I'd say hi

glad you did

So what helps you get sleepy? How bout if I send sheep emojis one after another hahahaha

I say that but I don't even know if there is a sheep emoji

must look

She found herself grinning at the screen.

I can send a noise file of the sound of waves?

Hahahaha thx but I can open my window to get those

Mmm true

Door dash you some chamomile?

Ur very cute. I'll be fine. This is actually helping

Me distracting u?

Ha yes

Good

It's just hard to turn my brain off enough sometimes, so, thx for the help

Any time

Night Lucas

Night K

Lucas

HE LOOKED DOWN AT his phone and smiled. He walked across his kitchen to the fridge to refill his water bottle and dropped his phone into the pocket of his joggers. Taking a swig from the water bottle, he crossed his living room and stepped out onto his balcony. It was a cool night, but it felt good on his skin after the workout. He leaned his forearms against the railing and looked absently across the creek towards the marina.

It was ridiculous to be so excited about her texting, but he was. He had been rethinking the night of the friends and family party. He'd felt awful how little he'd been able to speak to her. He was pretty sure she liked him, or was at least liking getting to know him, maybe? He really wanted to ask her out, but he felt like he fumbled the party, and on top of that, she was going through so much. She was grieving. If being here at her family cottage was her escape—her process for healing, it seemed wrong to mess with that. He really wasn't sure what his next move should be. And she hadn't reached out either.

Until now.

As his body cooled down, he started to feel a chill, so he stepped back inside. He was still smiling, though, as he climbed the stairs towards his room and the shower.

Kaya

KAYA BLINKED AWAKE AT the early spring sun coming through her window. She chose this room in the southeast corner of the cottage because it got the best morning light. When she suffered insomnia, it was almost a comfort to see the daylight breaking around the edges of the curtains. The night was over, she didn't have to lie awake and think about how she should be sleeping.

She got up, made coffee and oatmeal, and sat at the counter. She checked her inbox and formatted a few *Cool Cape May* postings that had come in. She saw some responses to her queries on land records predating the Admiral Hotel. She reviewed them and made some notes for herself.

She was pleased to see a request for a small feature in the *County Herald*. The editor wanted her to report on the departing high school band teacher and do a short profile on the one coming in to replace him. *Fun*.

After dispensing with all that, she checked the weather forecast. *Wow*. It was going to be uncharacteristically warm for late March—sunny and maybe up to sixty. She had been itching to get out and do something.

She'd meant to drive up to the canal and try kayaking in the wetlands. It was always something her family talked about doing, but when they were only at 1506 for a week, all their other favorite activities took precedence. And then when they had the cottage, all the new things they added to their favorites were down on the Point or further afield. Today seemed like a good day.

She pulled on some joggers in a quick-dry fabric, so if she did catch some splash, she wouldn't be too uncomfortable, and a lightweight, long-sleeve quarter zip in a deep berry color. She added a vest that she could take off if she got too warm. She pulled her curls back into a high ponytail, grabbed her sunglasses, keys, wallet, and phone and hopped into her car.

She headed through town and over the bridge at Spicers Creek. Before the canal bridge, she turned left and pulled into a dusty parking spot on the side of the road in front of Miss Chris Kayak & Paddleboards. She rented a kayak and the staff pushed her off the launch ramp. She steadied herself and paddled past the whale watcher boat, the marina, and back into the wetlands. It was quiet. Not just off-season quiet, but alone. Peaceful.

She saw turtles darting around the tall, reedy grasses. She kept following the main creek route as it got narrower. She wandered down offshoots until they became too narrow or shallow, backed out, and continued on the main creek. When she got to the old railroad trestle, she turned around and rested. A few beads of sweat rolled down her cheek. She shed the vest and pushed up her sleeves to the elbow. She was comfortably warm, not hot. She was tired, in that satisfying, well-worked way.

In the stillness, she felt the familiar tears roll down her cheek and mingle with the sweat. She felt very close to them, in the quiet, with a light breeze with that intoxicating, early spring mix of cool mist and the hint of summer warm entwined blowing against her face. "Hi guys," she said quietly, eyes cast into the water in the middle distance. "I'm alright," she breathed. An image of her parents faces, smiling, took shape in her mind. "I'm gonna be alright." Holding the paddle with one hand, she brushed her cheeks with the other, readjusted her sunglasses, and paddled back.

Her shoulders, biceps, hips, and calves ached, but in a good way. She was in a slow, steady rhythm as she made her way back. The staff spotted her approaching and came out to haul her boat up the ramp. An athletic teen staffer helped her out and off the floating dock to the top dock. Kaya walked towards the entrance, but then paused and leaned against the railing to appreciate the view of the back harbor.

She saw another lone kayaker coming up from the opposite direction she'd gone—in the wetlands towards the canal. He was using smooth, efficient strokes, like he was well-practiced. He had broad shoulders and was in a t-shirt displaying the corded muscles in his arms as he cut the boat through the water towards the ramp. He had a visor on, but her heart raced. That hair, those shoulders. *Lucas*.

Lucas

HE WAS MOVING FAST back towards the ramp. He thought he saw Kaya pull in and didn't want to miss her. He didn't break stride at all, and slid up the ramp at full speed. Jen was still standing there from helping Kaya out.

"Thanks, Jen," he called as she held the boat.

"You got it," the teenager replied and grabbed the front of his kayak. Lucas grabbed the back and they started walking towards the parking area, and *towards where Kaya was standing. She's still here.*

He kept his eyes on Kaya as they approached and couldn't stop a smile from breaking across his face. Her brows were raised and head slightly cocked.

"Well, hello there!" Lucas called, not breaking stride. "Give me one second," he said as he passed her. Jen and Lucas laid his boat on its side at the front of the deck, and Jen jogged back into the office. Lucas came back to Kaya. "You were out there today," he said, gesturing his head towards the water.

"Yes, God it was beautiful...therapeutic," she added with a laugh. "Do you need help getting that on your car?" she asked, gesturing to the boat.

He glanced at it. "Oh…no, that's okay," he made a dismissive gesture. "I'll come back for it later. Are you hungry?" Kaya looked up to meet his gaze. She took a big swig, draining her water bottle.

"I am, actually," she replied. "I haven't eaten since seven this morning and it's…" she glanced at her fitbit. "Gosh, almost two. Are you getting food?"

"Yeah, I was thinking Lobster House? Back deck?"

Kaya smiled. "Perfect."

Lucas pulled his sweatshirt from around his waist over his t-shirt and they set off on foot, up to and across 109 and down Schellenger Street to the Lobster House. They passed through the breezeway to the back deck overlooking the fishing boats and the condos across the creek. They placed their orders at the takeout window.

"Why don't you wait for our order, and I'll go get some drinks. Do you want something? I'm thinking I might have a beer," Lucas said.

"Sure," Kaya said, "If they have a dry white wine, maybe? And a water," she added hastily.

"For sure, waters all around. Gotta hydrate." He smiled. Lucas turned into the open-air bar. It wasn't crowded. It was still out-of-season, and the lull between lunch and dinner. There was no wait for him to get the drinks. He emerged and took the drinks to an empty table on the deck. He jogged back to where Kaya was waiting. "You can go sit—I'll wait for the food."

"I don't mind," she said, but just then their number was called. Kaya laughed as they went to the window to collect their trays. Lucas led them to the table. "It's so nice in the off-season," she said as they sat down. "I mean, we always come here anyway at some point in season, but it's such an ordeal to find seats. I always feel sort of awkward loitering around trying to get position near whomever might be getting up next."

She tipped her sunglasses up onto her head. Now he could see her big, brown eyes again. Her curls were piled on top of her head, glinting a little reddish in the afternoon sun. A few had escaped and framed her face.

He laughed. "Totally. Awkward as hell. Makes me enjoy it now so much more." They were quiet for a beat. "So, you said earlier that the kayaking was therapeutic. Anything in particular requiring therapy today? Or just...life?"

Kaya looked away at the water and then back at him as she picked up a french fry. "The usual," she said, like she was trying to keep her voice light.

"Please don't feel like you have to spare my feelings, but also you don't have to answer," he said, squeezing ketchup into the lid of his sandwich container.

Kaya smiled. "I'm not necessarily super sad today," she confessed. "It's just that quiet places, especially outside, sometimes make me feel like I'm...closer to...wherever my parents or, or their spirits are. It feels good, like they can feel what I'm feeling and thinking, maybe. I can't really explain it. That probably sounds weird." She laughed lightly and popped the fry in her mouth.

"Not weird at all, actually." She smiled at him.

A seagull alighted boldly on a nearby post and seemed not at all intimidated by them. Lucas tensed and slid his seat to be between Kaya and the gull. The gulls could get pretty aggressive around food.

Kaya laughed and put a hand lightly on his forearm. The contact snapped his gaze away from the gull and back to her. "It's okay, Lucas," she laughed. "I'm just as capable as the next girl in hurling something at a gull if I have to." Her eyes were dancing. He took a breath as he looked at her. He took off his visor, set it on the table and ran a hand through his hair.

"I hope you don't think I see you as some sort of damsel in distress, because I don't," he started, looking down. She removed her hand from his forearm and he glanced to the spot it had been, then up at her. She took a bite of her shrimp roll.

She chewed and swallowed. "I don't. But you do seem to be a very enthusiastic helper type...not that that hasn't been to my benefit several times already!" she quickly added.

"I'm working on it," he said, still looking down, but the edges of his mouth curved slightly upward. "I'm an only child. And my dad, well, he's sort of a savior-type—really helps people, sort of larger than life. His work is...important. There's always been this expectation, I guess, to emulate that. My mom and I are close, and I don't want to paint this like I had any kind of tragic childhood…" Kaya placed her hand back on his arm. He wasn't mad about it.

"It's okay, I'm not judging," she said. He glanced at her hand then back at her face.

"I guess helping people is my MO, which I guess I learned because I thought it would make my dad proud, but I have gotten…um…*feedback* from people in my life that I sometimes take it to a fault." His mouth quirked up again. "My friend, Casey, you know the one with the dog?"

"Yeah," she said, again removing her hand and sitting back in her chair, taking another sip of her wine. "Molly, the exuberant golden retriever." He rolled his eyes and chuckled.

"When he first got that dog, she was a rescue and needed a lot of attention. He had to go to a conference and asked me to dog sit. Well, she had this slight limp I noticed, and I sort of freaked out that Molly had gotten injured on my watch so I drove to a pet hospital in Vineland because I couldn't find one closer that had night hours. They did an x-ray and everything, and were like, 'she's probably just pulled a muscle' and said to just observe her for a couple days. And, yep, the next day, she woke up just fine. Man, Casey never let me live that down. He was like, 'she was eating and pooping and otherwise fine, bruh. You could have waited a day or two to see what happened'." He laughed and took a sip of his beer. Kaya laughed too. The silence settled comfortably between them, against the crying of the gulls and occasional fishing boat horns.

"Anyway," continued Lucas, "I don't think you can't handle yourself. Far from it, actually."

"Is that right?" she asked, a smile playing around her lips, as she paused her glass against the bottom one, before taking a sip. He needed to stop thinking about her lips.

He shook his head. "Yeah, I mean...God, everything you've been through with your parents and the asshole ex, and then you come *here*. Like, a lot of people could never be that brave. To leave everything behind, to know what you need to do for yourself and have the courage to do it...that's badass," he finished. He thought he saw a flush spread across her cheeks. She looked down.

"I have a confession to make," Lucas said, looking out at the water. His pulse quickened.

"Oh?" replied Kaya.

"I went out today because I thought I saw you...I mean, I wasn't sure. I was reading on my balcony, and you were wearing sunglasses, but I thought it looked like you. And it was such a nice day that I thought I'd see if I might run into you."

Kaya cocked her head and looked at him, then smiled. "Really?"

"Yeah, sorry. Does that make me a total creeper?" He laughed, but he was searching her face.

She paused, then shrugged. "No. I think creeper has to include creepy intent. This didn't feel like that, and I'm happy to see you."

He felt himself beaming.

"Wait," she said, "where do you live that you saw me?"

"Here," he said.

"The Lobster House?" she asked, laughing.

"Haha, no. Not at the Lobster House. Here at the marina—in those condos across the road." He gestured back toward the kayak rental shop. "Wanna see?" he asked. *Was that weird? I mean, I've been to her house.*

Before he could second-guess himself too long, she answered. "Sure! I have to go back to my car anyway." They finished their drinks, stood and bussed their trays, and walked back across 109.

Kaya

"SO THIS IS WHY you said you'd be back for your kayak later."

"Yeah, actually, do you mind if we grab it now?"

"Of course not, it's easier with two people, I imagine." They walked back to Miss Chris' and grabbed his boat, toting it towards a cluster of four-story condo buildings, relatively new, lining the creek. They had the vibe of sort of coastal townhouse feel. Lucas unlocked a storage shed on the ground level of one of the units and they slid the kayak inside.

"Want to see the inside?" he asked, tipping up his chin.

"I'd love to—these look really cool," she replied.

He gestured towards the unit. "They're all built with parking underneath on the ground, one big one-story unit up on the next floor, and two units above that are both two-story. I have one of the upper two-story ones." He led her up an outside staircase alongside the building, and then another. "There's an elevator, but I only use that when I have a lot of stuff to carry. It's slow," he explained. She nodded.

He unlocked the door and dropped his visor and keys on the counter. She looked around. It was beautiful, modern, small, and sparse, but not empty. He kept a neat place. This floor was an open room with a sleek blue and white kitchen with a marble waterfall island and a sitting area with an L-shaped sectional couch in grey-blue upholstery, a chair, coffee table and TV. There was a staircase against the right side of the room, leading up, she assumed, to the bedroom level. Her heart fluttered a little at the thought of picturing where he slept. Where he presumably...*well.*

She snapped her attention back to the room. An artist's rendition of the Point lighthouse hung over the sofa, and there was a collection of large potted plants in the corner.

Straight through the sitting area were French doors that led out to a small deck. She was drawn towards the water, crossing the room. She stepped out on the deck, and looked to the right. "So," she said, "I can see where you have a view of where I would have paddled past going into the wetlands. But," she said looking back at him, "when I saw you afterwards, you were coming from the other way."

"Well," he said, ducking his head but still looking at her, "I didn't want to be a total creeper, remember? I just thought, if it's meant to be, we'll run into each other. If not, then, well, it's still a good day to paddle." At the words *meant to be*, Kaya found herself suddenly flustered. Little butterflies buzzed happily around inside her. It had only been one glass of wine, but she was happy, emboldened by the sense that this thing might really be taking shape.

"I have a confession too," Kaya blurted.

Lucas was leaning against the door frame with his hands in his pockets, and smiled a slow, lazy smile. "This I have to hear."

"When I brought my sister around to the hotel over Christmas, it was not a coincidence, running into you. We went to Beach Plum to look for you. They told me you were at Congress Hall." Kaya blushed and looked down.

Lucas chuckled. "I kinda figured. Or...at least, I hoped," he said with a small shrug.

She smiled as she looked up and caught his gaze. She paused and said, "This is really a nice place, and today has been so much fun. Thank you." He stepped aside to make room for her to walk back inside. She crossed the room heading for the front door. He walked her out to the second—really, third-floor deck, since the first floor was up on pilings. She turned and looked at him, saying nothing. He looked at her. She waited, trying to be patient but her heart fluttered madly.

And then, she saw it. His eyes dropped for a second from her eyes to her mouth and back to her eyes. *Yes!* She waited. His eyes darted again. She let her eyes flit once to his lips and back to his eyes. He looked deep in concentration, like he was working to hold back.

It was almost like an out-of-body experience. She liked to think of herself as someone who was honest and authentic, but she was not usually *forward*. That said, her recent life experience taught her that life was short. Very short. And now she was making decisions that might appear reckless—like quitting her job and moving here— which might actually be working out for her. *And he called me brave. He thinks I'm a badass.* All these thoughts added up, in this moment, to a courage that startled and thrilled her.

She took a chance. She lifted her right hand and placed her fingertips lightly on his chest. The butterflies celebrated at the firmness under her touch.

His breath hitched. He didn't move, hands still in his pockets. "So, Lucas," she started, holding his gaze. "I really like you, and I think you like me, so..." There. She said it. Well, she said *something*. She left her fingertips in place and it was everything she could do to just wait, and not turn and run. Her heart was pounding in her chest.

His jaw worked a little before he spoke. "I do like you," he said. "I really like you. I just...don't want to be the guy who takes advantage of you when you're grieving. I don't...want to be that guy...not with you."

She smiled. "That's sweet, and frankly, from what I know of you, completely consistent with who you are, but here's the thing," she said, her eyes darting back and forth between his. "Yes, I'm grieving, and yeah, I'm going through some stuff, but I'm also out here living. If I pressed pause on living my life until there was nothing hard to process, I'm not sure I'd ever un-pause it. And I don't think that's how I want to live."

He gazed at her, with something close to naked admiration. She waited. Very slowly, he took his left hand out of his pocket and touched her waist. He stepped closer, canted his face down to hers, and very gently brushed her lips with his. It was light, and soft, and feathery. She pressed her palm fully against his chest, and his hand tightened on her hip. The kiss slowly deepened until their lips parted and tongues intertwined. She could taste the traces of his beer and vinegar from his sandwich. His right hand came up to cup her neck and cheek, his top two fingers wound into some errant curls that had come loose. Her left hand went to his lower back as she pulled them together.

She lost track of time because this was a *really nice kiss*. She started to note a warmth below her belly that she hadn't felt in quite some time. Then, she felt him also reacting between them, and it was like they mutually agreed to slow down—they slowly pulled back out of the kiss, keeping their hands on each other, but putting just a little distance between their bodies.

She smiled up at him, holding his eyes...the color of the ocean on a stormy day. Light blue towards the center but rimmed in a light grey. He rubbed his thumb on her cheek. He closed his eyes and leaned down to rest his forehead on hers. "I do. Really like you," he breathed. "It's going to be nice again tomorrow. We should do something. I'm free after two."

"Great idea," she replied. "Let me see how much work I have to do and I'll text you some thoughts?"

"Deal," he said, but still didn't let go. Finally, she sighed a happy sigh and stepped away.

"See you tomorrow," she said, turning towards the stairs and she just knew that she was smiling the goofiest smile.

As soon as she pulled out of view of the harbor, she called Callie.

"*Oh my God oh my God he kissed me!*" she shouted as soon as Callie picked up.

"Wait, stop. I was connecting my ear buds—what are you saying—did you say something about kissing?" Callie breathed out.

"*Yes*," Kaya said, her heart racing. She grinned ear to ear. "He saw me out kayaking, and so he went out kayaking, he said, to try to run into me, and then we got lunch at the Lobster House, and he wanted to save me from a seagull, and we went back to his condo because he lives right by there, and it's a beautiful place, and when I went to leave he told me he likes me and he kissed me!" Kaya knew she was rambling but she couldn't help it. She was on too much of a high to attempt to make any sense.

"*Well*," Callie said, pausing to process. "This is some serious shit right here. I mean, in a good way.

This is *not* something I thought I would hear today. Was it good?"

"It was beyond fantastic," Kaya confirmed.

"And how were things...left?" Callie asked.

"We're gonna do something tomorrow!" squealed Kaya.

"Well, then I expect another update tomorrow, young lady," said Callie in her best teacher voice.

"An update you shall have," said Kaya laughing.

Lucas

THEY HAD MADE PLANS to meet at the lighthouse and ramble around the maze of nature trails in the adjacent park. Lucas pulled his Subaru into the parking lot right on time. She was already there, sitting on the table part of a picnic table with her feet on the bench. She was wearing jeans, some type of striped t-shirt and a zip-up hoodie. Her hair was down today and falling over her shoulders.

He locked his eyes on her as he approached.

"Hi," she said, hopping down off the table.

"Hi yourself." He strode up to her, encircled her waist with one arm, lowered his head to her and kissed her. It was a sweet, short kiss, and it made him ridiculously happy that he got to do it.

As they turned toward the trailhead, their hands brushed against each other, sending a zing through his heart. He grabbed her hand and intertwined their fingers. Kaya smiled at him as they walked into the woods.

"Hey, can I say something?" he asked. He glanced sideways at her.

"Of course," she answered.

"I feel so badly for the shitstorm in your life, and I'm really sorry for all the sadness you have to experience, because I always was so happy to see you all...you know, back then...the joy that seemed to envelop you guys. I keep wondering if there's anything I can do or should do to...not erase your grief, but try to do things that would make you happy?"

She stopped walking and turned to face him, looking quizzically at him, her gaze darting between his eyes.

"Wow," he said, laughing and looking down. "That last part sounded way dirtier than I intended."

"Lucas." His gaze came back to meet hers. "You said, 'back then'. What do you mean 'back then'?"

He tilted his head to the side. "From when we were kids?"

"I'm sorry, what?" she stammered. "Did we...do we *know* each other?" She was looking at him in total confusion. *Did she really not know?*

He took a step back and dropped her hand. "Um, yes? You rented a place where I lived." She blinked at him. "At 1506 New Jersey?" Her jaw dropped and her eyes went wide. She looked to the side and touched her fingertips to her forehead. "We were the unit in the back on the other side." He stopped talking and watched her. She looked up at the trees, then shut her eyes.

"The owner-not-renter family!" she exclaimed, her eyes flying open, like maybe the memories had snapped into place. "With the black truck! That was you?" Lucas nodded and held his palms up as she kept speaking. "Your dad grilled burgers on Sundays! Honestly, your dad scared me a little. He always seemed so grumpy when we were playing in the driveway area. But I was always a little...okay, a lot, jealous of people who owned places at the beach. Especially 1506. That was *so* my happy place. Wow. That was...you. I didn't...I didn't put that together," she said smiling and shaking her head.

He chuckled. "Well, I was always a little...okay, a lot, jealous of people like you, too."

"What do you mean?"

"I was jealous of the joy in your family," he responded. He turned and resumed walking, and she fell in step. He picked up her hand again. "I have been very fortunate, and I know I walk through the world with a lot of privilege, but I can't honestly say there was a lot of joy at home. Of all the renters who came through that place, you guys seemed the happiest—I mean, everyone's happy at the shore, but you guys were *always* laughing, joking. When you were out in the driveway space, you were blowing bubbles, drawing with sidewalk chalk—and yeah, you're right, my dad was *definitely* grumpy about the chalk!" He laughed and continued.

"I remember one time you got mad at your sister because you thought she knocked you off your bike on purpose when she was really just turning around. I was like, 'oh no, this will be bad, I need to do something', because you were kinda like, 'what the heck' but then she was all, 'wait, are you ok', and your mom came out with the recycling and said, 'everybody good, yes?' and you and your sister looked at each other and burst out laughing. Always so much laughter. And, oh man, the year your dad got sparklers for the Fourth of July. I basically wanted to be adopted by your family."

"So that's what you meant," she said slowly, "with me and Callie, when you said, 'it's nice to be introduced to you'. We both were like 'that's a weird way to say nice to meet you'."

He chuckled, and absent-mindedly rubbing their joined hands with his thumb. "You must have thought I was crazy. You really didn't know it was me?"

"No, not until just now, I had not put that together. The first time I saw you at Beach Plum, I just thought you looked familiar from seeing you with your friends on the beach with Molly." They walked a bit in silence as the path became a wooden boardwalk over the marsh. "So," she ventured, "Is that why you like me? Because you remember me?"

He laughed and she looked startled. He stopped walking, but kept her hand in his as he turned to look at her. "Because I '*remember*' you? Come on, Kaya, there's a million reasons I like you, and I don't even know you as well as I hope to."

Kaya looked down. She turned away and started walking again. She squeezed his hand lightly. Then she looked sideways at him. "Wait, how old are you? I always thought the boy in that house was *old*."

He laughed deeply again. "I'm thirty."

"Huh," she said. "I guess four years felt like a much wider gap when you're a kid than when you're this age."

"Indeed," he agreed, smiling down at her.

Kaya

SHE RUSHED TO PROCESS this. This man knew her—well, sort of—then. In the before times. He knew her before all was lost. He knew—well, sort of—her parents. And Aunt Peggy. He was there the whole time. She wished she could tell them.

"You've known all along," she mused, still trying to wrap her mind around this new information. The trail opened to join with a path around the pond. She looked at him. He was wearing jeans, a t-shirt, and a button-up flannel as his outer layer, hanging open. Her heart fluttered when his eyes met hers and he smiled.

"I've known all along. Well, ever since you came in to Beach Plum. Even though it had been, what, almost ten years, I was ninety-nine percent sure and then you told me your name. That settled it, because I knew your names. You and Callie would call out to each other. Your parents would call for you." They slowed their pace and Kaya turned her face up to the sun. "I can't believe you *didn't*. Well, actually maybe I can. You guys were focused on each other."

"I mean, I remember knowing you existed. I just didn't pay any attention. You were older. And a boy. And you never came outside to play with us."

"I wasn't really allowed," he admitted.

"To *play*?" she asked incredulously.

"To play with people my parents didn't know and approve of. And my father would *definitely* never cosign on fraternizing with renters."

Kaya looked to him to see if he was kidding, but his face was awash in sincerity. Kaya's heart keened a little. What had he missed out on as a kid? They had circled back and returned to the parking lot.

"This was fun," she said slowly, squeezing his hand. She was loving how his hand was warm and his broad palm captured hers. She didn't want the afternoon to end.

"It was," he said, rubbing his thumb against her hand. It was sending little zings through her. "I wish I didn't have to go," he added. Her heart dropped a little.

"I wish you didn't either," she heard herself say before she could think better of it.

"I originally thought I was completely free this afternoon and evening, but I forgot I made plans to go to the gym with Casey...which I would normally be fine bailing on, but I also have to meet up with him to take Molly. He's going away again for a few days."

Kaya laughed. "You take Molly a lot?"

Lucas looked at her. His eyes were such a dreamy shade of blue in the bright sunlight. "I do," he said resignedly. "I mean, I don't mind, really. He travels a lot for work and it's a hassle if he has to board her."

"And you're a compulsive helper," she added.

"Entirely." Kaya held his gaze. He let go of her hand and brought his arm around her waist. He cupped her face with his other hand. Her heart fluttered happily. She lifted her hands to rest on his chest as he lowered his face and kissed her. "Have dinner with me," he said softly, breaking the kiss.

"Okay, when," she replied, a little breathlessly.

"Thursday?"

"Okay, text me when and where."

He bent down and kissed her lightly again. "See you then." As he stepped away, her body was already missing the warmth of his. She turned to walk towards home.

It took some phone tag before she could track down Callie, but they finally connected. Callie called back very shortly after Kaya sent a text saying, "big update."

"Spill, girl," said Callie.

"You thought the last update was a bomb; wait 'til you hear this one!" exclaimed Kaya.

"Oh, my God, did you sleep with him?" Callie practically shrieked out.

"*No!*" squeaked Kaya. "Oh my *God*, Callie. Ewww."

"Don't 'ewww' me! That dude is hot and you are hot for him. It's a fair question."

"Oh, totally, yes, all those things, but I just kissed him for the first time yesterday. I think you know me as *not* a person who jumps into bed with someone she hardly knows," Kaya said defensively.

"I do," allowed Callie, "and yes, I would have been a little concerned if you'd said 'yes' to that question. You've only known him since December and haven't really spent a ton of time with him."

"Well," Kaya said, "about that..."

"What?"

"Here's the thing—do you remember the family who owned unit two at 1506?"

"With the black truck and the grumpy dad?" Callie asked.

"Yes!" replied Kaya. "Well, it turns out, that was Lucas."

"The kid in that family was...*Lucas*?" Callie asked, clearly also processing like Kaya had had to.

"Yup." Silence for a beat.

"I am trying to think back..." Callie mused. "I want to say that he looked a little familiar at Congress Hall, but we met him so briefly. I'm trying to picture that kid at 1506. I mean, I remember there *was* one. But he never came out to play or anything."

"Yeah," allowed Kaya. "He said his family ran a pretty tight ship, and he confirmed his dad was super grumpy about our sidewalk chalk and riding bikes in the driveway. Just like we thought. So it would have been sort-of frowned upon to play with us little terrorizers, I guess. I gather he spent more time watching us than we spent seeing him. But also, he said he ran around with his local friends, went to their houses, that type of thing. But yeah, he's known who I was since I got here. You know how I told you that when he dropped off the Christmas tree, I spilled my guts to him?"

"Yeah," Callie answered.

"He said that he assumed I was so open with him because I knew who he was, and knew that he sort of knew Mom and Dad, or at least who they were."

"Well...wow," said Callie.

"I *know*."

"So why do you think you *did* spill your guts to him?" Callie asked.

"Great question. He just felt so...safe to me. I can't explain it."

"Try."

"Okay...he's so intensely kind. He's compulsively helpful and in a weird way, it makes me want to protect him. Like not have him always helping people. Give him a break, you know? Also, he's not afraid to sit with my grief and sadness..."

"That's rare," interjected Callie with a sigh.

"It is," Kaya agreed. "But he also draws me into happy. Like happier than I've felt or maybe let myself feel in a long time. Being around him it's like my heart is remembering how to be safe and healed, even while it isn't. He makes me believe it's possible."

"God, you're so cute. So I assume there was more making out today?" stated Callie, matter-of-factly, apparently having processed this large piece of the puzzle and moved on.

"There was no *making out*," groaned Kaya. "There was a very nice kiss hello, which if I'm being honest, was pretty cool—like, this is how we are going to greet each other now? He held my hand, kissed me goodbye, and we have plans to have dinner this week."

"Excellent. Carry on," said Callie.

"How are *you*, Cal?"

Kaya heard another deep sigh. "Good days and bad days. It's funny that you said he's okay sitting with grief. I feel bad always dumping my feelings on Juan. He has his own grief for Mom and Dad."

"They loved him," murmured Kaya.

"They did. But I feel like he deserves a break from me and my Big Sad sometimes. Like, when he comes in on me when I've been crying, I know he feels like he has to drop everything and comfort me, and that's not fair to him. So, I'm out with Tina getting coffee and I tried to talk to her about it—just like, confessing that there are recipes that I love but I can't make anymore because it's too painful—reminds me too much of Mom. And she just...she just changed the subject to some new thing on *New York Times Cooking* she wants to try. I mean, I wasn't *really* talking about cooking."

"That stinks, Cal, I'm sorry. I know Tina's otherwise a good friend to you."

"She is, but I mean isn't that what friends are supposed to be for?"

"In a perfect world, yes. I just think death and grief are so hard for a lot of people. I can't decide what's worse—avoidance, pity, or platitudes."

"Amen."

"I'm sorry that happened to you. It must have felt crummy."

"Well, I feel better now, so thank you."

"Any time, sis."

Kaya

AFTER MUCH DELIBERATION, KAYA chose slim black pants, flats, and a deep green v-neck tunic top. She didn't want to look too dressed up, but she definitely wanted to look good. She wore her hair down so her curls were falling just over her shoulders. She tried not to be too obvious with makeup and added gold hoop earrings.

"You look nice," said Maureen, as the older woman came into the Exit Zero work room.

"Thank you," said Kaya, looking up from her computer.

"Special event?" asked Maureen lightly, eyes dancing.

"Date," answered Kaya, flushing. "Going to dinner soon."

"Who's the lucky person?" asked Maureen, sitting down at the workstation beside Kaya. She unwound her homemade knit scarf from around her neck. Her green eyes held Kaya's gaze. "Is it Lucas?"

"Yes," confirmed Kaya.

"Oh!" gasps Maureen, clasping her hands together. "He's lovely! He overlapped in school with my daughter. Such a wonderful young man! I'm so glad."

"Yes," said Kaya, smiling broadly at the unexpected character reference. "It's still early. But I...really like him."

"Well," said Maureen, leaning back. "I like him for you. He's kind. He will be good to you, and you deserve some happiness." Kaya's heart swelled.

"Thank you," she said, simply, eyes welling up. "I really appreciate that."

"You're welcome," replied Maureen. She started to unpack her own laptop and notes.

"Can I ask you something?" said Kaya.

"Of course."

"Do you think I'm nuts...or...lazy...or selling myself short by doing this?"

"Doing what?" Maureen asked quizzically. "Having dinner?"

Kaya laughed softly. "No, this," Kaya replied gesturing around. "Like, I was a real rising star at my firm in DC." Kaya said it simply. Something about Maureen's warmth and the trust they'd built, Kaya knew Maureen would take the statement like a mom-figure, not interpret it as Kaya bragging. "I had a career that was on the fast-track. I'm not sure what I'm doing here, and if it's misguided...or I'm...giving up," she finished simply.

"Are you happy?" Maureen asked.

Kaya looked down at her hands. Her bottom lip trembled a little. She took a deep breath in and let it out. "Happiness is a fascinating concept for me," she answered, looking back into Maureen's eyes. "Like, there is a deep, aching, heavy feeling inside me all the time. I don't sleep well..." Kaya's voice trailed off as she looked away and down at the table.

"That's the grief, darling girl. That will take a good long while to dissipate and it may never fully go away. So let me ask a different way. Most days, are you enjoying where you are, what you're doing, and who you're doing it with?"

Kaya blinked at Maureen, and surprised herself a little when she answered, "Yes, I think I am."

"I think," Maureen started, then she glanced briefly out the window and back at Kaya. "That you need to trust your gut more. Something told you to come here, and you seem like you are generally at peace here, or getting there. I don't think we're defined by our job success, either."

"I think our lives are seasons," Maureen continued. "Some seasons are for rapid career growth. Some are for building relationships. Some for taking care of others. Some are for healing. Sometimes they overlap, but you've been through a lot. I think you can put the ten-year plan aside for a season and focus on you instead." She finished with a warm smile. Kaya held her gaze for a bit and then gave her a small nod.

"Now," added Maureen, "you have a date to get to."

Kaya glanced at her phone. "Soon. Yes, I do."

Lucas

WHEN KAYA WALKED UP to the restaurant, Lucas was waiting outside. He felt a smile spreading across his face as he watched her coming towards him. He couldn't help it.

"Hi," he said and kissed her lightly. He got a whiff of lavender from her hair.

"Hi," she said. She looked at him like she was suddenly shy. He opened the door for her. Inside, she took off her coat and hung it on the hook beside their booth.

"You look really nice," he said softly.

"So do you," she said, smiling as they sat down. He watched her, amused to see her eyes rove down and back up his body. *She's checking me out.* When her eyes came back to meet his, he smiled. A flush crept into her neck. *Busted.*

The waiter came up to them and they ordered. As she handed her menu to the server and he walked away, Kaya's eyes met his again. She quirked up her brows.

"God, you're pretty," he said. She laughed and looked down. He didn't mean to embarrass her, but the words had just come out.

The server came back with a bottle of wine and opened it. He handed Lucas the cork. Lucas politely inspected it and set it down. He swirled the taste the server poured, tried it, and declared it excellent. To be fair, though, unless a wine was actually skunked, Lucas was never going to send it back. As a fellow hospitality professional, he cringed to think of being that high maintenance. The server poured Kaya's glass, topped up Lucas's, set the bottle down and withdrew.

He heard Kaya clear her throat. "So, then...why didn't you reach out to me?"

"What do you mean?" he asked, looking at her over his wineglass.

"I mean, I know you didn't have my contact information until my birthday..."

"Correct," he said. "Plus, see above, under *creeper*."

"Okay, but then after my birthday?" she asked.

"I wanted to," he admitted setting down his glass. "But I wasn't sure what was in your best interest. I thought about it a lot. I invited you to the pre-season party because I wanted to see you, but then I was working and couldn't really talk to you. Tripp was such an ass hat, and I figured I'd totally botched things. I sort of was in my head about that for a week or so. It helped when you texted. I was trying to plan a move. And then I saw you in the kayak."

"Well, then I'm even happier I decided to go out on the water last week," she said. "And Tripp *was* an ass hat, but that's hardly your fault. How about less worrying on your own about what is best for me and just ask because I'm probably less fragile than you think and, anyway, I'm my own problem to solve." She said it with a laugh, but Lucas felt himself wince. She reached out for his hand across the table and caught his gaze. "What?" she asked.

"Sorry," he said, looking down. "I know I've told you about how helping people was sort of currency in my household, and I know I tend to go overboard."

"Yes," she said simply. He looked back up into her eyes.

"The only serious girlfriend I really had as an adult essentially broke up with me because she said I was always 'problem-solving' her. When you said what you just said, that kind of came back to me."

Kaya peered at him as if she were pondering this. "She broke up with you because you were too helpful?"

He laughed a sad laugh. "Essentially. The day Laura left, she said I took away her agency. God, Kaya, that has really haunted me. I loathe the thought of taking away anyone's agency, but especially a woman's." His eyes met hers.

"I am not sure that's fair," Kaya said. "I can see being annoyed if someone is doing things for me that I can do myself, but I've always thought it up to me to own my stuff, you know? I've got a lot of stuff that isn't ideal, but I like to think I communicate pretty clearly about what I want or need—when I know what I need, anyway. Did she give you anything like that?"

"I guess that's the thing," he said, looking at their clasped hands and tracing circles on hers with his thumb. "For a while, I tortured myself thinking back on whether she'd told me to stop, or communicated what behavior she didn't like, and I couldn't recall anything specific. It's like she just didn't like the person I was."

Kaya's face looked stricken. Lucas chuckled softly and said, "When you told me last week you were perfectly capable of taking on seagulls for yourself, I was so...*relieved*—like, here is a woman who's going to tell me what she needs...and what she doesn't."

"Well, that is true," she said, laughing. "You are so selfless and kind, but that must take a toll—always feeling like you have to say yes or make yourself smaller. I hope I never take advantage of that in you."

Wow. No one had ever articulated to him those things he felt. She was amazingly accurate. "How long were you together?" he heard Kaya asking.

"What?" he stammered, as his mind came back to the present. "Oh, a little over two years. But it's been a while—she left over a year ago."

"Well, cheers to her," said Kaya, raising her glass with her free hand. "Because I'm pretty thrilled to be with you now." Her face broke into a smile and he felt his relax too. "And I promise you," she continued, "if there's one thing I learned in therapy, it's how to communicate my boundaries."

"Then, cheers to that," responded Lucas. "Because I already have a feeling I'm going to fight for you in a way I've never wanted to fight for anyone before."

Kaya

KAYA FELT FLUSHED ALL over. The wine was heating her blood. Lucas was gazing at her, and he looked *good*. He wore jeans with a dark rinse and a crewneck sweater in a steel blue that matched his eyes. He was clean shaven and his hair was brushed back off his face.

And then calling her *pretty*? Kaya knew she wasn't unattractive, but Charlie always seemed more drawn to the fact that she was a team superstar with the bosses. He told her once that he knew she was too good for him because everyone at Alston knew she was going places.

Losing her parents caused a deep ache, a feeling alone in the world. But now she was gazing at this incredibly handsome, kind man telling her he admired her and was going to fight for her. Whole chunks of her heart were fusing and healing in that moment.

Whomever this Laura woman was, Kaya thought she was an idiot for having the love of someone as amazing as Lucas and throwing it away. She released his hand, braver now. "But since then, or before then, surely you must have dated," she said.

He looked up startled, but with a chuckle. "A little," he acknowledged.

"Because you're a total ten. Plus, you're nice and compassionate and..."

"You think I'm a ten?" he interrupted, sitting back in his chair, the sides of his mouth quirking up. *Adorably.*

"Shit, Lucas, you're an eleven and you know it."

He actually blushed a little! "You're kind," he said, looking down.

"Just facts," she replied, smiling. She sat back too, took a sip of wine and waited. "So? Girlfriends?"

Eventually he looked up again and continued. "Yes, I've dated. Flings with guests or, God forbid, coworkers, aren't exactly good for the brand, so that doesn't happen," he said sheepishly, "and this is otherwise a small town, as you know. But yes...a relatively serious girlfriend in college, and then later, Laura, but otherwise, you know...occasionally, here and there."

"Well, all of their loss is my gain," she said, feeling herself grin.

When they left and were outside and around the corner towards where she'd parked, he encircled her with one strong arm and pulled her in with his other, crushing her to him. This kiss was urgent and fierce and intense. She reached up and wove her fingers into his hair. His tongue was strong as he dove in. When he paused, both of them were a little breathless. "Fuck, Kaya," he breathed. "I have thought about this a lot." She smiled and kissed him again.

"Get a room!" a passer-by called, laughing. They pulled apart and chuckled.

"See you soon?" she asked, sliding her hands down his arms.

"Yes, please," he said.

Long after she drove herself home, she laid awake in the dark, smiling to herself, thinking about how Lucas had been thinking about kissing her.

Kaya

THE DAYS TUMBLED BY as March turned to April. Kaya and Alexis had fallen into a routine where they met nearly every week to run. One morning they met near Poverty Beach.

"Hey, girl," called Alexis.

"Hey!" responded Kaya. The weather was getting warmer. She had a running buddy. *She had a hot boyfriend who also happened to be the nicest person on the planet.* She couldn't contain her good mood today.

"*Someone* has a big smile today," teased Alexis. "I'm guessing loverboy has something to do with this."

Kaya ducked her head and flushed as they started running. "I am indeed rather happy about the Lucas situation," she confirmed. "But," she said defensively, "that's not the only thing!"

"I know, I'm just teasing," said Alexis. "What else is going on? Give me all the good news."

"I will, but you first today. Last time I rambled on like a lovesick idiot about Lucas, and you never told me anything going on with you."

Alexis smiled. "I didn't mind," she said, glancing at Kaya. "I love that this is working out for you. Plus, not much to report." They jogged down Beach Avenue. "My friend Sue got a new dog. Oh my god, Kay, it's so cute. It's a total mutt."

"Rescue?"

"Yeah, for sure. But he's only two, and so adorable. You should see his ears. When we're done, I'll show you a picture. We're gonna take him hiking this weekend and see how he does."

"Fun," said Kaya. "I know you wish you could have a dog, too."

"Yeah, I do..." allowed Alexis. "But with the hours I work, there's no way. I'd have to hire a dog walker and I don't want to do that. So, I just have fun at work, and with my friends' dogs," she said happily.

"And what's the latest on the trip?" Kaya asked. Alexis had mentioned that she and a group of friends were planning a trip to Costa Rica.

"Pretty much there with the plans. We'll be gone for two weeks in June. I'm so excited."

"That's awesome. You're gonna have so much fun."

"Okay, now you," said Alexis.

"Nothing much to say—I just feel...I dunno, recently, like my heart is just floating a little. It's been a while since I've felt this way."

"Well," said Alexis, "you've been carrying around some heavy crap for a while."

"Yeah," Kaya allowed. "But also, it's not just because of Lucas—although, that is pretty awesome," she said grinning. "I love the writing I'm doing. I love living at my happy place. I have new friends—like you!" she laughed, waving a hand in Alexis' direction. "I just feel lucky."

"We are lucky," Alexis agreed. "And I'm happy for you."

Lucas

LUCAS WAS WALKING THROUGH the hotel after having shadowed an acceptance of deliveries. Feeling his phone vibrate in his pocket, he pulled it out as he headed towards the stairs to climb to his office. He smiled to see Kaya's name pop up as an unread thread.

hey

He wrote back immediately.

hey beautiful

He watched the dots dancing on her reply. He had probably embarrassed her with that greeting and he so didn't care. She was so earnest that he loved playing with her. And he fucking *loved* complimenting her.

Can I ask a favor? Do you have some time this weekend? I need some help

> absolutely. you're speaking my love language

I need to replace a ceiling fan and I'm out of my depth on this one. Sorry it's not something more exciting

He smiled to himself as he took the last staircase two-at-a-time. Walking down the hall to his office, he typed,

> Seriously? How can you think that's not exciting? Proper air circulation is of critical importance

Haha well I'm glad you think so. This one's old and warped and I wanted to get the new one up before it gets hot but it's not a one-person job—at least not this one person

Well I will be there to help

He kept messaging her, hoping her neck and cheeks were getting nice and red.

But I have to tell you

If you're there, it's already hot

He smiled dumbly at his phone, awaiting her reply.

Kaya

TURNS OUT THAT, WITH Sloane's blessing, talking to all kinds of businesses in Cape May provided plenty of opportunities to also inquire about summer employment. Kaya made a lot of inquiries and was thrilled when she came upon the need for a bar hand at the Chalfonte. The Chalfonte was the oldest original hotel in Cape May. It hadn't had the multi-millions-dollar upgrades the Congress Hall had, and it didn't try to pretend it was fancy like Congress Hall. Every few years it got a fresh coat of white paint, and the green and white striped awnings were always in good condition. There were white painted Adirondack chairs on the lawn, and green painted rocking chairs strewn along the long wrap-around porch. But the floors sloped a little, the stairs creaked a little, and aside from having added air conditioning at some point, the Chalfonte felt like stepping back in time.

The pub, the King Edward—or "Eddy's" as the regulars called it—was on the edge of the original hotel building. It opened out onto a breezeway connecting the original hotel to a large addition. At one point, the addition had been a separate house, but the owners purchased it, painted it white, added green and white striped awnings, and made it part of the hotel.

The Chalfonte attracted fewer of the short stay tourists, and more families who—some, for generations—had summered in Cape May. They came and stayed for weeks, year after year, and the Chalfonte was like their home. That's not to say that Eddy's wasn't crowded. It was well beloved by the guest-residents as well as the locals. Most days, from the time it opened at 1 pm until it closed at midnight, it was a convivial experience within the dark paneled pub, and spilling out onto the porch.

Kaya was thrilled to get the King Eddy's job—it would be great pay, and even though she was comfortable in solitude, the job would provide variety in terms of human interaction. The manager, Randolph, an endearing mix of kind and grumpy, had told her that, yes, he did actually need some help because not as many kids were coming from overseas for summer jobs since the pandemic.

She ended the call and texted Lucas.

> I got a summer job!

> tell me

> King Eddys

She watched the three dots appear, disappear, and reappear

You're killing me K haha

what bc it's the Chalfonte?

The competition?
Really? Lol

Well I can't work with u...pretty sure that would violate some HR policy to be dating one of the bosses

Probly yeah

But seriously, I'm happy for you

Thank you. And there's something in it for you

Oh yeah? tell me

The money should be really good which means I will hopefully be able to save a lot and can afford to stay here all offseason

Kaya watched for his response. She expected some silly or flirty response. He seemed to love messing with her. But she was surprised—and touched—when his message appeared.

That is good news for me. The best news actually

Kaya

THE MONTH OF MAY meant more people in Cape May. The days were noticeably longer. It was still bright out when Kaya met Alexis for a run after dinner. Kaya told her about her in-season job.

"That's fun!" enthused Alexis.

"It is, and I'm excited because I should be able to save a lot of money to last next off-season." They jogged silently for a few minutes. "I will say, though," Kaya started, "it may be harder to run as much with this schedule."

Alexis laughed. "Because of *Lucas*," she teased.

"Because of *wo-ork*," Kaya mimicked back, laughing.

"Whatever you say, girl," laughed Alexis. "We'll figure it out."

"We will," agreed Kaya, smiling.

Lucas

LUCAS PULLED INTO HIS parking spot at Congress Hall, pulled his phone from his pocket and typed.

> Today is a very big day

Kaya wrote back immediately. This made him smile.

> Really?

> Yes now that you are a year-rounder I must inform you of a new (to u) holiday we celebrate

> Call me intrigued. What is today

> Opening day

Of...?

DRYDOCK

Omg omg omg YES

Picking u up at 8. Wait til u see—it's a whole thing

Wear something that pairs with moosetracks

You mean peanut butter cup sundae

Pick your poison, babe. This is happening.

☺

Kaya

IT WAS A BEAUTIFUL early May evening, and Kaya and Lucas sat on the deck at Lucas' place, dinner dishes cleaned up, sipping wine. Lucas was sharing that he moved to back-of-house rotations, moving closer to the center of business operations.

"So what's next?" Kaya asked, gazing at the sunset.

"I think I probably finish with a tour in actual property management."

"Amazing," she said. She turned to look at him. "This is so cool. You're going to own part of a Cape May institution."

"I know," he said, smiling. "And then the idiot brothers won't be able to pull rank on me since we'll be equals." He paused. "I'm pretty happy." He paused looked at her. "I'm pretty happy on several fronts, actually." She ducked her head.

When she looked back up, Lucas was gazing at her. "I like you like this," she said.

"Like what?"

"This—confident, optimistic, happy. It's one of many things that makes me want to be around you. It just feels so good being with you. I am not sure what I've done to deserve you, but I'm not going to question it."

Truthfully, she questioned it all the time. She thought constantly about why someone as amazing as Lucas would want to be with someone as broken as she was. She knew he was drawn to people and situations where he could help, and maybe that's why this happened relatively quickly. They had a connection she hadn't expected—she certainly didn't expect it so completely, so soon.

She thought her grief and trauma were like a moat around her heart but every time she was with him, she felt...safe. Even the brief interactions starting when she first moved out here, it was like he was locked in on her, holding the cold world at bay. Instead of running from the pain, he was building bridges over the moat and setting to work helping repair her tired heart.

"Come here," he said holding out a hand. She rose from her chair and took his hand. He pulled her sideways onto his lap and tucked a curl behind her ear. "These curls," he murmured, "drive me absolutely wild." Her face flushed with warmth. Lucas's arms came around her and she rested her hands on his shoulders and then circled them around his neck.

"Do you know how happy I am when I'm with *you*?" he asked.

"I'm getting a sense," she said, smiling.

"I'm serious, though."

"You mean it's not just that I'm a broken thing you are drawn to trying to help?" she tried to keep her voice light, but her heart raced as she looked at him, hoping for validation.

"Is that what you think?" he asked softly, his blue-grey eyes skating over her face.

"No...," she started, "I just...I don't know," she finished, looking down. He tipped her chin up to look at him again.

"When you first came back here and I recognized you, I *was* happy to see you because, to me, you had always meant joy."

"And now?" she asked. "Now it's because of my...pain?" She felt tears spring into her eyes.

"No," he said quietly. "Yes, I will always want to help you—whenever you need it. But you're the first woman I've been with who tells me what they need, but also when to stop...what they *don't* need. It makes me feel..." he looked away briefly and then back at her. "...free. Like I'm enough."

Lucas reached out and wiped a tear off Kaya's cheek before securing his arm back around her. She sniffed once and gently rubbed the back of his neck with her fingertips. "You are. More than enough," she whispered.

"And you're brave," he continued. "You're brave in the face of pain. You're strong. Despite everything you've been through, you still lead with your heart open to...new people, new experiences, new places. It's...incredible. You're not afraid to be your authentic self, to show your feelings—happy *and* sad."

She blinked at him, letting his words sink in. She *did* feel like she could be herself around him, she realized. It's not that she was "fake" with others—it was more that her trauma and introversion usually made her hold back, so she didn't make others uncomfortable. She didn't feel like holding back with Lucas. But she was someone people left, not someone people were drawn to, right?

Kaya pushed all her doubts away and let herself just feel. She bent her face forward and kissed him, softly at first, and then more deeply, slowly. She felt his hands roam around her back, sides, and hips as he kissed her. Her skin tingled where he ran his hands. She wound her fingers into his hair. His tongue got more urgent and his hands lifted at her hips. She swung one leg around, so her knees were on the couch, straddling him. He slid his hands down the backs of her calves, up her thighs and around her butt.

"Kaya," he breathed and kissed her again. He pulled her against him. Sensation was pooling quickly between her spread legs, and she felt him stiffen as well, starting to strain against his jeans. It was almost too much to bear. "Lucas," she breathed back.

He kissed her neck, her collarbone, and bent his head down to graze her breast through the fabric of her t-shirt with the tip of his nose, sending a pleasant shiver through her. "What do you want?"

he whispered into her ear. She sighed heavily and kissed him again.

She pulled back slightly and gazed at him. "I have what I want, which is you."

"Yes, you do. Can we go inside...?" he asked, nuzzling her neck.

When she didn't answer, he pulled his face back to look at her. His eyes were greyer and intense and sexy as hell. It was her nature to take things slow, especially when she had been so emotionally battered for so long. The way she felt right now though...

Kaya realized she was tired of hiding. She was tired of downplaying her brokenness. Lucas saw it all—and he *honored* it. But he also saw joy. And bravery. And suddenly, she was deeply, deeply grateful. *And*, she realized, completely head over heels in love.

"Yes," she whispered. She kissed him again. "Yes, we should absolutely go inside."

The edges of his mouth quirked up. "Are you sure?"

"I am."

Lucas

LUCAS LAID ON HIS side watching Kaya sleep. Daylight spilled through his bedroom windows. She talked often of insomnia, but she was certainly sleeping now. *Perhaps from the...exertion of last night.* If he was even partly responsible for her being able to sleep, he felt good about that. She needed to rest.

He watched her chest rising and falling. He could see the outline of her breasts under the sheet. Not quite able to believe his luck, Lucas thought about how she felt last night. His hands and mouth on those perfect breasts. Her legs wrapped around him. How right it felt to be inside her. The way she arched and cried out when she came...both times. *Well done, Lucas.* Of *course* he found her attractive. But it was much more than that. He admired how strong she was. That even reeling emotionally, she was honest and generous with her attention, compassion, and affection.

Kaya took a deep breath in through her nose and he saw her eyes flutter open as she yawned. Then her eyes widened and she clutched the sheet to her like she was just remembering what happened last night. Lucas propped himself up on one elbow and reached out his other hand to smooth her hair away from her face. "Morning."

Her face relaxed into a smile. "Good morning."

"Any regrets?" he asked softly, looking down at her.

"None. It just took me a second to remember where I was." Kaya reached out and ran her fingertips down his chest. "How about you. Regrets?"

"Only one." Kaya's brow furrowed and her hand stilled against him. Lucas smiled. "Just that I haven't yet brushed my teeth because I really want to kiss you right now. So, I'm going to rectify that." Lucas heard Kaya giggle as he hopped up and went into the bathroom.

Kaya

THE SUMMER BEACH SEASON was nearly here. Lynne made plans to come the week of the 4th of July. Callie and Juan were coming for two weeks towards the end of the summer. And this weekend, Melanie was coming. She was supposed to arrive around noon on Friday and Kaya was practically levitating with excitement. She worked from home so she could be there the minute Mel arrived. The deck doors were open to the screens so she could hear when the car approached.

Shortly after one, she heard the driveway gravel crunch and she flew down the inside and outside stairs. Squealing and hugging ensued.

As they got Melanie settled into her room, she teased, "So when do I get to meet the boy?"

Kaya blushed and looked down. "Tonight, if you want," she said, folding a set of towels that she set on the dresser for Mel.

"Oooooo, excellent. What are we doing?"

"Well, I figured you'd want to go out to dinner to one of my favorite places, so I can show you the Cape properly," Kaya said.

"Yes, of course, so is he coming with us?"

"He can if you want. I didn't know if you'd want it to be just us or not. He'll do whatever—and he won't be offended if you want it to be just us. He's sort of on standby for whatever."

"Wow," said Mel. "I'm impressed. I think this dude really likes you." Kaya just smiled. "Are you sleeping with him?"

"Melanie!" Kaya cried.

"It's just a question," replied Melanie, laughing. "Is that a yes?"

Kaya blushed hotly. "Yes, but just as of very recently. Like, two days ago."

"Oh, excellent. I'm happy for you. Just felt like time?"

"Yeah." Kaya sat down on the edge of the bed. "I realized I'm just totally wrecked for this man. I couldn't fight it any more."

"Why would you even want to fight it?" Melanie sat down beside her.

"It's hard to explain. When you're deeply sad, it is sometimes hard to remember it's okay to also be happy. And to some people—like, Charlie..."

Melanie scoffed and muttered, "That idiot."

"...my pain was a burden. Lucas...he, I don't know. He acts like it's a *privilege* to be in this with me, and I just stopped wondering why and gave into it."

"Good for you. You deserve happiness and great sex with a hot guy."

"Well, you haven't met him yet to know if he's hot, and I never said the sex was great," Kaya teased.

"But I've seen a picture of him and I bet if I asked if the sex was great, your answer would be yes." Kaya blushed again and looked down, although a smile broke across her face. "So that's a yes."

Kaya looked back up. "You know, I had boyfriends in college, but Charlie was my...first. All I can say is..." her face and neck were getting so hot. She could feel it. "Let's just say I didn't know what I was missing. Now I do."

"I *knew* it."

Later, the three of them were eating on the back deck of the Lobster House. Lucas had been all graciousness, having Kaya and Melanie sit while he got the food and the drinks. Kaya smiled as he approached. He was wearing khaki shorts and an untucked button-up plaid shirt. His hair looked a little wilder than normal in the breeze. She could never get used to how handsome he looked to her. *Yep, she was in deep.*

"This is so cool!" enthused Melanie, snapping Kaya's attention back to the present. "You'd never even know all this was back here when you're looking at the building from the street!"

"I know," said Kaya. "My family found it because my dad was toodling around on his bike. He was always an early riser and one morning he wanted to look at the boats, so he went around back of the restaurant and discovered this. Since then, it's been one of our favorite places, but we didn't find it until, like the fourth or fifth year we were here."

Lucas took a swig of beer. "Honestly, I grew up here and I didn't discover it until I moved in across the road," he said gesturing with his head back towards his condo. "Like, I knew the fish market and sit-down restaurant were here, but not this whole back deck situation. I have to assume my parents knew it was here, but it just wasn't their style, I guess."

"Do your parents still live here?" asked Melanie.

"No," he answered. "They still own a home here, down on New Jersey Ave." He glanced at Kaya and they shared a smile. "They use that when they're visiting, but they're basically retired now. They've got a place in Philadelphia on the Main Line around their friends."

"Philadelphia," scoffed Kaya. Her formative early career years in DC put her firmly on the Washington side of the DC-Philly rivalry. Lucas chuckled and looked down.

"Ah, Philadelphia," said Melanie, wistfully. Then she got a mischievous gleam in her eye. "This one got into it once at a conference up there." She pointed to Kaya. Kaya groaned and rolled her eyes.

"You make it sound like it was just me," Kaya complained.

"It *was* just you."

"*Everyone* was drinking," she whined.

"True," said Melanie. "But only one of us decided that singing 'Livin' on a Prayer' loudly was the move." Kaya groaned again. Lucas sat back, beer in hand, watching them with amusement. Melanie laughed. "It was hilarious. There were no clients there, so no harm no foul," she concluded.

Kaya chuckled. "In my defense..." she started while Mel said, "Yeah, yeah, yeah..."

"*In my defense*," Kaya began again, "you all should have been more careful with me. No one told me those drinks Matt kept bringing were doubles and I wasn't asking anyone to get them for me. It was loud and I didn't realize there were new drinks! I thought I was still drinking the same one."

"I know," said Melanie laughing. "It was very cute."

"I've never seen you drink spirits," Lucas said to Kaya, smiling.

"That's why!" she shot back.

Kaya

"SOMEONE'S IN A GOOD mood," observed Callum, when Kaya arrived, smiling broadly. It was the week before Memorial Day and the Exit Zero work room buzzed. Summer was officially kicking off soon and spirits were high. Everyone was in today, even Lucy, Mateo, and Adam.

"It's true," confirmed Kaya, flinging herself into a chair. "I made deadline."

"On *Cool Cape May*?" called Mateo from the graphics station.

"Yep," she replied, popping the last 'p'. "Just closed the last one. Had to go there in person because no one *ever* answers the phone at Jake's Pizza. But they gave me the money—cash, if you can believe that," she said gesturing towards her bag. "And I had the writeup with me, so they approved it on the spot."

Sloane came out of her office. "That is great news," she said, causing Kaya to turn and look in Sloane's direction. "I thought we might have to go to print without them. Really good work."

Maureen looked up with a warm smile. "And so many of your write-ups are just really rather...inspired, Kaya. It's *so* good this year," Maureen added.

Kaya flushed. Maureen's words filled her up. "Thank you. I'm just happy to do my part." Kaya knew Melanie was always happy with her work at her old firm, but Melanie became more of a peer over time. She hadn't felt the way she felt with Maureen since...well, not in a few years.

"While you're all here," Kaya heard Sloane start. She turned back towards Sloane who was leaning against her door jamb. Vance stood up from his desk and came out, and put a hand up on the doorway of his office. "We have some news," said Sloane. "Well actually, it's Maureen's news to share." Everyone turned and looked at Maureen.

"Thanks, Sloane," said Maureen warmly. "I love you all and this is hard for me, but I wanted to let you know that I'm leaving at the end of June." Kaya's heart sank and the back of her throat plummeted and squeezed. Her chest tightened. Her brain flooded. She squeezed her eyes shut and barely heard the rest. "I love it here, and this was a really hard decision for me, but I'm going to move up to Jersey City to be near my kids. My daughter is going to have a baby, she needs the help, and I know I will want to be very near my grandkids. It's time for me to officially retire."

It felt like a steel cage dropped around Kaya's heart. She opened her eyes and they'd hardened, deadened. She fixed an empty stare on Maureen and said nothing. Callum, Lucy, Mateo, and Adam hugged Maureen and told her how much they're going to miss her. Kaya turned back around.

"So," Sloane said, "we wanted you all to know first. We're looking for another researcher, but also if any of you want to pick up more work, let me know over the next week. Maureen is irreplaceable, but we're so grateful for all the wisdom she's shared over the years."

"For *sure*," Callum said. Kaya heard him and she knew too, how much she learned from Maureen. But Maureen was leaving, so. Nothing more to say.

"Are you okay?" Lucy said quietly, as she appeared at Kaya's elbow.

"Yeah," Kaya said, not looking at her as she picked up her bag. "I'm heading out for today."

That afternoon, she couldn't concentrate on anything. She went for a long walk on the beach to try to shake the heavy blanket of dread enveloping her. When she was almost back to the Coral Ave access point, she dropped down in the sand, hugged her knees to her chest, and just stared at the ocean. She didn't cry. She was just...empty.

She sensed someone coming up behind her and turned. It was Lucas.

"Hey," he said, sitting down beside her. "I saw your shoes at the stairs, so I figured you were out here."

"Hi," she said. Then, "Oh! We had plans tonight! I totally forgot. I'm so sorry."

"It's okay," he said. "It wasn't anything fixed. I was just going to take you to dinner. What's wrong?" he asked, searching her eyes. She didn't answer; just turned her gaze back to the ocean. "What happened?" he prodded gently.

"Nothing," she said. "Just that Maureen is leaving to move up north." He looked at her, silently.

"How do you feel about that?" he asked.

"It's fine. I feel fine. Let's eat." She stood abruptly and dusted the sand off her shorts. He jumped up beside her.

Lucas

"KAYA…" HE STARTED, PUTTING a hand on her arm. She gently shook him loose and headed toward the stairs. At the bottom, she slipped on her sandals and crossed the street to the cottage. Lucas followed her silently and stayed quiet as they both rinsed their feet with the hose and headed inside.

"Drink?" she asked, taking an open bottle of white wine from the fridge and pouring herself a glass. "This? Or something else?" she continued. He watched her.

"I'll get a beer," he said walking over to the refrigerator and taking one out. "Are you sure you're okay?"

She ignored the question but came to stand beside him at the open fridge door. "How would you feel about eating in? I got some good shrimp yesterday at Central Park, and I have everything for paella."

"That sounds great," he said. "I'll clean the shrimp," he offered, taking them out of the fridge. As he worked, he eyed her carefully. She said nothing, but set about measuring her rice, chopping her vegetables, zesting her lemons, and measuring out her spices. He watched her absent-mindedly wipe her fingers against the bottom edge of her t shirt. He stayed quiet too, observing her, almost like watching a skittish animal. His approach was finally rewarded when she spoke.

"I'm sorry I forgot you were coming over," she said, measuring out the broth.

"No worries," he said. "You're processing some big news." He scrunched up the butcher paper on which he'd collected the shrimp shells and veins. He tried to keep his voice light. "I'm going to take this outside to the trash, so it doesn't stink up your kitchen."

She glanced up. "Oh, okay, thank you." When he came back upstairs, he saw she had the rice seasoned, covered, and simmering. She turned away from the stove and leaned back against the sink. "I don't do well when people I care about leave me," she said, looking intently in his eyes, with almost a challenge in them. Lucas ran a hand through his hair. His mind clicked through what he knew about her lived experience in terms of loss— her aunt, her parents, even that shitty ex-boyfriend. She ran here to recover from repeated trauma. It was one of the things he loved most about her—how she took her recovery into her own hands and put one foot in front of the other every day. But he never considered how the pain she carried could flare up when she least expected it. Everything suddenly made more sense.

He crossed the kitchen in a couple long strides and gathered her to him. At first, she didn't reciprocate—it was like he was hugging a stiff form. But his gut told him he shouldn't let go and he didn't. Eventually he felt her arms come around his waist. She was not crying, he noticed. It was like she was not feeling...anything.

He rubbed her back. She hugged him tighter. When he took a step back, he looked at her, his hands on her upper arms.

"I get it," he said. She looked at him and then, with just a slight motion, nodded once. She turned back to the stove and started sautéing her vegetables and the shrimp in another pan. When both were done, she combined them, plated some portions, and they ate. The conversation turned back to other things. She seemed more relaxed, and so he relaxed, trying to remind himself that she was not his project to fix.

After dinner, Lucas realized he should probably go. He really wanted to stay the night—to hold her in his arms, get wrapped up in her legs, make love to her so thoroughly she'd forget her pain. But. She was in a fragile state. When they finished cleaning the dishes, he took her hand and said, "Walk me out?" Kaya's eyebrows shot up slightly, but she followed him downstairs to the door. She looked so beautiful, her dark eyes glimmering in the glow of the porch light. He took her face in his hands and kissed her. He felt her hands come lightly to his hips.

She pulled back slightly. "Stay," she said. He stilled, trying to read her.

"Are you sure?" he asked. "I don't want to take advantage of the rough day you've had." He felt her rub her thumbs against his hips.

"It's not taking advantage of me if it's what I want," she said, and he felt one of her hands creep up under his shirt to the skin of his waist. "You said it yourself—I always tell you what I need." His heart started to race at the intensity in her voice.

He scanned her face, silent. He let her words and intention sink in. "I can't really argue with that."

"Unless you don't want to stay...that would be a different story, but don't use me as the excuse." She looked almost defiant, he noticed. He scanned her face; he felt his breathing get shallow.

"I really, *really* want to stay," he said, his voice catching in his throat.

She smiled, took his hand, and led him back inside and down the hall to her room.

Kaya

SHE AWOKE IN THE dark. There was pale moonlight filtering through the windows. She laid still, ticking through all the sensations. Slightly tired and sore, but in a good way. *Lucas.* His slow, deep breathing beside her. He was on his side, facing her, with the covers off his upper body. She gazed at him in wonder. *He's breathtaking.* She replayed last night in her mind. He was so gentle. So *attentive.* She felt her cheeks heat, thinking about how he made her feel like she was something he was worshipping.

Charlie had never made her feel this way. There were physical differences, sure, where Kaya was thrilled to discover Lucas was superior; but also, with Charlie, the vibe was *aren't we having fun.* Lucas treated her like something precious. It was intoxicating. Almost enough to make her forget about Maureen. Almost.

She carefully got up, pulled her robe from the back of her door and padded upstairs. She filled a glass of water and opened a door to the deck. The sound of the waves crashing calmed her. She stepped out and leaned her hip against the railing. The cool breeze felt good on her skin. At this moment in the wee hours of the morning, whatever that other plane was where spirits resided felt very close. She closed her eyes.

"You'd like him," she whispered.

After a while she went back inside, put her glass in the sink and headed back downstairs. She dropped her robe on her chair and crawled back into bed. Lucas stirred slightly. She couldn't tell if he was awake or not, but his arms came around her and pulled her close. She breathed in the smell of him—salt air and a faint pine. He was so solid. This felt so *right*. She felt her heart relax a little. And she fell into a deep, deep sleep.

Kaya

THE NEXT DAY SHE worked from home. He had only been gone for a few hours when a text came in.

> I love you, you know

Wham went her heart. The image of him filled her mind's eye. He'd said it last night in a whisper when their limbs were tangled together. It was lovely then, but it was also a beautiful sight in the light of day. Before she replied, she saw the three dots.

> and I'm not just saying that because we're sleeping together. I just wanted to make sure you knew and now you have it in writing 😊

> Thank you

> I am happy to have that in writing

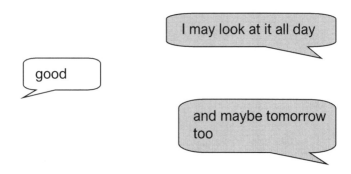

> I may look at it all day

> good

> and maybe tomorrow too

She wanted to tell him "I love you" back—because she knew she did. From the first moments of connecting with Lucas, it felt so natural. But she also felt so damaged, that she was not sure her heart was really working properly. But she did think another small piece of it just healed.

She was not sure if he would think she only said it because he did, and she felt like she should? *I should tell him in person.* Almost as if he could hear her, another text popped up.

> when can I see you next

Her thumbs flew to reply.

> tonight. I get off Eddy's at 7—too late?

> good

no not too late

my turn to cook

yay

but I'm not coming for the food 😊

oh I guarantee you'll be coming

Kaya flushed hotly and smiled.

Kaya

KAYA ARRANGED TO ONLY go in to Exit Zero on days Maureen was at the library. When they all picked a day for Maureen's goodbye dinner, Kaya initially agreed, but as the day got closer, she found she just...couldn't. She was sad and restless. Alexis had been away in Costa Rica. Kaya should go for a run to try to manage her energy, but it was not as fun by herself.

She asked Lucas if he had time to come over.

"Aren't you supposed to be at Maureen's goodbye thing tonight? I mean, don't get me wrong, I am always happy to be with you," he said, coming up the stairs to where she was making pesto.

She gave him a sad smile. "Yes," she said with a sigh.

"But...?" he came up to her and kissed her cheek, as she put pine nuts and basil into her food processor.

"I lied," she shrugged. He didn't say anything. She pulsed the food processor a few times and then said, "I told them I got scheduled last minute at Eddy's." She glanced up at him to see if he was judging her. He gazed at her intently, only, like he was trying to understand.

"What if they go to the bar to try to see you?" he asked.

"I doubt they would do that," she said with a wave of her hand. "I know you don't get it, Lucas," she said, holding his gaze for a few seconds and then looking back at her work. "But I just can't do goodbyes."

He stepped towards her, took her face in his hands and kissed her. "I get it," he said simply.

So, the day came and went, and Maureen left, and Kaya, as was her wont, never actually said goodbye. The next time she went in to Exit Zero, there was an envelope in her box with her name written in Maureen's handwriting. She closed her eyes and willed herself to open it. She couldn't yet, so she put it in her bag.

When she got home, she went out on the deck, sat down on the couch, pulled out the envelope and opened it. It was handwritten on one of Maureen's personalized correspondence notes.

Dearest Kaya,

I've so enjoyed getting to know you and working with you these last five or so months. I am sorry we did not get a chance to say goodbye, but I want you to know that I understand why. I want you to know that I see you. I see your pain; I feel it within you, and I hold grace for it. I'm also glad that the working and the writing has been healing for you—I've enjoyed watching you get lighter.

I'm sorry if my leaving has undone any of that lightness. And I know it doesn't feel this way now, but I don't think of myself as having left your life. I would welcome a call or a text or a visit, and I plan to bring my family back to Cape May often. But I also understand if that's too hard for you. Loss of any kind is difficult, I know.

I wish you all good things, you beautiful girl.

Peace,

-M

Now, Kaya wept.

Lucas

"I'M EXCITED TO MEET Lynne," Lucas said before taking another lick of the ice cream cone he held in his hand. They sat at Drydock at one of the outdoor table benches and his other arm was slung across her shoulders, resting on the bench back. They had been out with Tim and Casey and Casey's girlfriend, but the others had just left with Molly the dog, so now Kaya and Lucas were by themselves. A group of teenagers sat down on the empty benches at the other end of the table.

Kaya's ice cream was in a dish. "I'm excited for you to meet her, too," she said, as she held the cup against the table with one hand and wielded her spoon in the other. "She's amazing. I've missed her so much. And I know she'll love you. Of course, not in the same way *I* love you," she said grinning sideways at him.

"Obviously," he said, smirking. "And as soon as we're done here, I'm going to take you home and show you all the ways that I love you."

She flushed hotly and cast a shy glance his way.

"You're cute when you're embarrassed," he teased. "Your neck gets all red."

"Thanks?" she said, laughing.

Lucas felt his phone buzzing. He pulled it out of the back pocket of his shorts and involuntarily frowned.

"Everything okay?" Kaya asked. He looked back at her, and tried to relax his face into a smile.

"It's fine. It's just my dad calling." Lucas tried to ignore the tight feeling in his chest as he slid the phone back into his pocket and took another bite of his ice cream.

"You can answer if you want..."

"I know I can," Lucas replied, rubbing her shoulder with his free arm. "But I don't want to. It's a beautiful night, you're here, I'm happy, and I don't particularly want to change that."

Kaya scraped the last of her ice cream from the dish and ate it. He was mesmerized watching Kaya bring the spoon out from between her lips, although she seemed oblivious. "Does talking to your father make you...unhappy?" she asked.

Lucas exhaled, blowing his breath out through his mouth. Kaya turned her body on the bench to face him. He tucked a strand of curls behind her ear. "Lucas?" *God, her eyes were so pretty*, even when clouded with concern. "I know I always remember him as grumpy, and I know you said he was...controlling and had high expectations..."

"Yes," he said absently, turning back to take a bite out of the cone. The ice cream was melted, so he made quick work of finishing the cone. He wiped his hands on his napkin.

"Does he call often?" Kaya asked.

"No."

"So, shouldn't you see what he wants? I hope you didn't not answer because of me..."

"Kaya *stop*." He saw her flinch. *Shit* that came out sharper than he intended. "Kaya," Lucas tried again, more softly. He stood up, tossed her dish into a trash can, took her hand and drew her up to stand. Lacing his fingers in hers, he led her to the sidewalk where they started walking towards the marina. "He's probably calling to tell me he's coming down for some reason, or that he's getting an award, or he's been asked to do something impressive. My mom will eventually tell me, or he'll text. I don't need to talk to him live. I rarely enjoy it."

"He calls you to...brag?" Lucas could feel Kaya's sidelong glance. He exhaled forcefully. "I'm sorry, you don't have to answer that..." she added quickly.

"I don't think he sees it that way," Lucas replied. "I think he thinks he's just sharing news. I used to think he shared his accomplishments to inspire me to be...better. More impactful. But it turns out he's a bit of a narcissist. He hides it well under all the acts of service. But I have come to realize it's the other way around—the acts of service are to get the accolades."

Lucas felt weary saying this out loud. The learned behavior of compulsive helping was so deep. Doing anything for Kaya filled him up. But he had come to learn that capitulating to his father's need for flattery never filled him up. It drained him. He didn't want Kaya to carry his shit. He felt Kaya stop and squeeze his hand.

"Thank you for telling me. I'm sorry I pushed you," she said, rising up and kissing his cheek. "You're an amazing, gentle, and generous man, Lucas, and I love you." *This fucking girl.* She meant joy to him in his childhood, and she was still joy. He just gazed at her.

"And I think I was promised you taking me home and ravishing me."

Lucas felt a smile spread across his face as he turned to lead them across Lafayette Street. "Oh, that is definitely happening."

Kaya

THE NEXT DAY DAWNED muggy and warm. It was July third—Lynne was coming today! Kaya leaned over and kissed Lucas lightly. He murmured her name somewhere between asleep and awake. She reached out and smoothed his hair, then hopped out of bed. She got dressed, let herself out, and jumped on her bicycle to ride home. At the cottage, she showered and made herself breakfast. She'd woken early because she was excited to see Lynne, but she knew she still had hours to wait.

Lynne was many things—loyal, smart, funny, generous, quick with compliments for her friends and cutting with commentary on those who aren't. But she was not on time. Ever. So when she said she was aiming for a noon ETA, Kaya knew there was no way in hell she would see Lynne before two. Sure enough, just shy of 10 am Lynne texted "leaving now!"

Around 2:30 she pulled in. After hugs in the driveway, Lynne exclaimed, "Ok, I'm sorry I'm late but to make it up to you, I brought wine and I also stopped at a farm stand like an hour back and got these amazing-looking blueberries."

"Thank you, and you're not late. This is when I expected you," Kaya replied, laughing. "You forget that I have known you for quite some time!"

Lynne and Kaya had interned together when Lynne was at Georgetown and Kaya was in DC on her university's "Washington semester" program. They bonded over the long hours, the sketchy apartment building they were assigned to live in for the semester, and trying to live cheaply. They mastered the art of finding all the happy hours that served free appetizers to maximize their food budget. They had an unwritten rule that followed them into their post-college DC apartment— whoever saw the spider or roach first gets to freak out and the other one had to kill it.

When Lynne got a car before Kaya did, Lynne often volunteered to drive Kaya home to Poughkeepsie to visit in the years her mom was sick. There was sadness laced in the purpose, but the road trips were always fun. Lynne and Kaya never fought. It was odd, Kaya reflected. They'd had many, often hilarious, incidents where they totally misunderstood each other. Something like this was not uncommon:

"Do you want anything from the store or do you want to come?"

"Which store?"

"Safeway."

"No thanks."

"Maybe CVS."

"Not urgently."

"Like, you don't need anything urgently, or you don't want to go urgently?"

"No, I..."

"I can go later if that's better?"

"No, I just meant..."

At which point they would generally devolve into laughter. Conversations like those were easily—if not always efficiently—cleared up. But they never fought. They had an easy and deep friendship.

Later, after getting Lynne's things inside, they were out on the beach, sitting in low chairs, reading and then trading their *Us Weekly* and *People* magazines. "I do not understand how Kate Middleton runs around in stilettos on cobblestones," said Lynne.

"Yeah, agree," said Kaya. "Meghan does, too. And Euj, Beatrice and Sophie and Letizia—the whole lot of them. I mean, you also see them in wedges and flats at times, but the amount of time they spend in those heels, I would be tripping all the time."

"Same." They paused and continued leafing through the magazines.

Kaya turned her face to Lynne. "So, you've *finally* moved in with Evan?"

"Yeah," Lynne said, almost resigned.

"You're not excited?" Kaya queried, popping her sunglasses onto the top of her head and studying her friend's face.

"No, I am," Lynne said. "It is so much easier than driving back and forth and having my things in two different places. Especially with you gone, it was silly for me to not move in with him. I am all about it. It's just that my mother is not thrilled."

"Ah," said Kaya. "Well, I love your mother, but it's not her life."

"I know this, and we made the decision, we executed it. I just wish I wasn't doing something that bothers her."

"Well," said Kaya, "Evan just needs to put a ring on it pronto to class up the whole shacking up situation."

"Exactly," agreed Lynne. "So," Lynne turned her face to Kaya. "When do I get to meet Lucas?"

Kaya laughed. "Wow! You made it two whole hours before you asked. That's impressive."

"I am nothing if not restrained," scoffed Lynne, assuming a fake snobbishness. Kaya laughed.

"Tonight. He's gonna pick up some seafood and come over for dinner."

"Excellent."

Later that night, after dinner was over, and Lucas had gone home, the girls were sitting on the deck drinking wine in the deep dusk of mid-summer. "Oh, Kaya, he's so *cute*," breathed Lynne.

"I *know*," mimicked Kaya. She was a little tipsier than she had planned to be but she was just so happy. "Seriously, I'm like stupid lucky. I don't know what happened. It's like he just fell into my life, but then, he was always there across the driveway, I guess. But now... I can't explain it. I'm afraid I'll jinx it, but he's just *so* kind, and confident, and thoughtful, and totally without pretense...and I just feel so...*safe* with him." Kaya felt herself rambling. "And he's a super-hot kisser."

"Kay!" Lynne exclaimed.

Kaya burped a little and smiled. "Sorry," she said, laughing.

"No, I just meant..." started Lynne, as Kaya simultaneously said, "I just meant..." and they giggled chaotically. When they'd recovered, Kaya said, "I miss you."

"I miss you, too," Lynne said. "But I'm here now."

"You are. Thank you."

Kaya

A FEW NIGHTS AFTER Lynne left, Kaya stared at the ceiling fan rotating above her. There was no moon, so it was fairly dark. Weak shadows from hers and the neighbors' houses' porch lights came through the blinds. She glanced at the clock—almost four a.m. Her mind was preoccupied. She couldn't slow it down. She had been drifting between light sleep and awake, in and out of intense and strange dreams for the better part of an hour. Maybe Lynne's visit had brought a lot of memories into her present day...her past coming to find her here where she was hidden away. She had to clear her mind. She got up, went into her bathroom, and took a drink of water. She crawled back into bed and Lucas stirred.

"Ummm," he mumbled, putting an arm around her. She nestled against him, looped a foot between his feet and put her hand over his heart.

"Sorry if I woke you," she whispered.

"No worries," he said, sleepily. They fell back into silence, and she felt the rise and fall of his chest. She assumed he'd fallen back to sleep. But he spoke again in the dark. "Anything on your mind?"

His thumb lazily rubbed her shoulder along the ridge of her tank top strap.

"Not sure," she said. "Sometimes I just can't sleep."

"What are you thinking about?"

"My parents, I think," she ventured. Something about the darkness made it easier to say the hard parts out loud.

He cupped her cheek with his hand. At the touch, she opened her eyes and found him looking at her in the dark. "Kaya," he said, "will you tell me?"

"I don't know what it is exactly..." she started. She wound her hand around his arm. "With my mom, I mean, she was young and she lived longer than anyone with ovarian usually does. So I was back and forth between DC and home a lot. My dad was with her, and she was in the hospice unit of the hospital at the end, so, you know, she was well cared-for. But with my dad..." her breath hitched. Lucas rolled onto his back and pulled her to him. She laid her head on his chest and her hand on his shoulder. He ran his hand lightly over her forearm.

"Tell me," he whispered into her hair and planted a light kiss to her head.

She paused for a moment, listening to his heartbeat. Steady. "He was alone," Kaya said quietly. "He wanted to stay in our house, so we arranged for hospice care at home. We have very good friends and neighbors who were amazing, and we tried to come home as much as we could. Callie had school, and I...didn't have a lot of PTO built up. We weren't really prepared for how fast he would decline. I remember one night towards the end...after Callie and I had come home to stay until...until...anyway, we were there, and he needed to go to the bathroom. Of course, we wanted to respect his dignity...privacy...but when he was in there by himself, he fell..." she choked back a sob. "He was so frail...we failed him..."

He said nothing but tightened his arm around her torso to pull her closer. She clutched at his shoulder.

"We got him back in the bed, but were in over our heads, Lucas. We called the next day for more hospice care, but it wasn't long after, that...he died...a week or so later. The hospice aide who was doing his shaving and personal care came out to us in the kitchen where we were having coffee and said, 'I think you need to be with him. I think it's time.' And we went in...and it was." She was quiet for a beat. "We held his hands." She paused. "I just wish I could have been...better at all of it. For him."

Lucas kissed her hair and she thought she felt tears falling. Kaya raised her head and propped herself up on her forearm. She quietly scanned his face. He was looking up at the ceiling, as if he didn't want her to see him faltering. She took a thumb and gently wiped the tears from his face. "Thank you, Lucas," she said.

He turned his face to look at her. "For what?" he whispered.

"For being you. For being here," she said, holding his gaze. "It helps me—to be able to say the words out loud."

After a beat, he nodded slightly. "Your parents," Lucas said, "seemed so awesome."

"Thank you," she said. "They were."

He rubbed a hand over the small of her back. "You didn't fail them, Kaya. Life, it…it just happens. What matters is the love, and that you showed up."

She looked at down at him steadily in the dimness. "Thank you," she said again.

He sat up, leaned his face down and kissed her gently. Then he got up, went to the bathroom, and returned, enfolding her in his arms.

"I love you," he said quietly.

"I know," she said. "I'm grateful. And I love you too." She fell back to sleep.

Kaya

EDDY'S WAS PACKED. A buzzy, festive night in peak summer. Randolph was behind the bar with another server trying to keep up with demand several people deep. Kaya squeezed out the door to the wide porch with a bin to collect empty glasses. There was a large group of family or friends who had commandeered the corner where the porch turned and wrapped around the building. They stood and sat in rockers, laughing, and chatting animatedly with that raucous energy that comes when you're at the beach. You've let go, you're on vacation with people you love, and you've left all your cares somewhere else. Kaya smiled a little to herself. Their joy was infectious.

She edged over to them and collected empty glasses from the railings. She stretched to a side table to collect another, excusing her reach, when she heard someone say her name questioningly.

"Kaya?"

Kaya looked up. "Vanessa?" she replied. Vanessa was her first supervis-ee. As low person on the totem pole, Kaya was assigned to manage the intern. Then, after her graduation, Vanessa joined

Alston and she was joined at the hip with Kaya. Kaya was to Vanessa like Melanie was to Kaya.

A smile bloomed on Kaya's face, but Vanessa was looking at her more reserved...almost with a tinge of...not quite fear? Kaya couldn't place the expression.

"Oh my gosh, how *are* you? What brings you here?" asked Kaya.

"Oh. Um, my parents," Vanessa started, gesturing towards the other side of their group, "sold their place in North Jersey and bought a place here...on the bay side. And we're just...out tonight." She sounded hesitant, Kaya thought. *Weird*. Vanessa was never a shrinking violet when they worked together.

Kaya smiled again. "That's fantastic. I hope you love Cape May. It's magical."

Vanessa peered at her. "Thank you," she said simply. And then, "It's good to see you."

"Likewise..." Kaya responded. Vanessa's words seemed like a dismissal. Kaya gathered up another glass into the dish bin and turned to head back inside. That was strange. Yes, Kaya was on duty, and Vanessa was with her entire family—she remembered stories of the extended family beach week trips—so it wasn't the time to catch up but she couldn't shake the feeling that something felt off. They were *friends*. Why was Vanessa playing it so cool? They hadn't been in touch in a while, true, but...well, no time to dwell on it now. Over three hours until closing time.

By the time they closed and cleaned up it was around 1 am. The bike ride to Lucas' house was a lot shorter and better lit than back to the Point. And Lucas was there. So, she went there. He'd told her he'd leave the door unlocked. Sometimes he waited up for her, but she almost hoped he hadn't tonight. It was *so* late and she knew he'd have to get up for work tomorrow.

Kaya wearily climbed the outside stairs and eased open the front door. Lucas had left the under-cabinet lights on in the kitchen. She locked the door, turned off the lights, kicked off her shoes and padded upstairs to his room. She looked at Lucas sprawled out on his bed and she smiled. He'd left the light on in the bathroom with the door cracked. *So considerate.*

She tried to be as quiet as possible, but she *had* to shower. She was so sweaty and gross from her shift. She brushed her teeth, combed out her hair, and put on her pajama shorts and tank top. Turning off the bathroom light, she crossed the room, spread a towel over the pillow to guard against her damp hair and eased under the sheet with her back to him.

She felt him roll towards her and put an arm around her middle. "Hey, you," he mumbled into her hair.

She turned over to face him. "I'm so sorry I woke you up. Go back to sleep," she whispered.

He mumbled-scoffed. "How was work?" he asked, with his eyes still closed.

"Good," she said yawning. "A former coworker-friend of mine was there with her family."

"From DC?" he yawned too.

"Yeah," Kaya responded, preoccupied by her thoughts.

"That's nice. How was she?"

"It was odd..." she started, not really sure how to describe it. "We used to be really good friends, but she was almost...cold, sort of. I don't know. It was weird. I haven't seen her in a while, but it was just...weird."

"Huh," Lucas said, sleepily. His fingers were lightly stroking her hip bone over her shorts. Her mind was replaying the interaction with Vanessa, the look on Vanessa's face. She really didn't know what to make of it.

"Anyway," she said quietly, rolling away onto her back and looking up at the ceiling fan spinning in the dark, "it's late, sorry again for waking you. You need your sleep." Lucas flattened his palm and dragged it lightly across her stomach, slipping under the hem of the tank top. It sent a shiver through her and brought her mind very much into the present.

"I don't know how this works at whatever planet you're on," Lucas said, his voice suddenly thick. His hand roamed up to her breast and grazed over it before cupping it in his palm. Kaya moaned lightly. "But when the beautiful woman I happen to be in love with climbs into my bed in the middle of the night, what I do first is *not* go back to sleep."

Kaya smiled.

Kaya

BIKING HOME THE NEXT day, she put in her airpods and called Melanie.

"Hey! How are you? I haven't talked to you in a while," said Melanie when she picked up.

"I know. How are you? Are you in the car?"

"Yeah, on the way to a client, but I have another probably twenty minutes so I'm good. What's up?"

"Nothing," Kaya responded. "Just on my bike and thought I'd say hello." It was warm but the bike provided a welcome movement of air on her face. It was still early, so there wasn't a lot of traffic or people out yet. "Hey, you know who I saw yesterday? At my job at the bar?"

"I can't begin to guess," answered Mel.

"Vanessa Robey."

"Oh, wow, really? That's awesome. How is she? What was she doing in Cape May?"

"Yeah, it was pretty random," admitted Kaya. "She was with her family—I guess her parents bought a place down here. They were a big group— like, aunts, uncles, and cousins too—not just her immediate family. So, I didn't really talk to her. I was working, and she was with the group. We said hi, just exchanged a few words, really."

"Yeah, that makes sense," said Melanie. "When was the last time you saw her?"

Kaya thought about that. "At Alston," answered Kaya. "I haven't seen her since she left the firm, now that I think about it."

"I haven't seen her either, but I am not as close with her as you are...or as I thought you were," said Melanie. "I wasn't sure if you stayed in touch."

Kaya paused. "I never had a conscious thought about not being in touch, but...I guess...yeah, just haven't seen her since then." She paused again and Melanie didn't respond right away.

"Sorry," interjected Mel, "I had to double check I took the right exit."

"No worries. I should let you go. You're driving."

"Yeah, but thanks for calling. It's always great to hear from you! Be good. Talk soon."

"Yeah, talk soon," said Kaya, and she reached up and tapped her earbud to end the call. She was out on Sunset now, passing Exit Zero. She'd be back there shortly, but she needed to eat something and change clothes, so she turned onto Seagrove towards home. She mentally wrapped up her Vanessa thoughts and tucked them away for now.

Lucas

A WEEK OR SO later, Lucas left his boss' office. Mrs. MacFarlane had just given him what she believed to be wonderful, exciting news—a fantastic final opportunity before he became an investor and partner in the group.

As he quietly shut the door behind him, a wave of nausea hit him so hard he barely made it to the men's room before vomiting. When he thought he was sure that no more was coming, he steadied himself, washed his hands, rinsed his mouth, and splashed water on his face.

He went to his office, grabbed his bag, and went home. He couldn't be at work. He needed to think. He went for a long run, trying to sort his options, but he knew he didn't really have any, short of throwing away his entire plan for his livelihood he'd so carefully planned and executed. He paused on the 109, at the foot of the bridge going back over the canal, and took out his phone.

can I see u tonight? can I come over?

He started walking up the bridge to cool down and watched for the three dots to appear. Shortly, they did.

> Of course. You don't have to ask

> Around 6:30? I can bring food

> Don't worry about that. I have stuff to do a big corn & beans & tomato salad situation if that sounds okay to you

> I'm experimenting

> ok

> u ok?

> Yes see you soon. I love you

> Love you too

So, it was going to happen. He dragged a hand down his sweaty face. He had no choice but to wreck the woman he loved.

Lucas

HE LET HIMSELF IN and walked upstairs into her kitchen. The bright evening sun was flooding the room. She looked over her shoulder briefly and smiled when he appeared at the top of the stairs. God, her smile. She was barefoot and wearing a light blue sundress that hung below her knees. "Did you bring a bag?" she asked, which he assumed meant she hoped he would be staying the night. He sure as God hoped so too.

"Yeah," he said. He went to her and wrapped his arms around her from behind. He kissed the top of her head. He loved the smell of her shampoo— lavender and something else he couldn't place. It just smelled like Kaya. She put down the knife, wiped her hands on a towel and turned in his arms to face him. He took her face with one hand, keeping the other around her back and kissed her, slowly, intensely.

"Everything okay?" she asked. She pulled back slightly, looking in his eyes.

"Yeah," he said. He looked at her and kept holding her tightly. The way she searched his gaze twisted in his stomach. They slowly came apart and she turned back to the counter and tossed her salad. It was grilled corn, local tomatoes, fresh basil from her herb pots, red onion, cannellini beans, and feta cheese, all tossed with a dressing she had made from olive oil and freshly squeezed limes.

They sat and ate, and it should have tasted amazing, given how local and fresh everything was, but he had little appetite. He asked her about her day, what she was working on, how many shifts she had at the Chalfonte this week...anything...to put off what he had to say.

After they cleaned up, they went out and sat on the deck, nestled together on the cushions of the wicker loveseat. His arm was around her shoulders, his fingers tracing circles on her upper arm. Her head lay against his chest in the crook of his arm, and one of her hands rested on his thigh. They could hear the waves breaking just over the dunes. The sunset sky was bleeding with pink, orange and purple.

"You're quiet," she said. His fingers briefly stilled on her arm.

"Kaya, I need you closer," he said. His took her waist in his hands and dragged her across him so she was sitting sideways on his lap. She looped her arms around his neck and peered at him.

"What's going on, Lucas?" she asked, her big, brown eyes boring into him.

He wrapped his arms around her torso. Maybe, if he could just hold her tightly while he told her, he could keep her from running away—mentally or physically. He locked her to him with his grip and took a deep, fortifying breath. He wanted to trust that this thing between them was strong enough. He needed to. There was no other option.

"Kaya, I need to tell you something that's happened at work. And it's a good thing ultimately for me, but it's going to be very hard for you."

"Lucas, you're scaring me," she said, threading her fingers into his hair at the nape of his neck. "If it's good for you, why would it be hard for me?" The breeze off the ocean blew their hair. He pushed a shock of his hair away from his eyes and then tucked hers behind her ear, before resettling his hands firmly around her. The cheerful voices of children at neighboring houses floated through the air, along with the sound of the waves rolling ashore in their rhythmic pulsing. Two gulls soared overhead towards the dunes.

"Because," he said, staring intently at her, "for a little while...just for a short while...for work..." he hesitated and then rushed out, "I have to go away." He felt her flinch but kept his arms tight around her. He watched her closely as he held her, willing her not to shut down.

Her hands started to draw back from around his neck. "Kaya, stay with me here," he urged in a whisper. He thought he saw her eyes start to deaden. He leaned into her and rested his forehead against hers. "I'm *not* leaving you, Kaya. I'm coming *back*. Back to you. Back to us." He waited. Each second felt like an eternity. She squeezed her eyes shut.

"Where are you going?" she asked, finally, in a small voice.

"Shelter Island."

"New York?" Their eyes were closed and foreheads still rested together. *This is good*, he hoped. She hadn't bolted yet.

"Yes," he confirmed. "This is the last rotation—general managing the Cottages at Pridwin. In the Hamptons."

"For how long?" she said, even more quietly.

He exhaled slowly. He prayed that her asking questions meant she was processing and not pulling away. "I don't know," he admitted slowly, gripping her more tightly. "I mean, at least a few months, for me to really learn the role...but I'm coming *back*. It's temporary...I just...I just don't know how long."

"When do you...leave?" she whispered. Her breath felt like a caress on his face, but her voice broke a little on the last word.

"They want me to go soon—basically as soon as I can pack what I need, get my mail forwarded, that kind of thing. Actually, probably," he swallowed. "Day after tomorrow. But I can come back often, and you can visit me too, and we can talk every day, and then I'll come back, full time, and it will be like I never left." He rushed the words, hoping to get past them quickly to soften the blow.

"That's really great for you," she said drawing her face away from his as they opened their eyes and peered at each other. "You will be really good at that, and you'll get what you've been working so hard for."

So, it was going to be okay?... he searched her eyes. She moved to get up, and he tightened his arms around her to hold her in place, scanning her face desperately. She looked at him, gave him a small smile, and kissed him lightly. Then she gently pushed against him to stand up. She picked up her wine glass, and took it inside, placing it softly in the sink. He followed her and closed the French door. She turned and looked at him. He realized he was holding his breath.

"I'm pretty tired and I have a long day tomorrow, so I think I'm going to turn in," she said, holding his gaze briefly and then looking away. His skin prickled.

"Okay," he said, slowly, in a low voice. "I'll come with you."

"No," she said quietly, without any trace of emotion. "I think you should go."

"*Please,* Kaya," he whispered, as he stepped slowly, carefully towards where she was standing at the top of the stairs. He stopped just short of her. "*Please.*"

She didn't meet his gaze; she just stepped aside to clear his way to go down the stairs. She folded her arms lightly across her stomach.

Fuck. FUCK.

He looked at her for another beat, hoping, *praying, begging* the universe, that she'd look at him and give him another chance to make this okay. She didn't look up, she just stood completely still, her gaze resting on a spot on the floor off to her side.

He exhaled and dragged his hand down his face. "I'll call you tomorrow." She said nothing. He walked slowly forward, then down the stairs and out the door. When he got to his car, he turned around to look back at the door. She wasn't there.

Kaya

SHE LAID AWAKE. THE humidity had subsided today, so she opened the window, hoping the sounds of the waves and the cross breeze would soothe her raw nerves. She tried all her meditative practices— the systemic relaxing of her muscles from top to toe, her 4-7-8 breathing, picturing the waves rolling in and out on the beach. Her eyes stung with the lack of tears. Her mind was...blank. She closed her eyes and saw...nothing.

She got up twice to stretch, get some water, try to re-set and fall asleep. The second time it was nearly 3 am, and instead of going back down to her room, she laid on the couch in the living room. Her eyes caught an old family photo hanging on the wall. She and Callie were perched in one of the lifeguard rowboats at golden hour and her parents were standing behind it. Her dad was squinting in the setting sun, her mom's eyes were wide and clear, and she was beaming at the camera.

Finally, Kaya's own eyes drooped and she fell asleep.

In a vague dream state, she heard her alarm, but it was far away. In the dream, she was in Lucas' bed, and she wondered why he wasn't turning off his alarm. She opened her eyes, looked around his room, and it was empty. No other furniture besides the bed with a single white sheet on it; no clothes, no blinds. The ceiling fan turning slowly, and her, alone.

Kaya jerked awake on the couch and realized her actual alarm was going off, downstairs in her room. She was a little sore from sleeping on the couch, but she was glad she at least slept a little.

She washed her face and pulled on a cotton skirt and t shirt, grabbed her khaki shorts and Chalfonte polo for later, dumping those and her laptop into her tote bag, and headed over to the General Store. It was busy this morning so she didn't see Tess, and didn't want to ask for her given all the customers. She just grabbed her coffee and biked with one hand on the handlebars down Sunset to Exit Zero.

She set her laptop on the table and pulled out her power cord and phone. She saw Lucas had called already this morning—no voicemail, but he'd know that she'd see the missed call. She paused, looking at the screen for a beat. Then she mentally pulled the knife from her heart, shrugged inwardly, and went to work.

When she made the progress she wanted on the book project, edited something that Callum requested help on, and triaged her emails, she calculated that she didn't have enough time to go home before her Eddy's shift without having to turn right around again. But if she went to the hotel now, she'd be early. She decided to change into her uniform here and go hang out downtown to kill the time before her shift.

After she locked her bike around back of the hotel, she found a spot in the shade and pulled out her phone.

> I am hoping I can see you

That came in about forty minutes ago, she noted. And there was another one from about ten minutes ago waiting as well.

> I really really want to talk to you

She closed her eyes and opened them again, her thumbs hovering over the phone.

> hi lucas

The three dots immediately appeared.

> Hi! ty for responding!

My goodness, Lucas. Exclamation points deployed!

sure

Did u sleep well?

Huh. Not the swerve she expected.

Got a few hrs. u?

On and off, but I'll be fine.
Where are you?

at Eddys—abt to start my
shift. Was at EZ all morning

I'll come get you when
you're done at Eddys

it'll be like midnight

I don't mind

not a great idea

pls don't shut me out K

I love you

don't mean to hurt you—truly. Just this is how this goes

it doesn't have to

it does for me

I don't understand why I can't see you, talk to you. I'll be less than six hours away by car—much less on plane

sorry, Lucas. I don't know what to tell you. this is how I manage—what I need

I'll be back before we know it

I need you

Tears pricked her eyes. She squeezed them shut and then opened them again.

let's see where we are when/if you come back

The three dots appeared, disappeared, and appeared again.

when, Kaya. I promise you

Kaya

THAT NIGHT, SHE SLEPT like the dead. Between the sleepless night before and a long day of work, she was exhausted when she crawled into bed. She practically fell asleep in the shower before she put her head on the pillow.

She didn't dream.

A little after nine in the morning, she made her coffee and tracked down Callie, who was jogging as she talked to Kaya. Kaya heard the wind rushing past Callie's earbuds. Kaya found herself dispassionately—almost surgically—sharing the recent events.

Callie was quiet, lightly panting. "He's going."

"He is," said Kaya.

"When?"

"Tomorrow."

"But he's coming back."

"In theory."

"And he's not leaving you—this is a work assignment?"

"That's the story," affirmed Kaya. "And honestly, he didn't want to leave me. I mean, he definitely wants to, and needs to go do this job—it's the last piece of everything he's been working towards. But he's trying to say that we'll stay together—you know, that we visit each other and talk and shit."

"And you don't want to do that?"

"I don't know if I *can* do that."

"I understand. But don't you want to try?" Callie asked. A dog barked in the background. "You really love him."

"I do, but he's leaving...I just, I don't know how to be with him when I'm not *with* him."

"Do you want to date other people?"

"God, no!" said Kaya. "I only want him. But I can't pretend he's still here and everything is fine."

"So how did you leave it?"

"I told him we'll re-assess the state of things when and if he comes back." Kaya got the sense that Callie had stopped running.

"I see," she said. "That's what you want?"

"That's all I know how to do," Kaya said.

"Okay, well," Callie said. "I'm coming down."

"You guys aren't supposed to come for another ten days," Kaya responded.

"Yeah, whatever. I have all summer off anyway, so we'll just drive separately. You should not be alone."

"I'm *fine*, Cal."

"Sure, sure. But I've been really tired lately anyway. I could use some extra beach time."

"I'm *fine*, Cal."

"Okay, Kay. Then we'll just be *fine* together."

***

True to her word, Callie showed up two days later with herself, her bags, and provisions. "The drive took me forever," she whined. "I got too tired to drive and had to pull into a rest area at the top of the Garden State and take a quick nap."

"Are you okay, do you think?" asked Kaya.

"Yeah," said Callie. "Otherwise, I feel fine, I'm just tired. I'm looking forward to naps here. When I'm home, I feel guilty like I should be doing laundry, or finding new music for next school year, or paying bills. But here, I can just veg out." She released a huge sigh. Her light brown hair was tied atop her head in a messy bun. Kaya thought her sister had never been prettier in the late afternoon light.

They fell into a routine where Kaya did her Exit Zero work from home, and whenever she wasn't at Eddy's they hung out, cooked, walked, and talked. "You really haven't heard from him?" Callie asked one day as they walked on the beach. It was early evening, so they walked around the Point towards Sunset. It was that time of day when the families who had been there since the morning were packing up and dragging their beach toys and chairs away, and the sunsetters were coming out with chairs to set up for golden hour.

The wind blew her skirt around her legs. Kaya turned her face into the breeze and sighed. "I have. I mean, sort of. He calls. Usually around nine in the morning or nine at night. He never leaves a voicemail."

"And you never pick up?" Callie asked, stooping to pick up a rare intact seashell and dusting the sand off it before walking on.

"Nothing to say," Kaya shrugged.

"I respect your process and your feelings, but it's sad. He was so good for you."

Kaya said nothing for a few moments. "Yeah...but...he's gone," she said simply.

Callie looked at her thoughtfully. "Hey, I'm a little tired," she said. "Mind if we turn around?"

"Not at all," replied Kaya, turning around to head back. "Seriously, Cal, don't add worrying about me to your list."

Callie scoffed. "I know your old therapist used to say that worry is an unproductive emotion, but I have no idea how to stop. Some days I'm just going along about my business, doing normal things, and then pain and anxiety just rip through me."

"Yeah," Kaya said quietly. They walked a few moments in silence. "Did you ever think about therapy?" she asked her sister.

"Not really. I mean, I know I'm crazy, so I probably should, but it just sounds so exhausting to have to find someone, and the right fit, and then to start from the beginning and *share all* of this shit."

"It is hard, and it can be exhausting," Kaya confirmed. "But take it from this walking disaster, carrying it all around all the time is *also* exhausting."

Kaya

ONE DAY, CALLIE SUGGESTED they go to the General Store. "I want to meet Tess and Gerry," she said.

"Huh," said Kaya. "I forgot you don't know them." The Nevilles had become such a fixture in Kaya's life since she moved here. She popped in for coffee or a quick chat several days a week—it was part of her regular routine.

"I feel like I do!" replied Callie. "When are they least busy?"

The girls went over mid-morning—after the going-to-work crowd but before lunch. Sure enough, they asked for Tess, and she came right out of the office, beaming. Her reading glasses were perched on her head, so she'd probably been doing paperwork.

"I hope we didn't get you from something important," said Kaya, smiling. She couldn't help but smile when Tess was smiling.

"Morgan girls!" Tess exclaimed, shooing aside Kaya's statement. Tess reached out to each of them with an arm, collecting them into a group hug. "Let's sit!" she proclaimed and steered them to a table by the window. "Coffee? Tea?"

"You sit, Tess," said Kaya. "I'll get the iced teas." Kaya went to the counter and ordered from Tess' son who was working the register. She could hear the conversation at the table.

"Callie," Tess was saying to her sister, "it is so nice to see you again. I am so incredibly sorry for your loss. Your parents were just lovely humans. The nicest, most welcoming, sweetest, and friendliest people ever. And they were so proud of you. You went out and found your way. So smart, so giving. You're a gift, child. And," Tess lowered her voice conspiratorially, "your momma said you found yourself a prince of a man for a husband, so I assume he's a smarty pants too and just as kind as you."

"Thank you," said Callie, her voice catching with emotion. Kaya came back and set the iced teas on the table.

"Juan is awesome," said Kaya, nodding as she sat down.

"And how about our Kaya?" Tess asked, grasping Kaya's forearm. "She is quite the fixture out here on the Point. Writing stories about the community, working with the local business owners. I feel like your folks would be so happy about this."

"I know they are," said Callie. "They always loved it here, and they would want Kaya to be where she can feel her best and do good work." She smiled at her sister. "And," said Callie looking back at Tess, "I know they would be thrilled that there are people out here looking out for her. I always loved your place here," she said gesturing.

"Well that's very kind," responded Tess. "But the people make the place," she said with a smile towards Kaya.

Kaya

CALLIE AND KAYA WERE walking on the beach again, this time in their swimsuits, since it was mid-day, so when the sun got too hot, they could dip into the waves to cool off. They walked along in the part where the waves broke on the shore, so their feet and calves got wet as the waves crashed and receded.

"He called again," Callie said, side stepping further into the water to avoid a large gull on the beach. "I wasn't prying, I swear, but your phone was on the counter and I saw it light up with his name this morning."

"Yeah," said Kaya, absently as she looked out at the ocean and adjusted her visor.

"You didn't answer. I mean, I know you were working, but I know you saw it. I didn't want to interrupt you, but..."

"No," Kaya cut her off. "I didn't."

"I love you and you know that, but I mean, seriously?" said Callie, a sudden edge in her voice. She stopped walking, put her hands on her hips, and turned to Kaya.

Kaya's gaze snapped to her sister. "What do you mean?" she asked, crossing her arms over her chest.

"That dude is super into you. He's hot, he's the nicest human maybe *ever*, and you had a great thing going. You *know* he's coming back! Why are you fucking with him?"

"*Fucking with him*?" shouted Kaya. She quickly looked around to see if there were any kids in earshot. Then she looked back at her sister and more quietly, but just as intensely, repeated, "*Fucking with him*? You think this is a game to me?"

They stood at the water's edge, squared off like that for a beat. "No," Callie admitted. "Not a game." But her voice edged up again when she continued. "I just don't get why it's so hard to just pick up the phone or send a text! You're icing him out and it's just...mean!" They were just staring at each other as the surf rolled in and dragged out at their feet.

Kaya broke first, shaking her head. She dropped her arms with a resigned sigh, turned and started walking again. Callie hopped into step with her. "Shit, Callie, I thought you of all people would understand."

Silence hung in the salty air. "I just really like Lucas for you—he was good to you...for you..." Callie said gently, "and I don't want to watch it get thrown away. I don't understand why you can't talk to him."

They walked another minute or two and turned up towards the dunes, since they'd reached their beach access point. They stopped to shake out their towels, roll them up, and put them in the bag. Callie pulled her t-shirt over her suit, and Kaya shrugged on her cover up. They walked towards the access. The sand got hotter on their feet the further away from the water they walked. "I don't know how to explain it," Kaya started. "But, when people leave me, it's like I have to wall them off so I don't have to feel the pain of the...betrayal...that's maybe not the right word. But I don't know how to be halfway."

"Okay," said Callie finally. "I don't necessarily know that feeling. I guess I'm more of a hold-on-so-tight-it-hurts kind of person." They walked on. "Sorry, anyway...I shouldn't have attacked you. I think I'm just really tired." They reached the top of the stairs and picked up their flip-flops.

"And you still otherwise feel okay?" Kaya asked, relieved to relinquish the spotlight of the conversation. She shook the sand off her shoes and slid them on.

"Yeah. I mean, I don't sleep well, but that isn't completely new," said Callie as she slid her own flip-flops on and headed down the stairs.

"Same," said Kaya. "But there's nothing else it could be? I mean, have you seen your doctor for bloodwork or anything? Are you on your period? Because..."

Suddenly, Callie froze on the stairs and grabbed Kaya's forearm.

"What?" Kaya asked.

"My period is late."

"Stop it."

"No, I mean, you know I'm not on birth control like you, or as organized as you. I don't track this stuff to the minute and I've never been regular, but, I mean…"

"Well," said Kaya, grinning. "Looks like a trip to the CVS is in our future."

They practically ran back across the road. Callie bolted into the outside shower while Kaya ran to use the inside one. They dressed and hopped on their bikes.

"Am I not supposed to be biking?" Callie asked, looking back over her shoulder at Kaya.

"I don't think it would matter this early, but what do I know? We're going slow?"

"Shit, I've been drinking coffee! And wine!"

"It'll be okay! Not much and it's early! This must happen to everyone!"

They got what they needed at the CVS and pedaled back to the Point.

Kaya waited anxiously for Callie to come back upstairs. She appeared, holding the test. She took a paper towel, set it on the counter, and set the test gingerly on the paper towel.

"How long do we wait?" asked Kaya.

"The box said ten minutes."

"What are we looking for?"

"A line there just to show it's working, like a control…"

"I see it!!" squealed Kaya.

"That's just the control line," laughed Callie nervously. "If I'm...pregnant...there is supposed to be a plus there."

"Oh my God..." said Kaya. "I don't think we have to wait ten minutes..." As they peered at it, the plus sign emerged.

Kaya squealed again and hugged her sister. Callie looked a little shellshocked. "We have to call Juan!"

"We do," agreed Callie, a smile blossoming across her face.

Kaya

THE NEXT DAY KAYA was scheduled to run with Alexis. Callie was sleeping in, and didn't want to run now that she knew she was pregnant, so she had declined to tag along.

When they met up, Alexis immediately said, "What happened? Did something happen to your sister?" Her face was lined in worry.

"What? Why would you think that?"

"Just...something on your face, and I thought your sister was coming..."

"Ah," said Kaya, as they started jogging. It was hot today. A muggy, late July day. "No, she's fine. She's good even. We just found out she's pregnant."

"Oh, wow, that's cool," said Alexis.

"Yeah, I'm pretty sure I'm not supposed to say anything this early, but you don't know anyone who knows her besides me, so..." Kaya shrugged.

Alexis chuckled. "Sorry I won't get to meet her, though." They jogged along, slower, by some silent mutual agreement, due to the heat. "Hey, I know your schedule has been crazy, I've been busy, it's been hot, so I haven't seen you in weeks, but...can I just say you don't...look like yourself? Is everything okay?"

"Huh," breathed Kaya. "Sort of?"

"I mean," Alexis offered, "you don't have to tell me anything if it's none of my business." Kaya kept jogging, staring straight ahead.

"Lucas left," Kaya said simply.

"What?!" Alexis stammered. "He *left* you?" She kept turning to look at Kaya as they plodded along, to try to assess her emotional state.

Kaya kept her gaze straight ahead. "He didn't leave *me*, per se, but he's left for Long Island to work there."

"Permanently?"

"Supposedly no..." Kaya started. "In theory, he's coming back."

"Oh wow. When? Like, how long?"

Kaya pulled up and stopped running. Alexis followed suit. They stopped in the shade of an old, big tree. "Sorry," Kaya said. "It's just so fucking hot. Can we walk for a minute? My kingdom for a breeze," she said, trying to sound nonchalant, as she gestured in the air.

"We can absolutely walk," said Alexis loyally. Kaya felt Alexis glancing over at her.

As they walked, Kaya exhaled, "Ahhhhh!" and ground her palms against her eyes to stop the sweat stinging at them. *Yeah, just sweat, definitely not tears. Definitely.* "I don't know!" she groaned. Alexis stayed silent. Kaya reached up and adjusted her visor as they walked. "I'm sorry," she continued. "I just...I don't know how long, or when...or...if he'll come back. When he left, he didn't know the timing."

"What does he say when he calls?" Alexis asked quietly. "Does he know any more now?"

"Well..." said Kaya with a big exhale, "he calls, but I don't answer." She braced for a version of the criticism she got from her sister.

But Alexis just said, "How come?"

Kaya sighed. "This may not make much sense, Lex, but I was in therapy for abandonment issues after losing my mom, and it's really hard for me when people—especially people I care about—leave. I love him, but I don't know how to...engage with him...now that he's left. It's like, when people tell me they're leaving, my heart just...goes cold. I know that sounds crazy, and I'd totally get it if you...didn't get it." She finally turned and looked at Alexis as they walked.

Alexis was thoughtful, and then said, "I think I generally understand. And you need to do what you need to do to protect yourself. I don't know that there's any right or wrong here. It just really sucks." They walked on in silence for a few minutes.

"If it helps," said Alexis more brightly, "I will never leave. I'm from South Jersey, I have no plans to go anywhere else. I love my job. All I want to do is play with dogs and cats, do stuff outside, go to an occasional show or concert, drink beers with my

friends, and jog with you. So, you're stuck with me."
She grinned, and Kaya returned a small smile.

"I saw his friend Tim in the Acme the other day,"
Kaya said. "And I just turned around and bolted the
other way before he could see me. What's that
about?" she exhaled with a sad laugh. "I *like* Tim! I
have no beef with Tim!"

"I get it, though," replied Alexis. "You probably
just didn't want to have to talk about Lucas."

"Yeah. Probably. Let's change the subject," Kaya
said. "Let's talk about *your* love life. Any updates?"
She looked over and saw a goofy-ass smile on
Alexis' face. "*Lex!* What happened?"

"I was gonna tell you today anyway, but then you
were so sad..."

"*Spill!*"

"I am kinda seeing this girl. She's really cute,
and she's so nice, and she has the cutest puppy."

"The way to your heart," Kaya laughed. "What's
her name and how'd you meet her?"

"Amy, and boring—friend of a friend. I'm
surprised I haven't met her before, but we're really
hitting it off."

"That is so cool, and 'friend of friend' is not
boring—that is one of the most sure-fire ways to
meet people. Someone you know is solid thinks she
is solid. Win win...win!"

Alexis laughed, then earnestly said, "I'm sorry if
it makes you sad to talk about it, given everything
with Lucas."

"It absolutely doesn't," said Kaya honestly. "I want all good things for you. It makes me very happy."

Kaya

THE DAY JUAN ARRIVED was overcast and muggy, which was fine because Callie definitely wanted to be at the house when he arrived. Kaya laughed as her sister practically ran down the stairs when they heard the car arrive. Kaya followed and came down the outside stairs to find Callie and Juan in a tight hug. *Aw, Juan was crying.*

Kaya waited until they came apart to step in and give her own hug. "Congrats, bruh," she said into Juan's shoulder. When he pulled away, he wiped another tear away with his thumb, smiling.

"Thanks, Kay. I still can't quite believe it," he said, smiling down at Callie.

"That makes three of us!" laughed Callie.

During their visit, they spent time at the beach, eating seafood and drinking cocktails, per usual, except Callie's were zero-proof. The morning before they were going back to Providence it was cloudy again—not enticing beach weather. Callie had stopped any running and biking, so they were thinking of other things to do.

"Can you kayak?" asked Kaya.

"I don't think that's a problem?" Callie said, looking at Juan.

He shrugged. "I wouldn't think so, and we won't let you lift anything, but the sitting and paddling seem like it would be fine. Or we could ride together in a double."

Kaya drove as they headed to the back harbor. When she turned onto Lucas' road, her heart felt like it was flooded all of a sudden, and it took her breath away. She drove past his building and, with shaking hands, parked in front of the kayak rental. She dropped her forehead to the steering wheel and took some deep breaths. Callie reached over and rubbed her arm. Kaya felt Juan's hand on her shoulder from the back seat. After a minute, Kaya lifted her head, smiled weakly at her sister and back towards Juan. "I'm okay."

"It's okay if you're not," said Juan.

"Yeah, okay, you're right, I'm not," said Kaya attempting a laugh. "But we go on, yes?" She fixed her gaze on Callie.

Callie looked at her for a minute. "Yep," she said, reaching for the car door. "We go on."

They got out, got boats, and paddled into the wetlands. Kaya led them past the marina. As they made the turn to go upcreek, she couldn't help but glance up at Lucas' back deck. The decks surrounding his had towels hanging over the railings and bright furniture. On his, the furniture cushions were stowed away and the curtains inside the door were pulled closed. She turned away and kept paddling.

She led them deep up the creek until they were surrounded on both sides by tall seagrass and water. Dragon flies skipped above the water. The grey skies were a nice relief from beating sun, and the air was still.

"This is so cool," said Juan, with a slow stroke of his paddle.

"I know, right?" said Kaya over her shoulder. "When I found this last spring, I thought how much fun it would be to bring you guys back here." They paddled a little longer in silence. "Isn't it peaceful?" Some birds were chirping in the distance, but there were no other sounds around them.

"It is," agreed Callie. "So quiet." They got to where it started to get too shallow and narrow, turned their boats around and rested their paddles on their laps.

They were just floating when Juan spoke first. "I hate that we have to leave tomorrow. I don't want to leave you alone again, Kaya." Kaya smiled at her brother-in-law. She couldn't read his eyes from this distance and with them shadowed under his visor, but she could feel his care. What is it that their mother had called him? *A prince of a man.* Indeed.

"I'll be okay," she assured him, removing her own visor, swiping at her forehead and re-securing the back of it under her frizzy ponytail. "I have two jobs, friends, the beach, and an excellent running buddy. It's almost as good as therapy."

He looked at her for another minute and gave her a small salute. He lifted his paddle and looked over at Callie. "Ready to go back?"

"Ready," Callie and Kaya answered.

Kaya

ONE AFTERNOON, KAYA ANNOUNCED to the Exit Zero crew that she needed to stretch and was going to walk over to the Golden Stop for an iced coffee. Lucy leapt out of her chair. "I'll go with you," she said. "I'm totally dragging. I worked a late shift the other day and I still haven't recovered." Kaya so admired Lucy's nursing, and knew that she herself could never have the fortitude and patience to do that kind of work.

They headed out down Perry Street. Lucy stifled a yawn, then looked at Kaya and asked conversationally, "So, what do you hear from Luke?"

Kaya's head whipped around. "I'm sorry?" she shot back. Her cheeks flushed and her chest felt tight.

Lucy gave her a sideways glance, confused. "Lucas? How is he doing up in New York?"

"I have no idea," Kaya practically barked, more aggressively than she had intended. It was like Lucy's question had physically assaulted Kaya. The casual assumption that she and Lucas were in touch. Lucas' betrayal flooding her chest with pain. Kaya felt Lucy go quiet.

They paused to wait for the light at Broadway. The light turned green and they started across, when suddenly a car made a left turn into their path. "*Shit!*" screamed Kaya, grabbing Lucy's arm and pulling them both back. The car continued on like the driver didn't even see them. They were both frozen in place, breathing heavily. "Mother *fucker*!" screamed Kaya, to the back of the car as it drove away.

"*Shit*," she continued, after a beat. "I bet he was on his phone and didn't even see us. Are you okay?" she said turning to Lucy.

"Yeah," said Lucy. Her eyes were wide. "Thank you. That was...something." They both paused and took a couple more breaths, and then, after looking both ways again, crossed the street.

"Hey," said Lucy, tentatively when they got to the other side. "Are you okay?"

"Yeah," said Kaya, keeping her eyes straight ahead. "It was scary, but he didn't hit me."

"No, I know," Lucy replied quickly. "And that was, like, super scary, but I've just never heard you so...angry..." They walked on for a few minutes in silence. The form of a question hung in the air.

"Sorry if I scared you as well," Kaya finally said.

"No, it's okay. I just...wanted to know if you were okay, or if there's like...something going on."

Kaya huffed out a chuckle. "Gurl," she said. "I can't even begin to say, I guess." They continued across Perry Street towards the coffee shop. Lucy let it go, thankfully.

"Well," Lucy said as she held open the door, "at least there's coffee."

"Yes," agreed Kaya, "but I think after that, I better go decaf."

Kaya

ONE MORNING JUST BEFORE eleven, she wound her way through the customers in the Exit Zero restaurant and store. She waved to Sloane across the store and climbed the stairs to the office. Her shorts and t-shirt were a little damp with sweat from the bike ride over, and the air conditioning inside felt good. She was surprised to find the office empty, but then noticed Mateo behind the big monitor at the graphics station.

"Hi," he said, face peeking around the screen with a smile. He kept his dark brown hair short—a little longer on top, and fading down to shaved over his ears. Probably easier with the fire helmet. He was wearing a fire department t-shirt, jeans, and Birkenstocks.

"Hello!" said Kaya brightly. "Whatcha working on?" She set her bag on the table.

"Layout for the weekly. Callum went on vacation with his family this week, so I said I'd help out."

"That's nice of you," Kaya responded, coming around to look over his shoulder. She dropped into a chair next to him. "It looks good."

"Thanks," he said. Kaya swiveled back to the table and took out her laptop.

"It's quiet today," she observed, looking around.

"Yeah," agreed Mateo as he clicked and dragged his content around. "Vance had a meeting out somewhere. And with Maureen gone..." he shrugged and trailed off. Kaya cast her eyes downward. Mateo flicked her a side glance. "You okay?"

After a few seconds of silence, Kaya responded, "Yeah, I'm good. It's just..." her voice fell a bit quieter, smaller. She tested out saying the words again, "...it's hard for me when people leave me. Maureen..." Kaya gave a small shrug. The A/C and her lightly damp clothes were giving Kaya a slight chill. She pulled her old U of R hoodie out of her bag and shrugged it on.

Mateo took his hand off the mouse and swiveled to face her. He looked at her, his brown eyes warm and free of judgment. "Why? I mean, where do you think that comes from?"

Not meeting his gaze, she replied, "My old therapist would tell you I have an adjustment disorder in the form of an acute response to processing people's departures from my life, where I equate said departures to abandonment and devaluation of me as a person." She smiled weakly at him. His lips quirked up slightly towards a smile and his eyes crinkled a bit. She hesitated but decided to keep going. "It probably comes from losing my parents."

She watched for the familiar signs of someone getting uncomfortable, or rushing to say how sorry they were. But his face just relaxed to neutral. He tapped the fingertips of one hand against his chest. "Me too."

"You too?" Kaya asked.

"I mean, yeah, I also lost my parents."

Kaya looked at him thoughtfully. A feeling blossomed around her heart. A recognition. It was like a switch flipped. Like there was a secret language being spoken between their souls.

"How?" she asked.

"Car accident," he said simply, and she winced slightly and furrowed her brow. "Yours?" he asked.

"Cancer."

"Both of them?"

"Yeah."

"Sucks," he said simply. There was an unspoken, immediate ease in sitting with someone who—even when you don't know the details or their experience—you know has been through similar trauma.

Kaya nodded. "How does it play out for you?" she asked.

He smiled at her quietly and answered readily, "My profession. Being a first responder is important to me. My work feels like it has a purpose if I have opportunities to save people or prevent bad things from happening. Like, of course I know bad things happen..."

"You more than most," Kaya interjected quietly.

"Yeah. But if I have any chance to help things turn out better on any given day, I like that."

"Slay," said Kaya. "I like that too." He smiled at her and turned back to his monitor.

She had not spent a ton of time with Mateo, but she realized the exchange made her a little lighter. It felt good—taking a chance and trusting him with her truths, and him trusting her with his.

Kaya

KAYA AND ALEXIS MET up one seasonably warm afternoon in early September. They chose to meet by the ferry and run around the bay side, since town was still pretty crowded. Kaya was stretching in the parking lot when Alexis drove up.

"New running club rule," said Alexis, smiling as she approached.

"Okay," said Kaya. "What do you propose?"

"We go slower when someone majorly banged up her toe because her roommate left a giant box in the entry way for no apparent reason."

Kaya winced as she took off her sweatshirt and tossed it in the car. "Ready?" she asked. Alexis nodded and they started jogging. "So, ouch," said Kaya. "Does it hurt a lot?"

Alexis laughed. "It does, and I wasn't sure if it would hurt to run. But it feels okay now. Like, not any worse than just standing, so I'm good. What's up with you?"

The breeze was light. The sun was shining and felt good on her tanned shoulders and arms. It felt good to use her muscles, Kaya thought. Some days her quads felt like cinder blocks, but today the motion felt light. "Oh my gosh, I have to tell you about last weekend at King Eddy's," she said.

"I love a crazy work story," laughed Alexis. "Lord knows you've heard enough crazy stories about dogs!"

"Well, I do like to hear about all the ridiculous things your patients eat." Alexis laughed. Kaya continued. "I was supposed to open. Usually we open at one, so I have to be there by, like, 12:30. Wait, I need to re-tie my shoe," said Kaya, both of them stopping while Kaya tightened her laces. Then they picked back up running. "So I'm puttering around my house, doing dishes and stuff 'til I was supposed to leave, and my boss called me in a panic. This couple got married at the Chalfonte that morning, and apparently, the groom's family were literally pounding on the door to open the bar early."

Alexis started laughing. "Oh my God…"

"I *know*," said Kaya, also laughing. "I guess the groom's family are long-time regulars. My poor boss…he was all 'is there any way you can come in early', so of course I did, and, Lexi, it was hilarious. When I rolled up, there were indeed at least four old, white dudes standing *right* at the outside door to Eddy's. I had to ask them to move so I could get in! Meanwhile, the bride and what I assume was the bride's family were over on the lawn, looking low-key horrified, in like a what-kind-of-family-have-we-tied-ourselves-to-now way. I can't even tell you. The entire scene was *so* funny."

"Then were they rowdy?" asked Alexis, glancing over, "once you opened, I mean?"

Kaya chuckled. "No, actually, not at all. They were all very polite, and the bride was lovely, and it all wound up fine. They were actually all good tippers, too. Some of those old dudes were just *very* adamant that it was time to start drinking." They jogged along, starting to sweat and breathe harder now. "And hell bent on exercising their privilege," she added, her laughter coming out in huffs as they jogged.

"That's hysterical. I can totally picture it," laughed Alexis.

"But, yes," Kaya rejoined. "They were all nice to me."

After a few minutes of silence, Alexis said, "I haven't heard you laugh like that in a while."

A few more beats of silence. "I don't think I have," Kaya responded, glancing sideways with a sad smile.

Kaya

ONE EVENING IN LATE September, in that "shoulder" season after the tourists left but when the long-term rentals and owners were often still around, Kaya had a slow afternoon at Eddy's. Today, she was behind the bar. In her peripheral vision as she was drying glasses, she saw two women sit down at the end.

She approached them smiling as she grabbed a couple coasters to throw down. "Hi, ladies, what are you in the mood for?" As she dropped the coasters, she heard one of them say, "Hey, Kaya."

Her head jerked up. There, on the left, sat Vanessa.

"Vanessa! You're back!" exclaimed Kaya.

"Yes," she said with a small smile. "And this is my cousin, Abby."

"Hi, Abby," said Kaya warmly.

"What brings you back in September? Are you at your parents' place?"

"Yes," confirmed Vanessa. "I am between leases in DC and I can work remotely, so I'm gonna be here for a while. Can we...meet up?" Her face seemed...hopeful. "I'd love to talk."

Kaya smiled. "Of course. I would love that! I'm off day after tomorrow. Is that soon enough?"

Vanessa clasped her hands together and breathed in with resolve. "Yes. Excellent. I'll come to you. Just tell me when and where."

Vanessa arrived at the Point as promised, and five minutes early. Another thing that had made them kindred spirits in and outside of work—punctuality! It was a sunny day with a nice breeze, so Kaya suggested they walk around Lake Lily. "Are those shoes good for walking?" she asked, gesturing to Vanessa's sandals. Vanessa looked reliably chic, in crisp chino shorts and a flowy long-sleeve tunic top.

"Totally," Vanessa replied. "They're my go-tos."

"Fantastic, said Kaya, as she pulled on her sneakers and led the way back down the stairs to the street.

As they wandered towards the lake, Kaya asked, "So you said you're between leases…did you break up with Todd?"

"Yeah," Vanessa said matter-of-factly. "It was time. I need to either find a roommate or a smaller place I can afford, so while I do that, I figured there are worse places to hang out."

"Ha," said Kaya. "A page out of my playbook."

"Oh, so are you not staying? Are you planning to go back to DC? I knew you were here, obviously, but I haven't heard the full story. I don't talk to a ton of people at Alston since I left, and I wouldn't ask anyone else about your life anyway."

"Well, thanks for that," said Kaya. "At this point, I'm planning to stay here. I don't have any immediate plans to go anywhere else. I just meant that I also kind of fled here last year after my dad died. Work just seemed to not matter and I needed a break."

Vanessa nodded and was quiet for a moment. "I'm sorry about your father. Honestly, I hadn't heard that. All I heard is you and Charlie broke up."

Kaya let out a snort. Charlie, all things considered, felt like a lifetime ago. She hadn't even thought to mention him today. "Yeah, Charlie dumped me—which, believe me, is totally fine..." she hastily added when Vanessa shot her a look of concern.

"Charlie was never good enough for you," Vanessa said loyally.

"Thanks," Kaya said with a small smile and sideways glance.

They walked on in silence for a few minutes, and Kaya undid her ponytail and re-tied it to catch the tendrils that escaped. "Can I ask you something?" Vanessa said.

"Of course," said Kaya.

"Did I do something wrong?"

"What do you mean?" asked Kaya, forehead wrinkling in confusion.

"When I left Alston Group. I mean, I could see you being upset if I were going to a competitor, but you knew I wasn't. I wanted to try in-house PR. And I didn't leave you in a lurch—you know I finished or handed off all my projects and I even referred in another person to the firm...I just...I've never known what it was that I did wrong."

Kaya sorted her thoughts. "Why do you think you did something wrong?" she asked, although, if she were being completely honest with herself, she already knew. Maybe her penance was she needed to hear V say it.

"You shut me out. The instant I told you I might want to try in-house and had met someone whose company was interested. You just stopped talking to me outside of necessary business stuff...you stopped coming out for lunch or drinks when I was there...when I tried to talk to you, you were so short with me that it made it so intimidating." Kaya squeezed her eyes shut as she listened, all the memories of around the time Vanessa left the firm were being dragged to the front of her mind. *Yes*, she did do all those things.

"You didn't come to my going-away happy hour," Vanessa said softly.

"To be fair," Kaya said quickly, opening her eyes, "I never go to good-bye happy hours. Let the record show that I actually *did* go to yours."

"Sorry, yes, you came. For one drink and you didn't speak to me. It's like you came to say you came and that was it."

That is deadly accurate. Kaya's mind flew back to that day. Vanessa was her teammate, her friend, her first mentee. Her mate in the foxhole. She knew she had to show up at that happy hour. At the time, even as her heart was flooded with ice and pain, she'd known she owed it to Vanessa. Also, everyone knew how close they were. So she'd gone, and done the best she could.

Kaya knew she needed to say something. They were at the uphill, shady part of the road around the lake. Slowly she ventured, "You didn't do anything wrong, and I'm sorry my actions made you feel like you did."

"So, what was it?" asked Vanessa. "And I'm sorry if I'm prying, but you were my everything. You were my first boss, and you were so awesome to me. You taught me a ton, you championed me, you looked out for me. You shared my weird sense of humor and you matched me in sarcasm. I wanted—want—you to be my friend forever. I was sad that that seemed like it ended when I told you I was leaving."

Kaya stopped walking, so Vanessa stopped too. Tears welled in Kaya's eyes. Vanessa was quiet, maybe fearing she'd said too much. "What it was, V…was…not your fault. It was just that you left, and I know this is totally irrational, but I have abandonment issues. I was in therapy after my mom died, but I've still got lots of work to do. I can only tell you that when someone I care about pulls any kind of departure, I shut down. I'm not proud of it. Even knowing I'm doing it isn't enough to make it stop. I take it personally—like it's *me* who's being rejected, even when I know rationally that that doesn't make any sense. Like with you, I knew you weren't leaving *me*, but it didn't matter. I'm not proud of how I handled it, but it was at the time a sort of survival mechanism...if that makes sense..."

"Yes," said Vanessa simply. They started walking again. "Okay," Vanessa said thoughtfully, "so how come I'm here now, though, and you seem fine with me?"

"Yeah," answered Kaya, laughing weakly and wiping at her eyes with her shirt sleeve. "I can't really explain that. It's like the leaving itself is what triggers me. I never stopped loving and caring about you. And, actually, I've missed you," offered Kaya. "Like I said, it's not rational." She chuckled wryly.

"Well, *God*, I've missed you too. I can't tell you how many signs with bad spelling or grammar I've seen that I wanted to text you, but was afraid you didn't want to hear from me."

Kaya snort-laughed, "Oh, my gosh, yes. I literally saw one in the Acme self-checkout the other day that said 'this terminal does not accept cash'—but..." and before she could finish, Vanessa grabbed her arm and squealed, "they spelled 'accept' as 'except' with an 'e'! I saw the same sign!" They clutched each other and giggled.

"Okay, let's workshop this," said Vanessa, recovering.

"What do you mean?"

"Well, I am not going to stand for us not being friends. Unacceptable." *This* was the Vanessa that Kaya remembered. "But it's entirely likely that I'll go back to DC at some point. So let's practice. Role play!" V announced.

"Oh, Lord," Kaya said, laughing, trying to ignore the slight panic that even the specter of Vanessa leaving again had allowed to surface.

"Let's say that I moved...to Stone Harbor," said Vanessa. "What would our plan be?"

"Hmmm," thought Kaya, trying to take some deep breaths. She was working hard to get control over the fight-flight-freeze that she learned was happening in her brain. This was just hypothetical. And Stone Harbor was less than thirty minutes up the shore. A lot less if traffic was good. Breathe. "Maybe we make a plan to meet, like, once a week for dinner or breakfast."

"*Yes*," said Vanessa. "I like it. And having it set as a regular thing—that would help you know I was still here for you?"

"I think so," said Kaya thoughtfully.

"What if I moved, I don't know, up to Bridgeton?"

"Well, we could still commit to regular meetups, but if they are dinner we'd have to have it be a sleepover so we don't drink and drive."

"Okay, good. What about if I moved to Philly?"

"Well, then we really just can't be friends," Kaya quipped. They both laughed. Kaya felt the pressure around her heart start to subside.

"I promise you," said Vanessa, "when I go back to DC, that I will commit to whatever. Regular phone calls, cadence for visits, whatever you need to know I'm here in your life."

"You're a remarkable person, you know that?" said Kaya, smiling at her former teammate. "This is all very nice of you, and it shouldn't be your burden to manage my crazy."

"Small price to pay to have you back, friend."

Kaya

Now that Callie was back to school, their weekday meet-ups were usually fleeting while Callie drove from home to school. Kaya heard Callie's car Bluetooth connect as she answered the call.

"Good morning, sunshine," sang Callie.

"Good morning. Someone's cheery," she chuckled.

"What can I say. It's gonna be a good day," Callie said. Kaya pulled on a sweatshirt. *Was it?* She heard Callie ask, "Am I allowed to ask, speaking of good or not days...does Lucas still call?"

Kaya put in her air pods, but as the call switched from the phone to her ears, she caught the question and winced involuntarily. "He does not."

As she talked, Kaya went down the stairs to get her bicycle. She slung her bag across her body and headed out in the bright autumn sun. Callie was quiet.

"I can't remember exactly when it stopped, but no," Kaya said.

"And you never did answer, or...call him?"

"I just can't," confirmed Kaya, hoping they were not going to fight about it again. "Sometimes I wish

I could, but…I don't know. At first, I couldn't answer because I just couldn't go there. It hurt too much, and now…I don't know. Too much time has passed, maybe."

There was a silence and Kaya heard Callie's turn signal.

"Can I ask you something?" asked Kaya as she pedaled through the Point.

"Of course."

"Why are you not broken like this? Why do you not get triggered when people leave you?"

Callie snorted. "Well…it's true that that is not a particular trigger for me, but I'm far from unbroken. I don't know. Maybe because Juan and I were already together before Mom and Dad died. I had him by my side through all of it. Or maybe I'm just generally numb to everything. But don't worry, I'm totally broken," she laughed.

Kaya was on Seagrove Ave now, pedaling towards Exit Zero. "How so?"

"Well," said Callie thoughtfully, "I am paralyzed when trying to make important decisions. I am always thinking about what Mom and Dad would do."

"I get that," said Kaya, reveling in the cool fall air against her face.

"And if anything," Callie continued, "I think it's gonna be one hundred per cent worse when I have this kid. Like, I'm going to second guess every parenting decision, and wish like crazy they were here for me to ask for advice."

"Well, we'll figure it out together—you, me, and Juan."

"One way or another," said Callie. "Okay, I'm at school. Gotta go. Love you, bye."

"Love you, bye."

Kaya

IT WAS EARLY OCTOBER, and in the waning weeks of hurricane season, it appeared the season might not go quietly. The mid-Atlantic coast had been lucky this year so far, but a late-season storm was bearing down on the Outer Banks of North Carolina. Everyone at the General Store was watching reports and talking contingencies. There hadn't been a bad hit here since Sandy, but you had to be prepared.

It's surreal, Kaya thought, to be sitting here in this warm, calm place on this sunny Saturday morning, picturing a major storm possibly barreling towards them. Gerry said to her quietly, amid all the conversations swirling around them, "If you need any help buttoning everything up over there, or you don't want to be alone, just say the word."

Kaya smiled. "That's really kind. I think as of now, it doesn't look like it will be too bad. I've put away the deck furniture and the grill. Nothing else is out."

"Okay, well, let's see how today goes," Gerry said, giving her shoulder a fatherly squeeze before turning to pour everyone more coffee.

Later, Kaya went home and facetimed Callie.

"Will it be bad?" Callie worried, her brow furrowing. "Can you go off island? To your running friend, maybe?"

"Maybe," Kaya allowed. "But it looks now like it's heading out to sea. They're saying the Coast Guard haven't pulled boats out or anything, and everyone seems less worried now than this morning. I think it will be okay," Kaya said. She absent-mindedly traced circles on her jeans around her knee with her index finger, trying to sound reassuring and calm. She really didn't want her sister to worry and Callie, for all her strengths, was a worrier.

"I've got everything inside or well-tied down," Kaya continued. "They are saying now that we might not even get any rain; maybe just wind."

"Okay, well, keep me posted," Callie said. "And don't feel like it's a sign of weakness to take shelter if you have to leave the house."

"I promise," replied Kaya. She hit the end button and shot a text to Vanessa.

> All good over there?

Vanessa responded a minute later.

> Hey you

Yah tight as a drum. How's by u? if u want to hang in sturdy new construction on the bay side, or just want company, you'd be totally welcome. I'm on my own

I figured—that's why I'm checking in

Yah the 'rents called and walked through dad's 14-point spreadsheet of preparation

Vanessa dropped in the eyeroll emoji.

Ha! I bet. Thx for the offer. Think the way it's looking right now I'll ride it out on the Point. Just wanted to say hi

Got it. Well thx for checking in—let's compare notes tomorrow

Or if anything changes, come on out

Thx! Sounds good

Kaya checked the weather one last time before finishing the glass of wine she poured to help her hasten off to sleep. The storm was heading east over the ocean. The latest prediction was heavy wind overnight and some storm surge, but not a ton of rain. Kaya shut off the TV but didn't go downstairs to her room. She stretched out on the couch—not sure why. Just this sense that if the weather did get bad, she felt like she should keep watch.

She pulled up a throw blanket over her and closed her eyes. Clouds blotted out the moon, so it was dark, and she drifted off to sleep.

A little after two in the morning, a sound jolted her awake. Was it something hitting the house? Her heart raced. She jumped off the couch. The wind was howling around the house causing the clapboards to creak. She saw the tree branches bending aggressively in the back yard. She zipped her hoodie all the way up and stepped carefully out on the deck. The deck planks were wet but it didn't look like it was raining at that moment. The wind hit her face in a whoosh. She stepped to the right deck edge and looked over into the side yard. In the light of an exterior porch light, she saw the house next door's plastic trash bin had fallen over and got knocked into Point Taken.

Okay, nothing serious. She could right that tomorrow. She stepped back inside and secured the porch door. She stood, staring out into the inky, windy night. Her heart rate slowed back down and she felt oddly calm. She reflected at the irony, when she'd been through hell, it was possible to find resilience in a sense of almost numbness. *This all you got, world? Tropical-storm wind? Call me when it gets interesting.*

She went back to the couch and noticed her phone had lit up with a notification. *Huh.* She unlocked it. She smiled to see Juan's name pop up.

Hey there K. hope this didn't wake you but checking in

Kaya responded.

Dude it's almost 3 am 😊

I know—sorry—did I wake u

Nah, I'm up, and I put the phone on DND anyway

Funny—C went to bed early and I over-served myself on the whiskey, fell asleep on the couch watching football, just woke up. Crick in my neck— own damn fault lol

Hahahaha well time to get yourself to a proper bed

Yah for sure gonna go up, but just checked radar and weather channel and think you're in the thick of it so wanted to be sure ur ok. U? house?

Kaya looked up, blinking back happy tears. He thought to check on her.

Thx much. All good here. Neighbor's trash can fell against our house but that's the worst of it.

Not much rain either—just wind. Cape May bubble for the w

Thx for checking tho

Yah of course. I'll leave the phone off DND. If u need anything, call. Else check in in the am?

Will do. Thx Juan. And give my xo to Cal

U got it

She laid back down and pulled the blanket over her. She flexed her feet. She checked the weather again and then set her phone on the coffee table. It was great that Juan checked in. But there was something still tickling her consciousness. It wasn't fear. She just couldn't shake the sense that it wasn't supposed to play out like this. It was supposed to be...different.

Lucas. Lucas was supposed to be here. And suddenly, she was mourning him anew. Here in the dead of night in the middle of a hurricane, she couldn't push away the thoughts and feelings she could more easily compartmentalize during the day. Anger rose up in her heart that he left—he was supposed to be hers. He was supposed to be here. Deep inside she knew that was unfair—he had to take this assignment. But all she could feel was that there were promises made between their hearts in those heady months they were together. There was something *there*. He ripped out her heart and took it with him and the pain overwhelmed her. She turned on her side and checked the weather again.

The wind was predicted to be much calmer by morning. She pictured the beach, with waves rolling and receding. She let the wind become a white noise that finally sent her back to sleep.

Lucas

IT WAS NEARLY THREE in the morning. Lucas couldn't sleep, and he didn't want to just lay awake, so he made the perhaps questionable decision to go for a walk. He followed the pathway lights across the hotel's wide lawn. All the chairs had been secured for the windy weather—he'd made sure of that. The wind was whipping around him. He zipped up the sweatshirt he'd put on over his t-shirt as he headed towards the water.

He looked both ways out of habit when he got to Shore Road. Of course no one was out. He crossed the street and started down the hotel's long dock jutting into Shelter Island Sound. It was windy, but the water wasn't too wild. Of course, they were a little more protected back here in the sound, although Gardiners Bay and the open ocean were just around the other side of the island.

When he got to the end of the pier, he sat down on the wooden planks and let his legs dangle. He leaned forward slightly, gripping the edge of the decking with his hands, and looked out into the inky night. There were thick clouds blocking any moonlight. He listened to the sound of the water sloshing around the pilings below him. He gazed at the lights on the buildings in the distance across the sound.

His thoughts drifted—as they so often did—back to Cape May. It was his sweetest form of self-torture to indulge in thoughts of what she might be doing now. It had been unbearable when he first came. He was nearly too distracted to even do his job. But he had forced himself to compartmentalize—throw himself headlong into work, learning as much as he could and doing the best possible job he could to keep his mind off all things Kaya. First thing in the morning and last thing at night, though, he let his mind thoroughly drown in thoughts of her.

Mostly it worked, but of course not perfectly. He'd hear a song, or think of something he wanted to tell her. He'd see people take out kayaks and he thought of her. He'd see a corn and bean salad on the menu and thought of her. And then he'd be right back by her side in his mind.

At first, unwilling to accept that he still couldn't reach her, he'd call her. Not every day, but often. Once in the morning and once at night, during his indulged Kaya daydream time. He thought that if he kept up this sort of cadence, he might wear her down. She might change her mind and realize he was still here for her, thinking about her, loving her.

Pathetic. Lucas shook his head. He'd been delusional to think that had done anything but hassle her. She set her boundary—a very hard boundary. And he had proceeded to do the worst thing possible—the thing he promised himself he'd never do—fail to be helpful to her. He'd done the opposite. He caused her harm—once by leaving her—which, to be fair, he *had* to do unless he wanted to throw his life's work away. But then he crossed that boundary over and over every time he called her. What had he been thinking? Every call was probably like a stab to her, and he'd been wielding the knife.

He could still think about her, though, and right now, in the middle of the night, he let his mind run wild. His heart twisted thinking about the hurricane and whether she was alone. He'd looked at the weather and news coming out of Cape May about an hour ago. It looked like it wasn't going to be too bad, but you never knew. And her house was right at the dunes.

Every fiber of his being wanted to be with her. He wanted to snuggle with her in the dark and listen to the wind. To cocoon her in his arms and run his hands through her curls. To slowly take off her clothes, kiss his way down her body, and bury his head in...*damn* maybe he was letting his mind get a little too far out of safety. He reached down and adjusted himself through his sweats.

Lucas hung his head in the dark. *I've failed her*.

Kaya

AUTUMN WAS KAYA'S FAVORITE season. Growing up in upstate New York, falls were something special. The foliage along the Hudson valley, the apples, the cold that sneaked into the air, making everything crisper, brighter. She'd never had an autumn in Cape May, though. One year, they all met at Point Taken for Thanksgiving, which was a lot of fun. It was the first year after they'd bought the house, and Thanksgiving wouldn't be the same without Aunt Peggy, so they tried the cottage. In late November, it felt more like winter.

But here, in late October, Kaya felt autumn all around. She relished her bike rides and runs. Lynne came down for a weekend and they explored other towns' orchards and farmers' markets, as well as the back patio of Cape May Winery, adorned with fall décor.

It was still warm enough to sit on the beach... "sweatshirt weather" they called it growing up. The King Eddy's job was finished for the season, but she still went to town some days to wander Washington Mall, now with the lampposts decorated with dried cornstalks and pumpkins at their bases.

She wanted to throw herself into enjoying it all, and often, she could, but one morning she woke up and checked the clock. 3:26 a.m. She wasn't sure why she was awake and her brain was whirring, and then it hit her. The one-year anniversary of her father's death. It had snuck up on her, being in a different place, a world away. She picked up her phone. She knew Callie put her phone on DND when she went to sleep, so she wouldn't wake her if she texted. Kaya sent her a single heart. She put her phone back down and laid awake for a while with her thoughts. *Hi Dad. I don't think any of us thought I'd be right here right now, but I...do love it here. It's not perfect, there's some...shit that's happened...but I want to thank you for Point Taken...and for...watching over me. And I hope you and Mom are happy, wherever you are.*

She closed her eyes and took a deep breath. She picked up her phone to confirm her alarm for tomorrow was set and saw that she had a new message. From Callie. A single heart.

Kaya

ONE PARTICULARLY PRETTY AFTERNOON, Kaya was finishing up some work at Exit Zero and found herself gazing out the window, thinking the autumn was calling her. Time to end for the day and get out there. Sloane came out of her office and dropped into a chair beside Kaya, following her gaze towards the window and a tree just outside, with leaves in vibrant red and rust colors.

"Pretty out there today. This place really shows off in the fall," Sloane observed.

"It *does*," agrees Kaya, with a sigh, rubbing her hands down her thighs over the denim of her jeans.

"Vance and I are having a firepit tonight. You should come," said Sloane.

Kaya turned to look at her. "Really?"

"Yes," said Sloane with a smile. "Kinda a last-minute decision because the weather is perfect and there's not a lot of wind."

"Will there be a lot of people?" Kaya asked, with a slight hesitation. As an introvert, she didn't love large gatherings where she didn't know anyone. It was a little nerve-wracking. But the allure of the firepit called to her.

"No," said Sloane, "but Mateo and his boyfriend are supposed to come, so you'll know them. And I think the Nevilles too."

"Oh!" said Kaya at the mention of Tess and Gerry. "Maybe I can ride with them."

Sloane smiled. "Great idea. They know where I live."

"Can I bring anything?" she asked.

"Nothing but yourself. We'll have wine and s'mores and snacks. Starting around eight."

"Thank you," Kaya said, "for inviting me."

Sloane looked at her for a minute, her brown eyes warm. "We would love to have you. I know you're good on your own, but I also think it's nice, sometimes, to be with friends."

Kaya held Sloane's gaze. She felt so...seen. Connected. "It is," agreed Kaya.

On her way home from work, she stopped at the General Store and asked Tess if they could carpool, to which Tess enthusiastically agreed. Kaya bought a bottle of wine from the Store to take to the Spencers.

Later that evening, when they were heading back to the Point, Kaya found herself in the back of the Neville's SUV, reflecting on how nice it was. To just be easy among people, even though she knew only some of them, but in a beautiful backyard, in perfect fall sweatshirt weather, drinking wine, laughing, gazing at a lively, leaping campfire, and the bay beyond. She could listen to the conversations and only jump in if she felt like it. The evening was lovely.

Mateo's boyfriend, Michael, was a fellow introvert and wound up sitting next to Kaya. She enjoyed getting to know him better *and* passing comfortable silence beside him.

When the Nevilles dropped her off at Point Taken, she was feeling like her heart was a little more bright than it had been in a while. "Thank you," she said, getting out of their car. "I really appreciate the ride."

"Of course," said Tess, rolling down the window. "It was so fun to be with you in the wild."

Kaya laughed. "Indeed!" she said, and waved goodbye.

Kaya jogged up the outside stairs and let herself in. She climbed to the top level and went out on the deck. She listened to the crashing of the waves in the darkness. She took out her phone. She opened Instagram to see if any of her friends had posted anything interesting. She wasn't a big poster on social media, but she liked to see what her friends were up to.

She "liked" a story from Alexis of a video of a three-legged dog at the clinic jumping for treats. She "liked" a reel from Melanie of a dinner out with friends, and a post from Vanessa of her sunset over the bay. She knew Vanessa was still here but had found a new place in DC and would move back there soon. They had made a plan for calls or facetimes, and Kaya meditated most mornings to get ahead of the panic. It seemed to be working.

Kaya scrolled and was about to put her phone away when she froze and her breath hitched.

Lucas. Her heart felt a jolt.

Lucas was also not active in posting on social media, but this post was from Cape Resorts. It showed a confident, *handsome* Lucas standing in front of the Long Island property. He was at a door decorated tastefully with gourds and mums at its base, with one hand holding the door open in a welcoming gesture, with the other arm relaxed by his side. The post was highlighting him as Assistant GM, talking about his commitment to customers and strong representation of the Cape Resorts family.

He looked *exceptional.* Her pulse picked up. He was wearing a steely blue suit with a subtle windowpane pattern, with a dress shirt in the palest blue, open at the collar, no tie. The fit of his suit was perfect. His hair was fantastic. But she enlarged and examined the photo and observed that his smile didn't reach his eyes.

Same here, Lucas.

She peered at the photo. *He's there.* She reflected that when he left, to her, it was like he died. She didn't think about where he was and what he was doing now. He was just in a state of *gone.* She thought of him in memories, like how it felt when he held her—his mouth, his arms, all of him. His hand on the small of her back or wound in her hair. His smile. The smell of his aftershave. But all of it in the past. And yet, now, there he was. In the present. Today.

Kaya checked on her heart—literally, placed her hand over it, and looked out at the darkness. She went back inside and showered the campfire smoke out of her hair. She pulled on pajama pants and a light shirt, turned off the light and crawled under the covers. She laid on her side in the dark, and gently let herself think, for the first time since he left, about where he might be *right now*, and what he might be thinking about, and whether it might be her. She fell into a deep sleep.

Kaya

ONE BREEZY AFTERNOON IN November, Kaya showed up at the Wawa parking lot to meet Alexis for a run. The wind blew thick, puffy, white clouds across the deep blue sky, so the sun came and went. She zipped up her vest. In her peripheral vision, she saw a man approaching her. She glanced and clocked his appearance—expensive Barbour jacket, blonde hair slicked with enough product that it barely moved in the wind. Aviators.

"The business writer?" he said, slowing down in front of her. It was less a greeting, and almost like an accusation. "Andre's girl?" Kaya flinched involuntarily. She knew Lucas had nothing good to say about Tripp, and she felt even more exposed.

"Hi, Tripp, yes, it's Kaya Morgan. Nice to see you again," she said robotically.

He propped his sunglasses atop his head. His eyes narrowed. A light shiver rippled through her. "Seen him?" Tripp tossed off casually.

"No," Kaya responded. She really didn't want to be discussing Lucas with Tripp MacFarlane.

"Probably just as well," continued Tripp as he made no attempt to cover his looking her up and down. "You wouldn't want a front row seat to all the models and other rich girls out in the Hamptons, and the way they throw themselves at...shiny objects. Well, see you around," he said as he turned and strode over to his Range Rover and drove away. A sick feeling roiled in her stomach.

Ignore him. She closed her eyes, leaned against her car, and turned her face up into the cold breeze. She took a few deep, steadying breaths. *Innnnnnn and outttttt.* She willed herself to push the interaction with Tripp out of her mind.

"What are you thinking about?" asked Alexis, walking up to Kaya. Kaya opened her eyes and looked at Alexis. She smiled.

"Hat or no hat?" asked Kaya, cocking her head and holding out her knit beanie.

"I say hat. You're usually cold, there's wind, and if you get hot, you can always put it in your pocket."

"Yes, brilliant. Of course you're right," laughed Kaya. They started out down Pittsburgh towards the ocean. They jogged for a while in silence.

"You're quiet," observed Alexis.

"Am I?" said Kaya. "I ran into someone I know in the parking lot before you got there. But until then, I'd not said anything out loud to anyone yet today, so I really can't gauge properly," she concluded with a laugh.

"Really?" laughed Alexis. "You haven't talked to anyone? It's like, almost two o'clock. I have talked to Amy, about five thousand clients and all my co-workers, not to mention allllll the animals."

"I'm sure," said Kaya, smiling.

"Is that unusual?" Alexis asked after a minute. "To go all day and not talk to anyone?"

"Not necessarily. I mean in season it never happens. But now..." they were both starting to breathe more heavily as they warmed up. "...sometimes I'm alone at Exit Zero, or I do what I need to do from home, like today. And sometimes...sometimes I go to the General Store or something for coffee, and if I do that, I'll see Tess or Gerry. But if I don't...like, I didn't this morning...there's no reason to talk."

"Huh," said Alexis, shaking her head. "I just cannot imagine that. Like, even if I'm not at work or not with Amy, I always at least say good morning and small talk with my roommate. And you know me, I freaking talk to everyone. I say hi to all the neighbors' dogs. I learned this morning that the barista who made my chai is working a double shift today and also likes chai."

"Oh my God, Lex, that is so you," laughed Kaya.

"Yeah...but you don't mind being on your own, right?"

"Not only do I not mind," Kaya answered, "I rather like it. I mean, if I were a different type of person, I'm not sure I could have moved down here and made it work." They got to Beach Ave and turned right towards downtown. The wind was now fully against them. "Oof," breathed Kaya into the gust. "Don't get me wrong, it's not that I don't like people—I do! I just don't mind being by myself for stretches."

"What do you do? When you're alone?"

Kaya shrugged. "This...? I mean, I jog, or walk, or bike. I write. I read. I do projects around the house. I watch stuff on TV, listen to podcasts...like everyone else? And I like to look at recipes and cook and stuff."

"Makes sense. I do those things too, but I like doing them with other people."

"And I don't *mind* doing them with other people," Kaya responded. "As long as they aren't annoying people," she said with a laugh. "In fact, at this point, I prefer running with you than alone," she said, smiling sideways at Alexis.

"That's cool because I prefer it too," Alexis said, smiling back.

Kaya

FOR HER BIRTHDAY THE previous July, Juan had given Callie a gift certificate to the spa at Congress Hall. Before they left Cape May last August, Callie had pressed it into Kaya's hand.

"But this is for you," Kaya protested. "Juan wanted you to use it."

"Yes," said Callie, "but there will be time for that another year. I don't want to do it while I'm pregnant, and who knows exactly when I'll be back. You use it. I have a vested interest in Auntie Kaya's self-care." Kaya hugged her in thanks.

It was December before she got around to making an appointment. She figured she'd treat herself for making it a year. She loved Congress Hall decorated for the holidays. The massage was fantastic, and she made her way out from the spa, relaxed. She had on yoga pants, a sweater, and her hair up in a bun. She loved the feeling after a massage of her skin soft with spa lotion, so she always waited until she got home to shower. She was blissed out as she passed through the double doors from the spa back into the main hotel. She noticed a slender woman with thick grey hair cut in a severe bob approaching her. The woman was probably in her sixties and wearing a knit, cranberry-colored St. Johns shift dress, tailored perfectly, with gold button accents, and nude Louboutin pumps with small gold grommets.

Kaya never knew much about fashion or high-end clothes, but Lynne loved this stuff, and used to giddily point out certain brands on fancy women they encountered at various work and charity events. She would cheerfully clock shoes that neither of them could ever afford, but to which Lynne aspired someday.

Even if Kaya couldn't name the brand of the jewelry on this woman, the effect was probably the intended one. This woman was in charge. This woman owned the place. Kaya was suddenly very self-conscious.

The woman looked directly at Kaya and stopped just short of her. "Miss Morgan?" the woman asked.

"Yes?" Kaya replied, startled.

"Diane MacFarlane."

Okay, she literally *owns the place.*

"Pleasure to meet you," Kaya recovered, trying to sort out what was going on here. "Yes, I'm Kaya Morgan."

"I have been hoping to meet you. I took the liberty of asking to be alerted if you ever booked in at one of our properties." Kaya was so confused. "Walk with me," said Diane. They start down the long colonnade of shops between the spa and the lobby. Diane walked at a refined speed—fast enough to be with purpose, but not so fast to be uncivilized. Kaya threw her bag over her shoulder and fell into step.

"I believe you know Mr. Andre," said Diane.

Kaya's stomach plummeted and her eyes got wide. *Oh God what's happened to Lucas.* "Is Lucas okay?" she asked.

If Diane registered Kaya's anxiety, she didn't let it show. "Of course. Mr. Andre is quite excellent," she answered smoothly. *This is one serious ice queen.* "He's doing superb work at the Shelter Island properties and we are very much looking forward to him joining our management group."

Kaya stayed quiet because she wasn't sure what to say. Diane picked up her own conversation. "I have had the pleasure of working closely with Mr. Andre at times this fall. As I understand it, the two of you have or had some sort of relationship." *What the heck?*

Diane continued, "I do not wish to know specifics, but I resolved that if I had an opportunity to meet you, I would say this: Lucas Andre is a treasure. He is like another son to me. He is smart, efficient, has good technical training. But mostly he has, built into his character, an innate desire to help people. This is the secret to success in hospitality, and he's extraordinarily well-suited.

"He's far too professional to let any personal challenges affect his work, but the Mr. Andre currently at Shelter Island is a shadow of the one we normally know. I gather that he is out of sorts because he specifically wants to be of help to *you*, and has not been allowed to do so." They came to stop, near the base of the grand staircase in the lobby, but out of earshot of the desk and bell stand.

"Now, I will state again that I have no wish to know the specifics, but I will finish by saying that if I were the one with the power to restore the spirit of a man as lovely as Lucas Andre, I would wield it. You have this power." Kaya stared at her, mouth slightly agape.

"I don't expect a response, Miss Morgan, as I'm sure you can keep your own counsel. It was lovely to meet you and I hope you enjoyed the spa." Diane turned and started up the stairs.

"Mrs. MacFarlane?" Kaya called. Diane stopped and turned halfway, raising a single eyebrow in response. "Is Lucas coming back?"

"Of course," Diane replied. "Right after the new year." She turned and continued her ascent of the staircase, out of view.

Lucas

"Merry Christmas, bro," Lucas heard Tim say through the phone. Lucas was walking back to his office after checking in with the front desk team.

"Merry Christmas yourself," he answered. "Are you working?"

"Sort of," said Tim. "I have no idea if we'll get any emergency calls, but I'm on duty, so I'm going out if we do. Otherwise, it's not a work day, so I'm bored."

"What a compliment," said Lucas, laughing. "So happy to be your remedy for boredom."

"I mean, and I haven't talked to you in a while," Tim also laughed. "Are you in Philadelphia?"

"I am not. I'm still up on Long Island. I probably could have asked to have time off, but I'm almost done with this gig. I want to finish strong, and I want to support the staff who have to work today."

"And it's a good excuse to avoid your parents."

"That too," Lucas admitted. "Dad wasn't happy about it. I'm sure I haven't heard the last of that, either. I don't know if I made the right choice."

"Dude, I have known you a very long time, so I'm gonna be straight. Your dad's an asshole and I absolutely hate how he's broken you. And your mom is a perfectly nice person, but she doesn't really stand up for you. I'm actually *glad* you're not there."

"I see we're decking the halls with radical truth this year," Lucas muttered as he dropped into his desk chair.

"Tell me I'm wrong."

"Yeah, no, you're not." Lucas dragged a hand down his face.

"You know you're the best person I know, right?"

"Stop it, Tim. I don't need a Christmas pep talk."

"I'm serious, though. I know you think your inclinations to be helpful are pathological and maybe in certain situations they are. Certainly when you were chasing the approval of the narcissist that is your father they were. I'm glad you're turning that corner..."

"Oh, am I?" Lucas said, laughing through his nose.

"Well, okay, right, but I feel like you have fewer fucks to give than you used to. And what you've done for me, as my friend, has been invaluable."

Lucas stood up and walked to his window. "What do you mean?" he asked slowly.

"Seriously?" Tim responded. Lucas didn't reply. "You're the only reason I survived my parent's divorce."

"No, come on. I mean, I know it was a tough time for you..."

"Luke, stop. You were the only one who stayed with me during that time to know how painful it was. My mother was dealing with her own shit. I felt so rejected by my father when he left, and you were the one who stayed—who made me feel like I mattered."

Lucas was quiet, absorbing his best friend's words. "We were only sixteen," he said finally. "I hated seeing you go through that."

"I thought about taking my own life."

"Shit, Tim, I didn't know that." Lucas closed his eyes and pinched the bridge of his nose. He thought back to that year and how withdrawn Tim had been. Lucas had tried to just be around as much as he could. But he had no idea the depths of what Tim had been going through.

"I know. I didn't tell you. But in the darkest moments when I thought about it, I'd think 'what would Lucas do?' and it was to get up, go out, help someone. Reach outside yourself. That's your fucking superpower, dude. And it saved me."

Lucas exhaled. "I had no idea."

"Well, it mattered a lot to me—and I'll never forget it." They were both quiet for another minute. Lucas knew Tim was still there because he could hear him breathing. Lucas felt tears welling in his eyes. He didn't trust his voice not to shake and he couldn't think of a single thing to say. He had no idea he'd had that kind of impact on his friend. He had certainly never thought of his tendencies as a super-power. He'd always thought of it as a liability. This realization did something to his heart.

Tim spoke again. "Hey, are you coming home soon?"

Lucas looked out the window at the shimmering water of the Sound. "Yeah, right after the new year. Let's get a beer."

"Bet. So, anyway, Merry Christmas. Love you, brother."

"Love you too."

Kaya

KAYA WENT TO PROVIDENCE to spend Christmas with Callie and Juan. Callie was about five months' along and feeling really good, but Kaya was frankly happy for an excuse for a break. With the exception of her one trip to Washington to move, she hadn't left southern New Jersey since she got to the Point over a year ago. She loved having visitors, working, and making new friends, but she was finding herself happy to let her sister and brother-in-law do the entertaining. Plus, she figured they'd be starting new traditions, since next year, there would be a new little human celebrating his or her first Christmas in the family.

The day after Christmas, Callie and Kaya were strolling along the canal in downtown Providence. They had just come out of a coffee shop, and Kaya was enjoying the treat of a full-syrup peppermint mocha.

"Hey," said Callie, sipping on her decaf latte, "how's everything down there, really? It's been about a year now."

"Yeah," responded Kaya. "I am really glad to be up here with you. Thank you for having me. I realized I haven't left Cape May at all, and I was starting to feel...just recently...sort of, I don't know, jumpy. Restless."

"What do you think that's about?" They walked a little further and by some unspoken sister consensus, sat down on a bench facing the canal.

Kaya shrugged and zipped her jacket up higher. "Probably a lot of things, like is it okay to have an aimless career, how long can I hold out there this way...but also probably...if I'm being honest...Lucas." She put it out there. Callie said nothing but reached out and lightly brushed her sister's forearm.

"Hey, do you remember that last time we went out to lunch with Mom?" Kaya, asked, eyes cast out in the distance.

Callie swiveled towards Kaya, eyebrows raised. "Just you, me, and her? At that Irish pub?"

"Yeah, Timothy Patrick's," Kaya nodded. "Do you remember how I asked her if she was afraid to die?"

"Yeah, I remember," Callie responded softly. "And she said no. She said she wasn't afraid, she was just sad that she was going to miss everything we would become, what we would accomplish."

"The children we'd have," added Kaya turning to look at her sister with a smile.

"The children we'd have," Callie confirmed, absently rubbing her belly and returning the smile, even as a tear escaped from her eye and rolled down her cheek. "We held hands and we all cried, right there in the pub. She died just a couple months later." She paused, searching Kaya's eyes. "Where is this coming from, Kay?" she asked gently.

Kaya shrugged, took a sip of her mocha, and turned her face to look back into the distance. "Life is short," she offered. "At first, when I shut down and threw Lucas out, when I thought I had sectioned him right out of my mind and heart, it was easy enough to go about my life. I mean, it wasn't *easy*, but I sort of put him away. He was...just...gone to me." She paused and pulled her knit hat down a little. She took another sip of her mocha.

After a moment, Callie asked, "But that's changed?" She pulled a tissue out of her coat pocket and dabbed at her nose.

"That's changed," Kaya confirmed. "I obviously spend a lot of time alone and I think about this. Over the last couple of months, it's like my heart had been taken away...or...or stored away and now...little by little it's been uncovered...or, come back...I know that doesn't make any sense. I sound crazy," she added hastily.

But in hindsight, she realized how it happened, slowly. When Callie had come to visit and insisted on meeting all of Kaya's friends, it reminded Kaya that there were lots of people coming into and burrowing into her life. People didn't just leave, they came, too. Friends, co-workers, the best running buddy a girl could want. People in Cape

May who looked out for her, cared about her. The anticipation of a precious, little addition to a family that in recent years had just had subtractions. She had thought about all her DC friends who stayed in constant touch—the visits, but also the texts, the calls, the emails. She thought about Vanessa and what a lightning bolt that had been. And Diane MacFarlane. *Huh.* You just never knew where help getting your emotional shit in order was going to come from.

"It doesn't sound crazy," said Callie gently, jerking Kaya out of her reverie. "It just sounds like you don't want Lucas 'gone' to you anymore."

"No," replied Kaya with a deep sigh, still gazing out into the distance. "I really, *really* don't." Kaya turned and looked into her sister's eyes. "He's here. He's alive, somewhere on this earth. In fact, if we had a private plane I could probably get to him in a quick twenty minutes over Long Island Sound. I've been an idiot." She remembered how, just days ago on the plane to Providence, she had taken her phone out of her bag, pulled up the text thread, and stared at it for some time, until the plane started its descent.

when, Kaya. I promise you

She sighed again and smiled weakly at Callie. Without realizing it, she saw she had clutched her mittened hand over her heart.

"I think it's good that you're letting yourself feel these things again, don't you?" asked Callie, as she searched Kaya's eyes.

"Yes..." replied Kaya slowly. "But with those feelings come...anxiety, I guess. I'm really scared. Like, does he hate me? He *should*. He did nothing to deserve what I did to him. He took a normal, short-term job opportunity—one I actually want for him because it helps him accomplish his goals—and I punished him for it because of my issues. If he does come back, will he be able to forgive me? And even if he does, I mean, he could be seeing someone else. This guy he works with talked about all the, like, models and fancy people in the Hamptons. Sometimes I can't get the image of him with someone else out of my head. Or, he might just not want me anymore..." Kaya's voice caught at the end and her eyes stung.

"I think you need to cut yourself some slack," replied Callie. "I feel like, as Dad used to say, you've done the best you could with the cards you held at the time." They were both quiet for a minute.

"That's nice of you to say," Kaya said quietly. "Because you could have slung over an 'I told you so' and it would not have been even remotely misplaced."

Callie chuckled softly. "Are you going to call him?" she asked gently.

"No," Kaya said quickly, regaining her composure. "Too much has happened, too much time has gone by. I can't reach out now. Like, what would I even say? I can't just text now. Like, '*hey*' would be ridiculous. There is...too much to say...and I feel like...like it needs to be in person now. I really fucked up. I can't try to fix this over the phone or text."

"So, you're just going to…"

"I'm going to have a nice time here with you," said Kaya resolutely, setting her chin and looking her sister squarely. "Then I'll go back and…figure it out."

Callie looked quietly at her sister for a minute, until the edges of her lips quirked up. "I know you will," she said softly.

Kaya

ON THE SHORT FLIGHT from Providence back to Philadelphia, Kaya thought about the good times they had over the holiday. They stayed up until midnight on New Year's Eve, drinking champagne (or sparkling cider), and getting a wee bit sentimental.

"It's gonna be such a big year," Callie said, rubbing her just-showing belly. "But you know, I think it's gonna be big for you too. This is *your* year. Last year was just re-setting your life. Now it's time to live it!"

Kaya laughed. "Whatever you say, sis."

"I'm serious! I feel these things."

"Well, I'll drink to that!"

She landed in Philadelphia, made her way to the parking garage and drove back to the Point. It was quiet.

Three days dragged by. She made some progress on Sloane's next book projects and went into the office while it was still quiet and empty to start organizing the data for the next season's *Cool Cape May*. She tried to sort out how she'd know if Lucas came back. She couldn't stalk the Cape Resort properties because he would be fully management now—gone are the days of his being a barista or concierge.

With each passing day, she got more restless. How had she been so content keeping only her own company just a year ago? She did *not* want him gone to her anymore. She was desperate for him to come back so she could just get *started* apologizing...repairing...*hopefully*. Or if that wasn't going to be possible, then she wanted just to know that she had to get on with...rebuilding her life without him? *Oh God what have you done, Kaya?*

Her sleep hygiene, while never strong, was totally shot to hell. She was so anxious to get a read on where his heart was. Could he forgive her? How could she fix this? Would she be able to? She didn't know, but the desperation to try was starting to drive her wild, especially when tossing and turning through the long winter nights.

One late evening at the end of the first week in January, it was uncharacteristically, bitterly cold. She shivered as she jumped into her car. She was up in Rio Grande where she'd found a pharmacy with late hours to pick up a prescription she needed. She was making her way back down the 109 into town. She was only wearing a fleece for her outer layer, having underestimated the cold tonight. She came over the bridge, and like every time she drove by his condo, he flitted across her mind. She had just passed it, though, when light caught her eye.

Wait.

She turned left and doubled back around the circle, back over the Spicer Creek bridge to check what she thought she had seen. There *were* lights on in Lucas' condo. She turned left onto Wilson Drive and parked.

Her heart was racing as she shifted the car into park. The thought of being so close to him—if he was really in there—was overwhelming. She closed her eyes remembering his touch, his smile, how he held her. *Enough.* He might hate her, he might not forgive her, but one way or another she had to know. She should probably have made a plan but, well, she was here now.

She got out and jogged up to his building, the icy wind cutting at her. Her heart was pounding as she ran up the first flight of stairs and then the second. She tripped on a step but caught herself on the railing. She was out of breath, and before she could tell herself not to, she rang his bell. She felt like her heart was going to pound right out of her chest.

The door opened. *Lucas.*

His eyes went wide at the sight of her. They said nothing, but he felt the freezing air slicing in, so he opened the door and stepped aside so she could come in from the cold. Her cheeks were bracing. Her hair was most certainly a wild tangle of curls. She looked up at him in awe, like seeing someone come back from the dead.

His hair was shorter but still sitting in thick waves. He was wearing jeans, a t shirt and a pullover Flying Fish sweatshirt, and his feet were bare. He had maybe a day's worth of stubble across his jaw. He was so gorgeous it took her breath away.

"You're back," she said finally breaking the silence, rubbing her hands together rapidly to warm them.

"As I said," he replied, and she tracked a note of sadness in his voice.

Please, God. Don't let it be too late.

"What are you doing here, Kaya?" he asked quietly.

"I saw the lights on. I wanted to see you," she replied honestly. He held out his hands, palms up, as if to say, *here I am.* "I don't think there's any way I can make it up to you for what I've done, but I want to try," she said.

"You don't need to do that," he replied, shoving his hands into the pockets of his jeans. His blue-grey eyes were unreadable but didn't shy away from looking straight into hers.

"I think I do. I'm so ashamed of what I did to us—to you—and you didn't deserve it. It was awful of me."

"No need to apologize for anything," he replied.

"I disagree. It's taken me some time, and a lot of work," she said, "but I realized I missed you...so much...and I wanted to see you. Even though I don't deserve to." He still gave nothing away on his face.

"I appreciate that," said Lucas quietly, "but I think we know we're not right for each other." Kaya stepped back like she'd been pushed. Her eyes darted between his.

"Is there someone else?" she breathed.

"What? No!" he stammered. Both their chests rose and fell. The silence hung between them. "No. Kaya," he said more gently. "There is only you."

"So, we are then," she said.

"Are what?"

"We *are* right for each other," she said quietly. He said nothing. She was panicking inside. *Shit this wasn't working.* She was desperate. She *needed* to pull him back to her. Maybe if she could just touch him again—connect with him. She stepped to him and put a palm against his chest. He closed his eyes, motionless. She wound the other arm around his waist, snaking it between his torso and his arm with the hand still in his pocket. "I know there is a lot to talk about, and I want to do that...and I have a lot— so much—to make up for," she said. "But right now, can we just...be together?" She was flailing and she knew it, but she had to try everything she could.

He said nothing, perfectly still, and his eyes stayed closed. She was desperate to reach him. She used both of her hands to draw one of his out of his pocket. It was warm. She turned the palm up and kissed it, softly. He opened his eyes and watched her. There was a sadness in his eyes, she thought. Her heart keened. She kissed his palm again, slower, and rubbed her fingers against his hand.

When she looked up again, his eyes were hooded and darkening grey.

"I need you, Lucas," she whispered. Still holding his hand, she started to move towards the stairs. *Please come with me*, she prayed. She paused, their arms outstretched, looking at him. His jaw worked, and so much was going on behind his eyes, but she couldn't read it. She squeezed his hand. *"Please,"* she begged. After what felt like an eternity, he took a step towards her, towards the stairs.

Lucas

THEY WALKED, HAND-IN-hand into his room. It was dim since the blinds were mostly closed. She dropped his hand and they stood, looking at each other. Slowly, she took off her fleece and threw it on a chair. He didn't move. She kicked off her shoes and socks. He didn't move. His heart thudded. It was so surreal it was like a dream. Of course he knew he was coming back to the place where she was. But he hadn't expected her to come find him— to show up here, so soon.

He wasn't prepared for the pleading in her voice. He wasn't prepared to be standing in this room where they'd been so happy together, with her staring into his eyes like she was right now.

She took a step towards him and pulled her shirt off, tossing it on top of the fleece. *Goddamn.* His let his gaze slip briefly to the rise and fall of her breathing. She took another step closer so there were only inches between them. And then she stopped. There was a deep plaintiveness in her eyes, but he watched her stay perfectly still. *Was it his move now?*

He tried to summon his thoughts, his arguments, the logic he believed he'd so expertly woven for himself over the last four and a half months. But his mind was blank. All he could feel was the tug of this woman.

Slowly, as if in a trance, Lucas brought his hands up to her face. The instant his hands made contact with her skin, it was like a dam broke. Lucas grabbed her face between his hands and kissed her, warm, searing. A torrent of feeling *alive* flooded through him as she responded to the kiss. She clutched his torso. He brought his hands off her face and dropped to her back. He skimmed them down to the backs of her hips and lifted her, hiking her up around his waist. She gasped, tightened the grip with her thighs and threw her arms around his neck. He carried her to his bed and laid her down on her back. With one motion, his shirt and sweatshirt were gone, and he watched her shrug off her bra.

There was nothing restrained now. Clothes were shed. It was hands and mouths and hips and need. She was real and she was in his arms.

Kaya

SHE AWOKE REALIZING SHE'D slept. Hard. There was cold, milky early morning light coming in through the slight openings in Lucas' blinds. She was here. He was here. He was back. She looked at one of his hands, draped on the pillow, and flushed thinking about the deftness of those hands.

She eased out from under the sheets. She took her clothes into the bathroom, peed, and put on her jeans and shirt. She brushed her teeth with her own toothbrush that was still where she kept it when she brought it here last summer. She tiptoed downstairs and made coffee. She tossed her fleece on a chair and grabbed one of Lucas' sweatshirts hanging by the door. It was too big on her, but she breathed in the smell of him and smiled.

The sex had been...well. They hadn't talked much at all. It had been instinctual, desperate...primal almost. Her cheeks flushed as she thought about how natural and *good* it felt to be with him again. Like she was clawing him back into her heart and she hadn't been able to stop.

She poured the coffee and was looking out at the creek when she heard him come down. He froze at the sight of her, taking it all in, her standing with the coffee, wearing his sweatshirt, in his living room. After a beat, he came down the last two steps. He was wearing socks, sweatpants, and his hoodie from last night.

"You're still here," he said, confused. The smile that had been on her face dropped away.

"Yes, of course...?" she started.

"I just..." he stammered quietly.

"Lucas," she said, "I know I have work to do to get you to trust me again, but you know that I would never hit-and-run."

"Of course," he said, rubbing the back of his neck with his hand. "That's not what I meant. It's just that last night was..." he trailed off.

"...amazing?" she supplied, walking a few steps towards where he stood.

He looked at her. "It...it felt so good, *you* felt so good...but...it was...a...a mistake."

She stared at him, unblinking. "Explain," she ground out.

He dragged his hand down his face. "I'm not good for you," he said, looking pained.

"Disagree," she shot back.

"You deserve better," he said.

"*I* deserve better?!" she said, her voice rising rapidly. "I literally took the purest love of the best man I've ever known and pushed it away. I left you adrift for *months*. If anyone should be throwing around 'you deserve better's', I'm pretty sure that person should be me!" She was flushed now. Kaya moved to the island and set down her mug, afraid there was a scenario where she wound up throwing it in frustration. He looked at her and put his hands in the pockets of his sweats.

"You should be *livid* with me!" Kaya went on, plowing into his silence. "You should be telling me that you can't trust someone who was so cold. Or that you don't understand why I did it. But you should *not* be telling *me* that *I* deserve better!"

"But I *do* understand," he said plaintively. "I knew what my leaving would do to you, and I couldn't...I couldn't help you when you needed it," he said, eyes dropping down.

"Only because I didn't let you!" she shouted. His eyes flew back up to hers. "I gave you zero chance to even try!"

"I...I am not sure I can forgive myself for hurting you...for...not being able to help you," moaned Lucas. Kaya turned towards the windows and ran her fingers through her crazy morning-hair curls. She spun back around to him. He was still rooted in place at the bottom of the stairs.

"Let me make sure I understand here," she said, voice still edged. "I have some shit baggage that you did absolutely nothing to cause. Through no fault of yours, and certainly no intention on your part—if anything, you had every intention of trying to do the *right* thing by me and my shit baggage—but I got triggered. At which point, I literally sent you away and locked you out of my life since August. *August*! If anyone's looking for forgiveness here, it should be this girl!" She jabbed both thumbs towards herself. He said nothing.

Her breathing was ragged and her heart was beating wildly. She closed her eyes and forced herself to take a big inhale, and exhale.

"Look, Lucas," she started again, trying to keep her voice calm, even as she felt so shaky. "I can't make you forgive yourself. Even as I know with every fiber of my being you have nothing to apologize for. I've learned enough through therapy to know that's your work to do. But if I understand your position here, you're saying you would rather us *not* be together than do whatever work you have to do."

"I don't know what I'm saying...only that I don't want to risk hurting you again," he said, holding her gaze, but saying nothing else.

She breathed a deep breath in, and out, shutting her eyes. "You're hurting me now." She opened her eyes and her voice came to a quieter pitch. "Do you not love me anymore?"

"No!" he shouted suddenly, his eyes sparked blue and fiery. She waited.

"I love you so much it drives me insane," he said, curling his hand to a fist over his heart. She blinked at him a few times.

"Then let's do the work, Lucas," she said, gently now.

"I'm not sure where we would even start," he said, with a tinge of sadness in his voice.

"Figure out what *you* need and tell me," she replied. "Whatever penance that in your mind you think you need to do, let's do it. And me, I'm going to try to get you to see yourself the way I see you. I will do whatever I can, every day, to help you understand that everything you are, and everything you do, is enough. I know my shutting you out made you feel that it wasn't, but it is. The help you give me, the care you show me, the love you shower on me...it's all enough. More than enough." Tears started rolling down her cheeks.

He looked at her helplessly, soundlessly.

"You said once you would fight for me," she implored. A spark charged through his eyes. His jaw worked.

"I have put you through hell," she said, her voice shaking slightly. "I hate that I did it. But I want you to know I've been doing the work. I'm working to better manage my issues. And it's been through the help of people close to me that it's been happening. You should have been one of those people all along, and I really, really want you to be one of them now. I don't ever want my life team to not include you. I love you. I need *you*. Please fight, if not for yourself, then for me."

They stared at each other. Her words and the emotion hung in the air between them. Something fired through Lucas' eyes. Suddenly, he turned, stepped into a pair of his sneakers that were by the door and walked out. As the door slammed, Kaya gasped. She physically doubled over, her hands hitting her knees, like he had sucked the air out of her when he left.

"No..." she whispered aloud, but felt paralyzed, like she was frozen to the spot.

She forced herself to breathe...deep breath in...and out...to be able to physically unclench. When she did, she stumbled to his door, threw it open and looked around wildly from his front deck. She ran over to the stairs but didn't see him. Where were her shoes? Shit - upstairs. She turned to go up and get them, but was hit with the futility...it was impossible to know which way he'd gone—and by the time she went and got her shoes... she slowly went back inside and closed the door.

This wasn't happening. He had every reason to be mad at her. But he...left? She grabbed her phone and texted him.

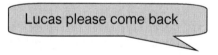

Lucas please come back

She heard the ping come from a charging station across the room. His phone was still here.

It was torture. She couldn't finish her coffee—the acid roiled in her stomach. She dumped it out and put her mug in the dishwasher. She went back upstairs, took a shower, combed out her hair, got re-dressed in her clothes, and went back downstairs, praying he'd be back. She looked around; he wasn't.

She sat down cross-legged in the middle of Lucas' living room floor, facing the creek. She tried to will the water to calm her. She thought about texting Callie. Or Alexis. But she was afraid. She knew it didn't make sense, but she thought if the next person she talked to wasn't Lucas, this whole thing might really be permanently broken.

He had to come back. He had to. What had he said? They weren't right for each other? But then there was last night, so on some level, he must still want her...? But then he said it was a mistake? She had no idea what was going on in his head and heart. She vacillated between being so angry at him for giving up and praying to a God she wasn't sure she believed in that he would come back. That, along with a healthy dose of cursing herself for driving him away in the first place.

After an hour, she realized she couldn't just stay there. If he was going to come back, he would have by now. She slowly got up, let herself out, and got in her car to drive home.

Lucas

LUCAS BOLTED DOWN HIS stairs and started sprinting. As fast as he could go. The cold air rushed into his lungs as he pumped his arms. He probably looked ridiculous, but he didn't care. All he could do was move. Anything to outrun the pain. He edged the marina and headed down Pittsburgh towards the ocean.

I love you. I need you. Please fight, if not for yourself, then for me.

He briefly squeezed his eyes closed and opened them again. He had dreamed of being with her again, loving her again, but he had promised himself he wouldn't. He *couldn't* risk hurting her again. But the pull had been so strong. He'd succumbed to a moment of vulnerability but it *had* to end there.

Lucas turned instinctively to do a loop to the Coast Guard base and back to Pittsburgh to continue towards the water. He wasn't really paying attention to the route; he just kept running. The pain was palpable. When he passed the main gate to the base, he thought about Tim being in there somewhere and promised himself he'd call him later today. He recalled all the surprising things

Tim said about how Lucas helped him through his dark times. That his "superpower" had saved Tim. Was he doing that now? Or was he causing more harm?

Why in the hell had he slept with her? *Well, he knew why.* Because he loved her with every fiber of his being and he struggled to deny her anything she wanted. But he needed to stop this now or he would risk hurting her again. Better to be out of her life than risk that. She'd survived over four months without him. She *said* she was doing better. *Leave it alone, Lucas.*

Unable to keep up the pace of the all-out sprint, without thinking about it, Lucas had slowed to a jog at his usual pace. He stopped when he got to Beach Ave to re-tie his sneaker that had come undone. He turned right and jogged along Beach.

Only because I didn't let you...I gave you zero chance to even try.

Oh, the irony. One of the things he had loved most about her was how clear she was about what she wanted and needed from him. All the pain of being apart was her boundary. She *had* shut him out. Never gave him a chance to love her from a distance—not that he'd stopped. He just hadn't been able to tell her. Lucas reached the boardwalk and crossed the street to climb the stairs up to it as he kept jogging.

And now she was saying she wanted him back. Could he really deny her that? Especially when he was still so in love with her? Wasn't his insistence not to be with her also hurting her? Which would it be? The certainty of hurting her now by denying her, versus the *potential* of hurting her in the future if they did get back together.

You're hurting me now.

He couldn't believe she asked if he was seeing anyone else, or if he still loved her. Did she really believe he would want anyone other than her? *Well, it was her own fault that she didn't know what he had been up to and if his feelings had changed*, he thought, and then immediately felt terrible for thinking it.

Kaya had done what she needed to do. She had a trauma response and acted the only way she could manage in that moment. He knew this.

He reached the end of the boardwalk at the cove. Without thinking about it, he kept jogging, onto the sand and along the water.

His planned strategy had made so much sense in the solitude of his suite on Shelter Island. But it was making very little sense here. Where she existed. Where he'd made love to her last night like his life depended on it. Where she was asking him to come back to her. Telling him she loved him. Telling him she needed him. Begging him to fight for her.

His calves were starting to burn from running on the sand. He dropped off the berm to the harder sand closer to the water as his feet kept pounding forward. Even in the cold air, he was sweating. His exhales were misting as he breathed.

It was useless. He had to give her whatever she asked for. He suddenly felt, deep in his core, that there was no way he was going to be able to deny her. And, he realized, he didn't want to. Yes, he feared hurting her again. But he also didn't want to hurt her now. She always told him what she needed, and she was doing it again now. And he wanted her. So badly. A life without her—impossible. He had to take this risk.

Lucas slowed to a stop and put his hands on the back of his head, breathing hard. He stared out at the ocean as his chest heaved. The waves crashing and receding. He wiped his sleeve across his forehead and dropped his hands to his hips. He hung his head. Finally, he turned around and looked up. The lighthouse. He'd run all the way to the Point.

Kaya

HER EYES WERE DRY and pricked like they wanted to tear up, and she drove home in a sort of trance. She made her way through town, which was empty at this early hour in January. She went down Sunset, onto Seagrove, and onto the Point. She felt like if she could just make it home, then she could let herself weep. The sobs were building in her stomach as she turned the corner and pulled into her drive.

She headed up the stairs to the door and when she looked up, there he was.

Lucas.

Sitting, breathing heavily, on the top step just outside the door. His arms rested on his knees. His head was hanging forward on his broad shoulders, but his gaze was fixed on her. She froze.

"How did you...how are you..."

"I ran."

"You *ran here*?"

"Well, I just started running. Anywhere. And I..." he gulped in a breath of air. "...wound up here." They stared at each other.

Kaya shook her head and willed herself to unfreeze. "You need water, and you're going to get a chill; let's get you inside." She bounded towards the door. He stood up, stepped aside for her to open the door and followed her upstairs. She threw her keys and pocketbook aside and grabbed a glass of water. She filled it and handed it to him. Then she backed away, watching him.

He leaned back against the sink like he had over a year ago, when he helped her with the Christmas tree, and gulped down the water. "Thank you," he said. She just nodded. She found it impossible to look away from him.

His breathing evened out. He carefully set down the glass. He looked up towards the ceiling and blinked. He locked back on her gaze for a beat, then closed the distance between them in three strides, and crushed her to him.

Kaya gasped in surprise and then buried her head against his chest, wrapped her arms around his waist, and exhaled in the solidness of him, the warmth of him, the *realness* of him. He tucked her head under his chin, and she felt sweat—or his tears maybe?—fall in her hair. She hugged him tighter.

"I'm sorry I'm sweaty," he whispered.

"There is no universe where I care about that right now," she whispered back.

She felt him lightly kiss the top of her head. She pulled back and looked up at him, keeping her arms around him. Lucas' gaze grew earnest. He reached up a hand and put it softly on her neck and cheek.

He rubbed her face with this thumb. "I do want to be among the people in your life. You have no idea," he said, his eyes darting back and forth between hers. "I want more than anything to be *the* person in your life."

Her heart leapt. The way he looked at her—there was no mistaking it. There was a warmth in his eyes she hadn't seen since before he left.

"You already are," she whispered. His face softened. "Can we re-start there? We can figure this out," she pleaded quietly. She hugged him a little tighter as she looked up at him. He parted his lips and slowly exhaled a breath.

"Okay."

"Okay?" She searched his eyes.

"Yes, okay," he answered. He exhaled a deep breath. "In the name of respecting your boundaries and trying to be helpful, I let you go," he said. She stayed perfectly still.

He took another breath, exhaled, and continued. "It was hell, Kaya." Her heart clenched again but she stayed quiet.

"But I did it because I told myself it was what you wanted and needed."

She nodded slightly and held on tighter to him. He continued to rub her face with his thumb. His other arm tightened against her back. "Please understand, though," he said, "that if we're doing this now, again...I will continue to try to respect your boundaries, but never again will I *ever* let you go."

A smile drove from inside her to the surface of her face. She couldn't help it. She could feel his heart beating against her chest.

"It's a deal?" he asked.

He wanted no other answer, nor did she have any other to give. She beamed at him. "Deal."

Epilogue—8 months later

Kaya

KAYA BLINKED SLEEP OUT of her eyes as she came upstairs.

"Heyyyyy," sang Callie softly.

"Good morning!" said Kaya, bending down to kiss the forehead of little Sofía Clare in Callie's arms. "And good morning to you," she cooed at the perfect little human. "Did you get any sleep?" she asked her sister.

"Some," said Callie, yawning. "I'm sorry if she woke you in the night."

"I didn't hear her," lied Kaya. They smiled at each other.

Kaya got her coffee and stepped out onto the deck. It was the typical warm of August, and a light breeze was coming off the ocean. She rested a hand on the railing, closed her eyes, and listened to the waves crashing on the shore. She heard the glass door open behind her. She felt strong arms come around her waist. She leaned back, relaxing against him. "Morning, baby," she heard Lucas' sleepy voice whisper against her ear. She placed a hand over his and smiled.

Later, as they were eating breakfast, Kaya looked around. She looked at the little diamond sparkling on her left hand. She recalled that warm day in early spring when they went kayaking, and deep in the stillness of the wetlands, Lucas pulled his kayak alongside hers and pulled out the ring. She'd never known what it felt like, until that moment, to be truly wanted, the power of someone saying they wanted to be your person, your family. And for it to be someone she loved so completely...it was almost overpowering. She remembered standing on her deck in the dark and whispering into the night, "I found someone to be buried with."

It wasn't perfect—nothing could ever be. But she and Lucas had both found therapists they liked, and they committed to each other that they would be honest when either of them was feeling triggered. It worked—enough of the time anyway. Enough that her heart knew it was safe with him—knew it now at its core. She was so happy.

She thought about how happy she was that Alexis and Amy got another dog. She thought about how good it felt to sit and have coffee the other day with Maureen when her old mentor visited Cape May...the relief Kaya felt at accepting the invitation. How it felt to let go of the fear and let people love you.

She looked at her niece. She ached with wishing her parents could be here. But she also thought about how full her life was, the five of them, plus all her friends and people who cared about her. She thought about trust, how much work it was, how scary it was, but what a gift it was. When her gaze swung towards Lucas, she found him looking at her. They smiled at each other. Her heart was whole.

Acknowledgements

Around January 2017, I realized I could only handle reading happy-ever-afters—a position that further solidified when the world shut down in March 2020. Wracked with the loneliness and anxiety of quarantine, immersed in romance novels, I realized I wanted to try to write one. The draft of *Whole in the Heart* came fast—like the story was writing itself. It took much longer, of course, for it to get here.

I love reading author's acknowledgements and am tickled to be writing mine, so here we go: To my editor, Meredith Bond, a huge thank you. I will always be grateful for the WRW crew and that meet-up at the library in Bethesda. I felt like I had something, but this wouldn't have happened without your encouragement. This gift you've given me brings me such joy. Thank you for making the story so much better, and for sharing your vast knowledge of storytelling and structure. (Look! Not an ellipsis in sight!)

The first (only) readers of this book will be my family and friends, and so to you I say: this is fiction. While some of these characters may do, say, and experience things similar to things that I and people in my life do, say, and experience, please do not interpret this as a memoir, even a veiled one. When starting out in a new format, you write what you know. I tapped into places, feelings, and motivations that felt authentic to me. That's it. Calm down everyone.

Thank you, Adam, for the beautiful cover art. I know you think you "suck at this," but truly, you don't. My heart is so full seeing my characters and places come to life.

Thank you, Ayesha, for encouraging me and being the first person to read it all the way through. Your opinion means more than you know. And thanks for indulging my trauma. Potlucks forever! Melanie, you GOAT, your enthusiasm and notes kept me at it. Thank you, all my family and friends who've been excited for me, even if romance isn't your jam. I used so many of your ideas. (You're right, Meg, she *did* need a running buddy!)

Finally, thank you Edgar, for supporting me and not thinking this was silly. You read the whole thing (twice!), and had great suggestions. Thank you for looking out for Juan and his sustenance, and for always cleaning the shrimp. You're a ten.

Made in the USA
Monee, IL
01 June 2025

18561687R00240